Shelter

A Blackbridge Novel

Claire Boston

BANTILLY
PUBLISHING

First published by Bantilly Publishing in 2019 as book 1 in the Blackbridge First Response series

This edition published 2021.

Shelter: Blackbridge Series 5

EPUB format: 978-1-925696-34-9
Mobi format: 78-1-925696-35-6
Print: 978-1-925696-36-3
Large Print: 978-1-925696-37-0

Cover design by Lana Pecherczyk
Edited by Ann Harth
Proofread by Teena Raffa-Mulligan

About the Author

Claire Boston is a contemporary romance author who enjoys exploring real life issues on her way to the happily-ever-after. She writes heart-warming stories, with resilient heroines and heroes you'll love. In 2014 she was nominated for an Australian Romance Readers Award for Favourite New Romance Author.

When Claire's not writing she can be found creating her own handmade journals, swinging on a sidecar, or in the garden attempting to grow something other than weeds.

Claire lives in Western Australia with her husband, who loves even her most annoying quirks, and her grubby, but adorable Australian bulldog.

You can connect with Claire through Facebook (https://www.facebook.com/clairebostonauthor) and Twitter (https://www.twitter.com/clairebauthor), or join her reader group (http://www.claireboston.com/reader-group/).

Also by Claire Boston

<u>The Texan Quartet</u>
What Goes on Tour
All that Sparkles
Under the Covers
Into the Fire

<u>The Flanagan Sisters</u>
Break the Rules
Change of Heart
Blaze a Trail
Place to Belong

<u>The Blackbridge Series</u>
Nothing to Fear
Nothing to Gain
Nothing to Hide
Nothing to Lose
Shelter
Shield
Harbour
Protect

<u>The Beginner Writer's Toolkit</u>
Self-Editing

DEDICATION

To all the volunteer fire and rescue crews out there who give up their time in order to protect and save the community.
Thank you.

Prologue

Jeremy Mendelson cut the last leg for his new desk and switched off the table saw, the high-pitched buzz fading in the night. He lifted his safety glasses onto his head, brushing his hair off his face and studied his design. Not particularly inspiring. It seemed pointless to make an office desk when he had his whole house to himself and could use the kitchen table.

The scent of smoke tickled his nose. He checked the floor and bench, but nothing was smouldering.

He sniffed again, the smell stronger this time and more acrid. Not a neighbour's log fire, but more the stench he associated with a house burning down.

His stomach clenched as he strode to the entrance of his shed and scanned his property. His porch light was a beacon against the heavy clouds obscuring the moon and stars. He shifted his gaze higher, above the trees marking his property border, and his pulse skyrocketed. An unmistakable glow. Fire. Too big to be his neighbour with a simple bonfire and far too late at night.

He grabbed his phone from his pocket, dialled triple zero as he left his shed and ran across the yard to his house. "I've got a fire on my neighbour's property, about ten kilometres east of Blackbridge, Western Australia." He gave the address as he raced into his bedroom, tripping over the boots he'd left on the floor. Where was his gear? Flung over the chair in the corner where he'd left it the last time he'd washed it.

He pulled on his pants while holding the phone between his chin and his shoulder. It dropped to the ground and he threw on his shirt before picking it up. "What was that?"

"What can you see?"

He strode into his living room. "Just a bright glow from here." His bulldog, Fetch was curled up snoring, his head hanging off his bed. He'd be fine. The fire wouldn't spread, they'd had a lot of rain in the past week.

Keys. Where were his keys? He scanned the piles of papers and models on the table, the clutter on the kitchen bench and finally saw them in the bowl by the door. For once he'd left them where he was supposed to. On his way out, his fingers brushed the frame containing a photo of him and his dad on a fishing trip. "Focus," he murmured and headed out to his ute.

"Is anyone inside?" the dispatcher asked.

"I don't know." He hoped not.

The drive to his neighbour's property took only a minute and as he pulled in, he swore. A lot of people milled outside the burning building, staring at the flames, a couple gesturing frantically. "It's an outbuilding, well alight. If anyone's inside, there's not much time to get them out." He parked at a safe distance and ran to the migrant workers. "Anyone inside?"

One Asian man yelled at him in another language and pointed, gesturing frantically. Not helpful.

Where was Henk? Jeremy scanned the area until he

spotted him. Henk stood apart from his workers, yelling to another man. Didn't he have a garden hose anywhere? Jeremy checked the outside of the building as he strode to him.

"Anyone inside?"

Henk jolted. "Jeremy, thank God you're here. I didn't hear the sirens." He glanced behind Jeremy and frowned.

"They're still en route. Is everyone accounted for?"

He shook his head. "No. Annisa is still inside."

Jeremy swore and told the operator, then asked, "Where would she be?"

"Probably her room – back, right-hand corner."

Of course it fucking was. The furthest away and closest to the fiercest flames. No sirens yet. "What's the layout? Doors open or closed?"

"Long corridor runs down the middle of both floors with rooms on either side. I think the fire started in the kitchen at the far end of the corridor. Ask the workers about the doors."

Jeremy threw his phone to Henk. "Update dispatch." He ran back to the group of Asian men. "Did you leave the doors inside open or closed?" Annisa might have gone into one of the rooms and become disoriented.

The men stared at him and one said, *"Annisa di dalam."*

Shit. That sounded like Indonesian. *"Bicara bahasa Indonesia?"*

"Melayu."

Close enough. He repeated the question in Indonesian.

"Buka."

Open. It meant the ventilation would feed the fire, but also prevent a build-up of gases that could cause a backdraft. The flames were already at the main door. Foolish to go that way without a breathing apparatus and a water hose.

Jeremy grabbed the ladder and a hammer from his work ute. He pointed to the man. "Hold the ladder," he said in Indonesian. To the rest he said, "Move back," and gestured.

They did as he asked.

"That window?" he yelled at Henk over the crackle of the fire and pointed.

"Yeah."

In the distance, sirens wailed but not close enough. The extra minutes could be the difference between life and death. He had to go. No one else would die on his watch. Pain washed through him and he gritted his teeth. Focus.

He shoved the hammer into a pocket and leaned the ladder up beside the window. "Hold it," he barked, pounding the sides of the ladder. The worker nodded and steadied the ladder.

He ignored the nerves humming in his stomach and climbed. No light inside from the fire, so he switched on the torch on his helmet and scanned the room. Empty. Damn it.

"Annisa!" The roar of the fire swallowed his words.

The window was open a crack, but didn't budge when he tried to widen it. Locked. At least there wasn't any smoke up here yet. He checked over his shoulder as he pulled out his hammer. No flashing lights. He had to go in. Lowering his helmet shield and leaning away from the window, he smashed it.

No backdraft.

Thank God. "Annisa!" He ran the hammer handle around the window frame, smashing as much glass as he could, and climbed through, testing the floor before he put any real weight on it.

It held.

An unmade single bed, a storage box against one wall and no room for anything else. He checked under the bed. Clear.

Shit.

Going further into a burning building with no means to communicate with the people outside was straight up stupid.

He scrambled across the floor to the door and peered outside. "Annisa?" he yelled. Smoke gathered on the ceiling, blocking the torchlight.

Something, maybe a sob, to the left. "Annisa, if you can hear me, yell out."

"*Tolong!*"

Indonesian again. "*Kembali ke kamarmu.*" As he spoke, he crawled towards her voice, keeping the wall on his left. He coughed, moving faster. The smoke could be deadlier than the flame. "Annisa."

A dark shape in front of him took form. Annisa huddled at the top of the stairs, her eyes wide, body shaking. She sobbed something but he didn't understand. Black smoke billowed up the stairs, and he turned his head, blinking his eyes. Too thick. Too easy to get lost down there. Better to go back.

His eyes watered and his lungs burned. "This way." He tugged her arm, gestured for her to follow him.

She shook her head, wrenched her arm away.

"*Cara ini, silakan.*"

When he got out of here, he'd practise his Indonesian.

She didn't budge.

He didn't have time to wait. His head already spun from the smoke. "Don't panic." He crouched down and hefted her over his shoulder. She weighed next to nothing. She shrieked and hit him, but he held her legs tight against his chest and double-timed it back to the room at the end. As he burst through the doorway, a masked face was at the window.

Lawrence.

Annisa stopped struggling as he passed her out the window to his fire captain. The floorboards under his feet bowed. "Move!"

Lawrence was already in motion, shimmying down the ladder. Jeremy lunged for the window sill to haul his arse out as the floor gave way.

The crack of disintegrating wood and a roar of flames with a huge burst of smoke and heat. He hung from the window sill, not daring to peer down at the inferno beneath his feet. He felt it fine.

Broken glass dug through his gloves and he hissed as he struggled to pull himself up.

Chin ups were also going on his to-do list.

Muscles straining, head spinning, he scrambled for better purchase and got his arms over the sill, his thick jacket protecting him from the broken glass. Strong arms dragged him further over and then the person lugged him over his shoulder and carried him down the ladder. He was dumped unceremoniously next to the ambulance.

"Anyone else inside?" Nicholas asked.

Jeremy coughed, shaking his head, sucking in deep breaths of fresh air. "Not that I know of."

Guy, one of the paramedics, pushed him back so he sat on the edge of the ambulance. Annisa lay inside on the bed, being attended to by Cynthia. Guy handed him an oxygen mask, and Jeremy put it on as he took stock of the situation.

Several team members hosed the flames, and the fire hissed in protest.

"Any injuries?" Guy asked.

Jeremy's throat and eyes burned and his hands hurt like a mother-fucker. Shards of glass stuck out of his gloves.

Guy swore. "Let me check that."

Jeremy gritted his teeth as Guy pulled the glass out and then slid the gloves off. A couple of gashes in his left hand were bleeding.

"You might need stitches," Guy said as he cleaned the cuts.

Jeremy grimaced. He had a full schedule of work next week.

"How's your breathing?"

Lifting the mask away from his face, he croaked, "Throat hurts, so do eyes."

"We'll rinse out your eyes in a minute." Guy bandaged his hand as Lawrence walked over.

"Is he all right?"

Guy nodded. "They both need a proper examination at the hospital, but there's nothing life-threatening."

"Good." He turned back to Jeremy. "What the fuck do you think you were doing?"

Jeremy shrugged. "There wasn't time to wait."

"Bullshit. Instead of hauling one person out of the house, we had to haul two."

"The top floor gave way."

Lawrence grunted, unimpressed. "I'll check on you when this is out." He walked away.

"That sounded like a threat." Guy laughed.

Jeremy shrugged. Yeah. He'd get reamed. But at least the woman had survived.

"You ready to go?" Guy asked Cynthia.

"When you are."

"Come on, Jeremy. Let's get you into the ambo and strapped in."

As Jeremy stood, dizziness washed over him. He swayed and put his hands out for balance. Guy steadied him. "Take it easy, mate." With an arm under Jeremy's elbow, Guy helped him into the vehicle.

As he was strapped in, Jeremy glanced out the door. Everything was under control.

"Ready?" Guy asked.

Jeremy nodded. Annisa was strapped onto the bed and she gave him a small smile.

That one smile made all the shit jobs Lawrence would give him worth it. He grinned at her.

"Wait for me." Henk climbed into the ambulance. "I can't have my worker going to hospital alone."

Annisa's eyes widened, fear crossing them.

Jeremy frowned. Henk could be a jerk, but why was she scared of him?

His gut clenched. Something wasn't right.

He'd keep a close eye on Annisa and make sure she was fine.

Chapter 1

"Zamira, what is this crap?" Zamira's colleague, Murray waved a policy document in front of her.

She flinched at the demand and squinted, her eyes adjusting to the brighter light outside the meeting room she'd been stuck in for the past four hours. "The new policy on the treatment of asylum seekers." She'd spent weeks writing it and another couple of months to get the approvals needed to make it policy. She gestured for him to accompany her and hurried towards her desk, distancing herself from the tedium of the meeting.

Murray rolled his eyes. "It's rubbish. We can't do all these things out in the field."

She straightened her spine. Be polite, be respectful. He was in charge of the operations team she wanted to join. "Those items came from recommendations in the recent review. It's best practice."

He sighed in exasperation. "Best practice but not practical. We don't have the time or the resources. It's obvious you've never worked out there."

She flinched at the accusation. Yeah, she hadn't worked in the field, but it wasn't through lack of trying. She wanted to work for Border Force's Task Force and stop the mistreatment of migrants and asylum seekers, but unlike him, she was stuck behind a desk writing policies instead. She bit back the desire to snap at him and said, "The document was available for comment for several weeks before it was approved."

"I've got more important things to do than read documents." He stormed off.

Zamira sighed and sank into her office chair. Now wasn't the best time to tell him how much she wanted to be part of the Task Force. But then again, there was never a good time.

She rubbed her thumb against the silver pendant her grandmother had given her. She was the reason Zamira wanted to work for the Task Force – to stop other migrants from being treated like slaves the way her grandmother had been when she'd first arrived in Australia. She had won her freedom by following the rules until it was the right time to act.

When was right? Zamira had been a policy writer for so many years, sticking to the rules, ensuring best practice, and she'd got a reputation for being a stick in the mud. Her parents' advice to keep her head down and do things by the book so she'd be noticed and promoted had certainly backfired. She wasn't moving anywhere. She hadn't even been short-listed for an interview last time she'd applied.

Zamira checked the time. Less than an hour until her leave started and she'd escape the grey winter dreariness of Melbourne and head for sunny Cairns. A week taking photos, doing yoga and reading the latest Marvel comics was what she needed. She'd have time to re-evaluate her job and decide where to go from here.

She dug her mobile out of her bag. One message. She logged back into her computer and then checked her voice mail.

It took her a second to recognise the frantic Malay words. "It's Annisa. Zamira, please help me. I'm sorry, I shouldn't have run away, I should have told you I was coming. But it's too late. Henk won't let me go so I lit a fire. I'm in hospital in Blackbridge. Help."

Zamira's heart beat fast as she grabbed a pen and replayed the message. Her second cousin, Annisa had run away from her small village in Malaysia a month ago, leaving only a message to say she'd got a work visa and gone to Australia. She hadn't been heard of since. Annisa's mother had contacted Zamira's mother and Zamira had spoken to her supervisor. No visa had been issued in Annisa's name. If she'd been telling the truth, the documents must have been forged.

Zamira googled Blackbridge, her chest tight. Her family blamed her for Annisa running away. She'd met her cousin six years ago when she'd gone to Malaysia with her grandmother to meet family and explore her heritage. Annisa had been twelve at the time with big dreams of what she'd wanted to do with her life. Zamira had kept in touch with her, encouraging her to study and expect more from life than being a wife. When Annisa had spoken about coming to Australia, Zamira had sent her books to help her learn English and Annisa's parents had put a stop to their correspondence. They hadn't wanted Annisa to leave. That had been over a year ago.

The search results appeared. Blackbridge was a coastal town in the south of Western Australia. The other side of the country. She rang the number back and it went straight to message bank. "Hi, you've called Fleur. Leave a message and I'll get back to you."

Zamira hesitated. She didn't know who Fleur was or whether leaving a message would get Annisa into trouble. She hung up and called the hospital number instead. "Can you please put me through to Annisa Ramanan's room?"

"I'm sorry, she was discharged this afternoon."

Zamira's heart sank. "Thank you." She hung up. Think. At least she knew what town Annisa was in. She walked to her supervisor's office, nerves fluttering in her stomach. Just outside she stopped, took a deep breath and then tapped on the door frame. "Vince, I just got a message from Annisa."

He didn't look up from his computer. "Later, I'm busy."

She swallowed her nerves and her frustration, took a deep breath. She'd catch more flies with honey, even if she wanted to swat him. "I'm so sorry for interrupting, but it's urgent. I told you my cousin is missing after she left a note saying she was going to Australia."

He scowled, glancing at her and gesturing for her to continue.

"She's in a WA town called Blackbridge. The man she works for won't let her go."

"How do you know?"

"She left me a phone message. There was a fire and she was in hospital, but she's been discharged."

Vince typed a few things into his computer, his frown deepening. "You said Blackbridge?"

"Yes."

"I'll make some calls." He gestured towards the door.

Dismissed. She bit her tongue and returned to her desk, playing with the silver pendant around her neck to calm the annoyance. She had a bunch of emails to respond to before she left, but after each one she glanced towards his office. Finally, her phone rang.

"My office."

She hurried in, wrapping her necklace around her

finger as she entered.

"Close the door." His tone was grim.

Her muscles tensed as she did as he asked.

"What I'm about to tell you is strictly confidential — got it?"

"Of course." She had the appropriate security clearances and had signed a confidentiality agreement when she'd started.

"Someone in Blackbridge has been identified as a person of interest by the Task Force. They're watching him and gathering evidence. I've got to assume it's the guy your cousin is with."

"Can they get her out?"

"Eventually. If they go in now, it will ruin the whole investigation and they've been working months on this."

"But she might not be safe."

Vince swore. "I'm sorry, Zamira. It's out of my hands."

Not good enough. "Vince—"

"I've done all I can."

"What about the police? Can't we call them?"

"Not without tipping off the guy." He stared at her. "Don't even think about calling them. This is Border Force business. It's confidential."

Her chest squeezed, and she slowly breathed out before she said something that would get her into trouble. "Thank you for trying." She kept her back straight as she walked out of the room. She'd lose her job if she called the police, but she couldn't leave Annisa there alone. Annisa had been a sweet, optimistic girl full of enthusiasm and the wonder of life. She had little experience beyond her small village and must be frantic and afraid. And it was Zamira's fault she'd decided to run away.

Zamira checked the time. Five o'clock. The desire to walk out without finishing her emails was strong, but it wasn't fair to take her dissatisfaction out on her colleagues. Tension settled onto her shoulders as she responded, answering questions about policies, procedures, and legalities of certain actions, but all the while, the image of Annisa, a teenager who was a little too bony, but still with a wide grin, hovered in her mind.

What could she do?

She knew no one in Western Australia, but she needed to talk to Annisa, reassure her help was coming.

Zamira sat straighter. That was it. She was going on leave. She could change her flight from Cairns to Perth. No one here needed to know.

The idea hummed through her along with fear. She googled the town again — small, right on the south coast not far from the regional port of Albany. It wouldn't be hard to find Annisa in such a small place. Zamira could talk to her, and then report her situation to Border Force and they could intervene sooner.

And by using her initiative, perhaps she'd finally attract the attention of the Task Force.

It felt right. It was time for her to act.

She shut down her computer and picked up her bag, flicking through her phone to find the airline number as she walked to the exit.

"Have a great holiday, Zamira," someone called.

She smiled and waved. "I will." Stepping outside the building, she dialled the number she'd found. "I'd like to change my flight."

***

Zamira's headlights illuminated the big green sign declaring, *Welcome to Blackbridge.* She sighed. Finally, after a four-hour flight and a five-hour drive, she had arrived. Heaviness hung around her eyes. She'd barely slept on the flight and twenty-four-hour service stations were almost non-existent on the drive down. Now at just after six in the morning, coffee was high on her list, but her first stop had to be the hospital. She might be able to get some more information about Annisa there. She parked in the small carpark and followed the winding well-lit path past the lovely hedged gardens, to the building and the unmanned reception desk. She pressed the bell and waited. A nurse appeared wearing blue scrubs and smiled at her. "Can I help you?" Her name tag read Fleur.

Zamira blinked rapidly. Was this the woman whose phone Annisa had borrowed? "I'm looking for Annisa Ramanan. She was in a house fire Thursday night."

"I'm sorry, she was discharged yesterday afternoon."

Zamira frowned. "She told me she was being discharged today." She crossed her fingers behind her back as she lied. "Do you know who picked her up?"

"Henk took her home."

Henk. That was the name Annisa had mentioned. Her tired brain tried to process what to do next. She needed an address. Zamira ran a hand through her hair. "It's been a long night. I've been travelling since she called me, and I've forgotten her address. Could you give it to me?"

The nurse looked apologetic. "I'm sorry. We can't give out patients' personal details."

She was so close. "Annisa used your phone to call me, didn't she? I could call your number and prove it."

Fleur shook her head. "I still can't give you the address."

Damn. It had been worth a try. "I'll call her later," she lied. If only she had a phone number for Annisa.

She walked outside, closing her eyes against the frustration threatening to overwhelm her. Stupid to think it would be that simple. At least she had the right town. Time to regroup and find coffee, sugar and somewhere to stay.

She drove back into the centre of town and pulled into a small carpark surrounded on three sides by little shops. The sun peeked above the horizon, changing everything from black to grey. The lights inside *On The Way* bakery caught her attention. A bunch of bikes took up a parking bay outside and a group of cyclists sat at a table inside chatting and cupping their mugs of coffee. Perfect. She pulled her jacket tighter against the chill and hurried to the door.

Zamira inhaled deeply as she walked inside and the aroma of fresh bread, hot coffee and sugary baked goodness assailed her.

Praise be to Allah.

Aside from the cyclists recovering from their early Saturday morning ride, a couple of parents looking as tired as she felt bought hot chocolates and croissants for their young children. As she waited for her turn, she scanned the cafe. Over two dozen round wooden tables spread out across the wooden floor, windows made up three of the walls and two doors allowed easy access from both the carpark and the street. The large display cabinets had wide, round sheets of glass to reveal the delectable treats and powder blue name tags identified each treat. On the wall behind, baskets hung with a range of breads and there was a small stack of white boxes ready for takeaway treats. The whole place had a comforting, homely vibe. Several staff served customers and a short Asian woman with her long black hair tied back in a bun came out from the kitchen carrying a large tray of fresh croissants. She added them to the display cabinet and replaced the tray in the kitchen before approaching Zamira with a smile. "What can I get you?"

"I need the biggest mug of coffee you've got and whatever sugary pastry you recommend."

"Tough night?" the woman asked. "My fiancé's favourite is Mai's Delight and I made a batch this morning. It's part pastry, part custard and all good." She pointed to it.

"Sounds perfect." Zamira opened her purse as the woman plated up the dessert and gave her coffee order to the teenager behind the coffee machine. Zamira handed over a twenty. "Does that make you Mai?"

"That's right." She smiled and handed over the change. "This is my bakery. Why don't you take a seat and I'll bring out the coffee when it's ready?" Mai returned to the kitchen.

Zamira settled in a seat by the window. Sunlight gradually illuminated the wide street and mismatched buildings. A couple of people braved the cold rugged up in thick jackets and beanies and walked their dogs.

She closed her eyes, resisting the temptation to lean her head on the table.

"Here you go." Mai placed an enormous mug of coffee – more soup container than coffee cup – on the table.

"Wow."

Mai glanced around and lowered her voice. "I got a mug from my personal collection because you look like you need all the caffeine you can get."

"Thank you." She curled her hands around the mug and took a long sip of the glorious nectar. "I had a late flight last night."

"Where from?"

"Melbourne."

"And you drove to Blackbridge this morning?" Mai frowned.

She nodded.

"You must be exhausted. If you're too tired to drive, I can call a friend and we can drive you and your car to wherever you're staying."

Zamira blinked and warmth spread through her. "That's really nice of you."

Mai shrugged and slid into the seat opposite her with a sigh. "It's part ulterior motive — I don't want any of my crew called out when you crash your car."

"Crew?"

"I'm second in charge at the volunteer Fire and Rescue."

Zamira's eyes widened. "My friend mentioned a fire somewhere here a couple of nights ago."

Mai nodded. "Out at Henk Jennings' place."

A surname. She was getting somewhere. "I hope no one was hurt."

"No one badly, but the building might have to be knocked down."

Zamira's brain clamoured with questions. "Were you at the fire?"

"No, I was here baking, but my fiancé responded. They rescued a woman trapped inside." Mai shook her head. "Jeremy went in without the proper gear to save her. He was lucky he didn't kill himself."

Excitement stirred. Was she talking about Annisa? "Why?"

"He lives next door to Henk. Smelled the smoke and called it in so he was on site before the rest of the crew. He didn't think he had time to wait for the truck to arrive." She sighed. "He was probably right. The floor collapsed as he was climbing out."

Zamira's breath caught in her throat. This Jeremy

had saved Annisa's life.

A large group of people walked into the bakery, talking and laughing. "There goes my break." Mai stood up. "If you need a lift, I'll be in the kitchen until around ten."

"Thank you."

Mai greeted the new group, squatting to talk to a couple of the young children who stared wide-eyed at the cabinet.

With such friendly people in town, how could Annisa be trapped here?

Taking a long sip of coffee, she searched the white pages. A couple of Jennings in the area. She clicked on the one that said H Jennings and swiped the map out to get her bearings. He had a property out of town. That would explain why people didn't know about Annisa. Zamira bit into her pastry and the custard, creamy goodness momentarily distracted her. The flaky outside texture combined with a soft inside with a bite of citrus — divine. She closed her eyes and savoured it, as a burst of energy hit her system.

Using her thumb, she panned the map around. Too isolated for her to stroll by and see if she could spot Annisa. A pin not far away stated Hideaway Retreat. She clicked on the link. A collection of cute, short-term accommodation cabins which blended into the native bush. Maybe she could stay there. She checked the website — fully booked all week.

Well at least she could pretend to get lost looking for it.

After finishing her coffee and pastry, energy surged through her. She'd scope the place and then find somewhere to stay. She stood and looked for Mai to thank her, but she was busy in the kitchen.

Zamira headed for her car, the carpark almost full

now.

The icy air through her open window kept her alert as she drove. She followed her phone's directions as she turned off the highway onto a smaller bitumen road and then onto a gravel road. Peppermint trees and bushes lined the road, blocking the properties from view. Occasionally a mailbox or driveway indicated a new place and she'd glimpse a roof. It would take a long time to walk into town.

"*You have arrived,*" her phone proclaimed.

Zamira stopped. A driveway twenty metres in front of her and another twenty metres behind her. Which was it?

Both had letterboxes, one shaped like a wooden cottage, and the other a simple metal one you could buy for under a hundred dollars from the local hardware store. The driveway with the metal mailbox also had a large metal security gate which currently stood open.

She drove forward but the metal mailbox had no name or number on it. Shifting into reverse, she checked the wooden letterbox. Nothing.

Decision time. Which road should she take?

The wooden mailbox had a much safer feel. The person who lived there cared about aesthetics and appearance. Her mother would approve. A neat yard denoted a neat mind. Zamira drove down the well-graded drive hedged by peppermint trees. It opened into a large gravel yard and her mouth dropped open. The centrepiece was the house. A dark wooden cabin much like the letterbox, but it had wide verandahs and a dirt path leading up to the front door. A smattering of flowers grew in the small garden beds either side of the path, as if the owner had shaken a mixed packet of seeds into the bed and waited to see which ones grew. Gorgeous.

Behind the house was a large wooden shed almost the same size. The wood was more faded, greying from age and the big double doors stood open. A large water tank sat at the side of the shed and next to it a fire hose and generator. This person was prepared. A truck and a ute were parked outside. No sign of any burnt building. This couldn't be the right place.

As she circled the open gravel yard, a man appeared at the shed door.

She stared.

Cave man. He had to be over six foot, with scruffy blond-brown hair that hadn't been brushed this morning, and a thick, full beard. Despite the cold morning, he wore only a black T-shirt and jeans, the cut of the top defining his firm biceps and broad chest. He frowned but lifted a hand in a wave.

Her muscles tensed. Mai had said something about the neighbour calling in the fire, saving Annisa. This could be him. But she was hopeless at speaking to men around her own age. Too little practice.

This wasn't for her, it was for Annisa.

Besides, it would look suspicious if she drove away, and she didn't want him to call the cops on her.

She parked, made sure her mobile was in her pocket and got out. Her mother would be horrified she was out here alone with a strange man.

"Can I help you?" The man wandered over. He was at least a half foot taller than her with muscles in his arms and chest that could easily overpower her.

She forced a smile and shifted closer to her car, keeping the open door between her and the man. "I think I'm lost."

His smile lit up his rich, hazel eyes and it took his whole appearance from Neanderthal to hunk. Wow. Her heart raced as he said, "Where are you going?"

Her mind went completely blank. "Ah… something retreat."

"You mean Hideaway?"

She nodded.

"You took a right when you should have taken a left. Hannah's place is over that way." He pointed. "If you turn right out of my place, drive to the T-junction, turn right again and then take the next left you'll find it."

His words barely registered, she was still reeling from the punch his smile had packed. She was obviously too tired. Blinking rapidly, she said, "Sorry, can you repeat that?"

Concern crossed his face. "Are you all right? You look exhausted."

She ran a hand through her short hair. "Long drive."

"Where'd you come from?"

"Perth."

His eyebrows raised. "This morning?"

She shrugged. "No point in paying for a night in the city when my plane arrived."

He shook his head. "You're lucky you didn't have an accident. Why don't I drive you over? I can walk home."

Huh? That was overly friendly even for a country town. "You don't know me."

"But I recognise your fatigue. I've seen it too many times in crash victims."

He had to be the fireman Mai had mentioned. The one who'd rescued Annisa. "Are you a paramedic?"

"Fire-fighter. Look, at least let me get you a cup of coffee." The crinkle of his forehead showed his genuine concern.

He could give her more information about Annisa. "That would be great. Thank you." She'd be sloshing coffee, but it was for a good cause.

"This way." He walked towards his house, his jeans stretching nicely over his butt. She'd never been into the scruffy, bad boy look, and her parents would never approve, but he was attractive. Or maybe her judgement was off because of her lack of sleep.

A bulldog trotted down the back steps towards them, its white face contrasting against its brown body, a huge sloppy grin on its face. Zamira slowed. Her mother's voice in her head told her dogs were dirty, don't touch them. She wrapped her hands around her waist as the dog passed the man and pranced around her. "Ah…"

The man turned. "Fetch, come here!" He took a couple of steps towards her and pulled on his dog's collar. "He won't hurt you, he just doesn't understand personal boundaries." With a groan, Fetch followed him back onto the verandah. The man took off his boots and opened the door. "Come in."

Zamira hesitated. She shouldn't go into a strange man's house by herself. She was thousands of kilometres from home and too far away from any neighbour who could hear her scream. No one knew she was here.

Understanding dawned in his eyes. "Why don't you sit outside and I'll bring it out?"

Relief filled her. "Thank you." A small round table sat on the verandah with two chairs next to it. She sat on the one facing the door and let out a deep breath. It was peaceful here. Quiet. No traffic noise, no people yelling or machinery at work. Just the occasional drip of water from the earlier rain. She inhaled. Damp soil and eucalyptus.

The verandah faced the back of the property. A couple of vegetable patches were close to the house and then nothing but low-cut grass for a good fifty metres before some shrubs and the bush proper — no yard or fencing. No big trees around the house and it must get hot in summer, but right now it was lovely.

"Do you have milk or sugar?" The man kicked the back door open and carried a steaming mug in one hand and his fingers looped through the handles of a bottle of milk and jar of sugar in the other. He placed the mug in front of her but knocked the sugar jar as he put it down, spilling sugar all over the table. "Shit, sorry." He bumped the milk bottle and managed to catch it before it fell. His face red, he stared at the table for a second. "Spoons. I'll be right back." His triumphant smile made her heart give another rapid beat in response.

It had to be the fatigue causing her to revert to her baser instincts. Men didn't usually affect her like this. Though social interactions with the opposite sex had been few and far between since she'd left university.

She added milk to the instant coffee, and he returned, handing her a spoon and then wiping up the sugar, throwing the granules into the garden. "I'm Jeremy by the way." He sat in the other seat, his own coffee in hand, and Fetch settled next to him.

She smiled. "Zamira."

"That's pretty. Where's it from?"

"It's Malay." She put two spoons of sugar in her cup to disguise the horrid instant coffee taste. As she lifted the cup to her lips she hesitated. Could he have slipped something into it? She rolled her eyes at the mental caution from her mother. Normal people didn't have access to that kind of drug. She took a sip. Get the conversation back to Annisa. "So, do you get many fires out here?"

He leaned back in his chair, crossed his legs at the ankles. "Not usually at this time of year, but my neighbour had a fire a couple of nights ago." He gestured towards the side of the house in the direction of the metal letterbox place, but the trees blocked the view.

Her pulse raced. "Was anyone hurt?"

He flexed his hand which had a waterproof dressing on it. "Not really. The woman I dragged out had a bit of smoke inhalation."

Zamira's eyes widened. "You had to go into a burning building and rescue someone?"

Jeremy shrugged. "All part of the job."

"Was she stuck?"

"I think she got disoriented and by the time she found the stairs, the ground floor was alight. She didn't speak a lot of English and my Indonesian's dodgy at best."

"Your neighbours are Indonesian?" Malay and Indonesian were similar languages, so maybe Jeremy was wrong.

"No, Henk's from South Africa. He supports migrant workers, finding them work and providing accommodation on his property. Annisa was one of them."

She bit down on her smile. She had found her. It *was* Annisa.

But if Jeremy knew Annisa was a migrant, did he also know about Henk's treatment of her? Best she not mention her connection to Annisa until she found out more.

Next stop, Henk's place.

Chapter 2

The beautiful Malaysian woman sitting across from Jeremy placed her mug on the table and pushed back her chair. "I should go. Thank you for the coffee."

Disappointment washed through him. It wasn't a hardship to sit in front of such a beauty and chat on a Saturday morning, even if she looked completely out of place in her black pants and matching blazer jacket. She probably couldn't wait to get away from the klutz in front of her. In his defence, he didn't have guests regularly. He stood up. "Are you staying in Blackbridge for long?"

"About a week."

Perfect. "If you need any recommendations, call me." He took a slightly bent and grubby business card out of his jeans pocket and handed it to her. "And if you want some dinner company, I scrub up OK." He winked.

Her nose screwed up and she took the card between two fingers. "Thank you."

Right. She was one of *those* women. Probably high society and didn't like to mess with plebs like him. Shame. Her cute pixie cut, deep brown eyes and flawless skin gave her a model quality. His mates would have been jealous and the limited time she was here suited him just fine. No possibility of getting too attached.

As she got into her car, he repeated the directions to the retreat and then watched her drive away. She'd interrupted him while he'd been working on his desk, but that held no interest for him. Her questions about the fire reminded him he'd been meaning to check on Annisa. After he'd been x-rayed, he'd been taken to a different hospital room and she'd been discharged before he'd had a chance to speak with her.

Wandering back into the house, he found his phone and the keys for his ute. Might as well go now. It wasn't like the desk was a priority.

As he drove up his neighbour's drive, the burnt remains of the worker accommodation drew his eye. In front of it, a dozen two-man tents had been set up. Not a great solution at this time of year with it being so wet and cold. If most of the migrants were from Indonesia, they must be freezing. He pulled up at the main house next to a little white hire car like the one Zamira had been driving. He frowned. There she was at the front door talking to Henk.

What was she doing here?

Henk moved closer to her, leering over her with a big grin on his face. Jeremy increased his pace as Zamira stepped back and glanced around. Spotting Jeremy, her hand flew to her chest and her tanned skin flushed darker.

Henk scowled briefly before stepping forward to shake his hand. "Jeremy, I never got the chance to thank you for responding so quickly the other night."

"No problem. I don't want to interrupt, I just dropped around to check how Annisa is."

"You're not interrupting. This lady was asking for directions to the Hideaway Retreat." He laughed and placed a hand on Zamira's shoulder. "She can't follow her sat nav."

Zamira cringed away from Henk and played with the silver pendant hanging around her neck, not looking at Jeremy. She couldn't possibly have forgotten the directions he'd given five minutes before. Betrayal stung him. She'd lied to him, but for what end?

"Annisa's resting. She's still feeling a little sick from the smoke."

Jeremy focused on Henk. "I hope it's nothing serious."

"Nah, it's not."

Zamira stood between the two of them, her lips pressed together, arms wrapped protectively around her waist.

"I see you've got some tents set up for your workers."

"Yeah, best I could do for now."

"Want me to go through the building? I can give you an idea if it's repairable or needs to be knocked down."

Henk hesitated. "That'd be great, but I'm on my way out. Could you come around tomorrow about ten?"

"Sure." He paused. "Look why don't some of your workers bunk at my place until the building's fixed?" He was surprised Henk didn't have them sleeping in his house.

Henk frowned. "Thanks for the offer. They're more comfortable staying together and it won't be long."

"Offer's open if you change your mind." Jeremy shook Henk's hand and then glanced at Zamira. Whatever she was up to, she looked nervous of Henk. He couldn't leave her alone with him. "Want me to show you the way to the retreat?"

Her smile was pained. "No, it's fine. I've got it now." She slipped past him and hurried down the path.

Yeah, she was definitely hiding something. "I'll see you tomorrow," he said to Henk and returned to his ute. They'd had some weird drug-ring related stuff happening in town a couple of months ago and he couldn't ignore his gut. He followed her down the drive and paused outside his own driveway to see which way she turned at the end of the street. Left.

Either she was really shit at remembering directions, or she had no intention of going to the retreat. And if that was the case, what was she doing here?

On a whim he followed, staying out of sight, following the light dust trail left by her car. At the main highway he lost her, but he took a gamble and headed towards Blackbridge. She'd visited him and Henk which meant it probably had something to do with the fire the other night. But an arson investigator would have been upfront and so would an insurance assessor. He'd dealt with both a number of times.

So what then?

He accelerated, creeping over the speed limit and was soon rewarded by the little white car on the road ahead. He slowed again and followed her through town to the tourist centre where she parked and went inside.

He found a parking spot and got out, rubbing his arms against the cold. He hadn't grabbed a jumper before he'd left. Inside the centre, the heating was on and he sighed as he scanned the room. He waved to Barbara behind the desk and then spotted Zamira over by the accommodation pamphlets.

She'd definitely lied about the retreat. He hated dishonest people.

He walked over. "Got lost again?"

She shrieked and whirled around, her hand on her

chest. "Jeremy."

"Either you've got a shit sense of direction or you lied to me." Why was he so mad? Pretty women rejected him all the time.

She drew herself tall, all a hundred and seventy centimetres of her and glared at him. "If you don't stop following me, I'm going to call the police."

His mouth dropped open. He couldn't deny it.

"Leave me alone." She stalked out of the tourist bureau with her head high, looking every bit a wronged woman.

She suddenly reminded him of his mother. Pain compressed his chest. Definitely best he stayed clear of her. He didn't need that kind of grief.

But he'd mention her to Adam at football tomorrow.

That way at least the cops could keep an eye on her.

****

Zamira hadn't packed expecting to do something illegal, so the dark blue pants and her deep red rain jacket would have to do for camouflage at night. After Jeremy had confronted her at the tourist centre she'd driven around town until she'd found a little bed and breakfast with a vacancy and then she'd slept for most of the afternoon. When she awoke, she was far more refreshed and able to plan.

She needed to get onto Henk's property and talk to Annisa without Jeremy or Henk seeing her. Jeremy was definitely suspicious and if he called the police, she'd be in so much trouble.

She should have returned to town after speaking with Jeremy and planned her next step instead of heading straight to Henk's. Then she would have come up with a better idea like reviewing Google maps and seeing that a fire access road ran right behind his property. She could have wandered through the bush with her camera and pretended she was looking for the perfect shot.

Too late.

Now her best option was sneaking onto the property at night. She'd bought a decent torch and some night vision binoculars that afternoon, but hadn't considered appropriate clothing.

She hoped her little car could handle the fire access track without getting bogged. She couldn't easily explain that. Knowing her luck, Jeremy would be part of the local mechanic call-out crew as well. She shivered. He'd seemed so trustworthy when she'd stopped at his place but then he'd followed her next door and into town.

Super creepy.

Maybe he was involved with Henk. He'd offered to help fix the building and had known about the migrant workers, and yet he'd done nothing to stop their exploitation.

It didn't matter. The Task Force would figure it out and if he was involved, then he deserved to be arrested.

She checked her handbag — torch, night vision binoculars, phone.

She headed out to her car, nerves brushing her skin. Her mother's voice again – this was not the way a woman behaved. It was far too dangerous, it should be left to the men.

Zamira was tired of letting men rule her life. Though she loved her father, he had certain beliefs – which were half a century out of date – on a woman's proper role, and then she'd had to deal with Vince treating her like she was nothing more than a glorified typist.

No more.

Night had settled over the small town, the street lights were on and warm light spilled out of house windows and puffs of smoke escaped from pot belly fires.

Her headlights barely made a dent in the darkness even on high beam as she drove out of town, and other cars were few and far between. She hadn't spent a lot of time in the country before. It was disconcerting to have no street lights, no headlights behind her or coming up ahead, no neon lights from shops and service stations. She slowed when her navigation told her, even though she couldn't see a road. Suddenly the turn appeared out of the dark and she braked sharply to make it. Why wasn't there decent lighting at the intersection?

More cautious now, she crawled along at half the speed limit and as her phone told her to turn right in a hundred metres, a kangaroo bounded out in front of her. Heart in her throat she jammed on the brakes and her car slid, fishtailing as the 'roo bounded into the bush. She got control of the car and stopped, her heart thumping hard. Was that an omen she should turn back?

Her grandmother would tell her yes. Her mother would be appalled she'd even considered coming out here.

She couldn't desert Annisa. Still she rubbed her silver pendant for luck.

More cautious now, she drove to the fire break, her headlights illuminating the soft grey sand road that would bog her little car before she got ten metres.

She checked her map. A couple of kilometres to Henk's place. Her Doc Martens were sturdy enough, she could walk. She pulled onto the road shoulder and switched off her lights.

Darkness plunged around her and she gasped. It was

like all the light and sound had been sucked out of the world. Melbourne was never this dark, or silent. What the hell was she thinking? She had no idea about the bush. There'd be snakes, spiders and wild foxes out there. She'd probably twist her ankle and be stranded.

No. Annisa needed her. She'd identify Annisa's tent and then sneak in to talk to her when everyone was asleep.

Zamira opened her door and the automatic light was a comforting beacon. Sound returned as insects chirped around her. She retrieved her torch from her bag, switched it on and then locked the car.

She took a deep breath in and walked forward.

The cold settled around her, so Zamira zipped up her rain jacket to keep some of the warmth in. Above her clouds blocked out the moon and the stars, and the large gum trees added shadows. Before long she was puffing, the soft sand pulling at each footstep. Her breath clouded in hot gasps. She should have spent more time at the gym.

A loud rustle in the bushes to her right. She swung her torch around and peered into the darkness, her muscles tight, hand shaking.

Nothing.

Her skin crawled and she breathed slowly to calm herself. Probably a wallaby or a smaller marsupial. She walked faster, glancing behind regularly.

She really should have told someone where she was, but she hadn't wanted to hear she was foolish. She knew she was.

But there had been few other choices.

She reviewed her map again. Not far from Henk's property. She retrieved her night vision binoculars from her bag and then hesitated. Switching off the torch would plunge her into darkness. Gritting her teeth, she pressed the button and dropped the torch into her bag. She quickly lifted the binoculars to her eyes, scanning the area.

A large man-sized shape appeared in the bushes not five metres away from her.

She shrieked, leaping backwards.

Chapter 3

Zamira's heart raced faster than a racehorse as she stared, frozen in place. Her skin pimpled and she clenched the binoculars. They could do as a weapon. Which way — back to her car, or into the bush?

The car.

The figure moved, bending over to nibble at a plant. Her breath left her in a whoosh.

Kangaroo.

Her imagination was running away from her. She breathed deeply for a minute to calm her racing heart. She'd come this far. Keep going.

With a renewed determination, she continued towards Henk's property until the map showed her she was opposite it and then scanned the bush she had to walk through. Were snakes active at night? Or did they hibernate in winter?

It would be her luck to be bitten and die out here.

She swallowed hard. She'd be careful.

Moving into the low scrub, her footsteps were muffled by the wet grasses. She walked slowly, keeping her binoculars trained on the ground so she didn't trip. She halted in front of a wire fence stretching either way in front of her. It wouldn't be hard to climb through. The wires ran parallel to the ground with enough gap between them for her to squeeze through. Then she'd be on Henk's property, though there was still bush as far as she could see.

As she reached out to separate the wire, a male voice said, "You touch it and you'll get a hell of a shock."

She shrieked, whirled around and lost her balance, falling towards the fence. She dropped the binoculars and strong hands hauled her upright.

He held her close, his chest firm, arms tight and she struggled, hitting him, her pulse pounding in her head as fear took control. "Let go of me." It was more of a sob than the order she'd wanted.

"Just to be clear, the fence you almost touched is electrified." The deep voice sparked a memory and as he let her go, she said, "Jeremy?"

"Yes. And no, I'm not following you this time. I was investigating who was sneaking along the fire break." He chuckled quietly. "Imagine my surprise to find you. Should I call the police now?"

"No. Please, don't. I can explain…" Except she really couldn't. Not without knowing if he was involved with Henk. If he was, he could give everything away.

"I'm listening."

The first spit of rain hit her cheek and she glanced at the sky.

"Zamira, give me one good reason not to call the police right now. We've had all sorts of dodgy things happening in Blackbridge this year and I won't ignore you sneaking around. Too many people died." His tone was rough.

The police would call Border Force and she'd be in so much trouble. Another drop of rain hit her face, and then another. His expression would tell her if he was involved. She bent down, felt around until she found her binoculars and picked them up. His face wasn't clear enough.

The rain fell faster now and she pulled up her hood with a sigh. "Can we talk at your place?"

"All right." He flicked on a torch and the light made her blink. "This way." He gave her a long look, jaw set and then moved ahead of her.

She couldn't outrun him and he'd likely track her down. Someone who ran into a burning building to save a woman couldn't be all bad — right?

He turned. "You coming?"

With another sigh, she followed, drawing her phone out of her pocket. She'd send her sister a message so that if she disappeared, someone would know where to look for her.

As she typed out a message, her shoulders slumped.

No signal. Goosebumps leapt to her skin.

If Jeremy was in on this, she was screwed.

***

Jeremy led the way to his place, but kept a close eye on Zamira in case she tried to hit him over the head. When he'd seen the light bobbing through the trees he'd thought he was imagining it for a minute. But then he'd realised it was a torch and had decided to investigate. He wasn't calling the cops if it was kids playing spotlight. The guys would never let him live it down.

He'd been stunned when he'd recognised Zamira in the glow of the torch. He'd followed at a distance and when she'd switched from torch to night vision binoculars — who the hell carried them for legit business? — he'd kept close to the trees, but she hadn't checked behind. Instead she'd nearly freaked out at something in the bush nearby and when she'd continued on, he'd noticed the kangaroo.

She was obviously no expert at sneaking around.

Which meant he couldn't be cruel enough to let her get zapped by Henk's electrified fence. Though it would have served her right.

No, whatever was going on, she wasn't a seasoned criminal. Perhaps he could help, stop her going down a similar path that had killed or imprisoned so many of his friends.

As they left the bush at the back of his property, he slowed so she could walk next to him. The rain had begun in earnest now, still light but constant, the type of rain that deceived, appeared soft but would drench you in minutes. The back porch light shone in front, killing his night vision and illuminating the drops. He looked at Zamira.

What was her interest in Henk?

She glanced at him but didn't say a word.

"Where's your car?"

She was silent a moment. "At the entrance to the fire break."

A straight stretch of road so it shouldn't cause a hazard.

Fetch lay on the verandah where Jeremy had left him. He lifted his head as they approached, and his tail thumped on the wood. Jeremy rubbed the dog's head, then glanced over his shoulder at Zamira. "Come inside."

He stripped off his soaked jumper and undid his boots, leaving them outside.

She hesitated and he raised his eyebrows. "If I was going to do anything to you, I would have done it in the bush, away from my house." He was the one who should be worried. She was doing something dodgy and if she had a gun in her bag, he'd be stuffed. "This way."

He led her through to the laundry, handing her a towel for her hair. She'd been sensible enough to wear a rain jacket at least. He hadn't grabbed one before he'd left and the cold was seeping into his bones. "Hang your jacket over the sink."

He didn't wait for an answer but continued through into the kitchen where he switched on the kettle. When he turned she was there. "Mugs and tea are in the top cupboard," he said. "I'm going to change." If she ran, he'd report her to the police.

When he returned to the kitchen, the kettle had boiled and she had poured two mugs of tea. He paused in the hallway. She had a weird sense of what was appropriate clothing for sneaking about. A long-sleeved blood red shirt, the type most girls would wear out to dinner and blue office pants — slacks, his granny would have called them. She wore Thor socks on her feet, which was kind of cute. With a sigh, he got out the milk and handed it to Zamira.

"Thank you." She looked more subdued tonight, though she no longer had the dark fatigue circles under her eyes. She must have found somewhere to sleep.

He cleared a space at the dining table, moving design notes, files and models to the kitchen bench, and then gestured to a seat. "What are you doing in Blackbridge?"

She glanced at him through her eyelashes, worry in her eyes, and slowly sipped her tea.

"Are you in some kind of trouble?"

She shook her head. "No, but my cousin is."

Cousin? Zamira was Malaysian and had asked questions about the fire. All at once everything clicked. "Annisa?"

She gasped and then nodded. "She's my second cousin, she called me from hospital…" She paused.

"You rescued her. How did she seem?"

He frowned. "Distressed. A little scared of Henk."

Zamira studied him and then placed her mug on the table. "Annisa told me the man who brought her here wouldn't let her go. She left Malaysia a month ago and no one has heard from her since."

Jeremy leaned back. "You think Henk kidnapped her?" It made no sense. People knew she was there.

"Not exactly." She closed her eyes. "I work for Border Force. We monitor foreign workers and migrants to ensure they aren't being exploited. Annisa thought she had a legitimate work visa, but nothing has been registered in her name. She could virtually be a slave."

He shook his head. "Isn't that going a bit far? We don't have slavery in Australia."

Her gaze hardened. "You'd be surprised at the number of people prosecuted each year for what amounts to modern day slavery; from paying incorrect wages to giving no annual or sick leave and not allowing them to leave the premises. And they get away with it because the migrant workers don't know their rights, don't speak a lot of English and are threatened with deportation if they do question it." Her voice rose with passion as she spoke.

He whistled low. "I had no idea."

"Not many people do."

He rubbed his beard. "You think Henk is doing this?" He hated to think his neighbour was capable of it, but after what had happened a couple of months ago with a close mate, he wasn't ready to discount it. You never really knew someone.

She nodded.

"So, you're here on a reconnaissance mission for Border Force?"

She glanced at her mug. "Something like that."

He expected the people hired to protect the country to be less jumpy. "Are all the workers next door slaves like Annisa?" Henk had arranged work placements for them all over Blackbridge. The bus with the workers drove past every morning.

"Possibly. Annisa's scared. Desperate, even. She lit the fire on purpose."

His eyes widened. That was very risky. She'd almost been killed. He sipped his tea. If what Zamira said was true, then he couldn't do nothing. He couldn't let anyone else lose a loved one. "I'm going over there tomorrow to quote Henk for repairs on the building."

Zamira raised her eyebrows. "You're a builder?"

He nodded. "I can ask Henk if I can talk to Annisa and give her a message."

She brightened with a huge grin and the sparkle in her eyes hit him straight in the gut. Shit. Where did that come from?

"That would be great."

He stood, needing the distance, and took a notebook from the bench. He flicked to a blank page and handed it to her with a pen.

"Thank you." She gazed right into his eyes, her expression full of thanks before she bent her head to write the note.

He let out a breath. He always fell fast for a pretty face. A psychologist would probably say he was searching for the affection he'd lost, but he knew better. Caring too much for anyone was just asking for heartbreak and he had enough pain to deal with.

He shouldn't get messed up in this more than he already was. Besides, Zamira had more important things to deal with than him making a move on her — *if* she was telling the truth.

Zamira ripped out the piece of paper and folded it in half and then half again before giving it to him.

He unfolded it. He could understand the gist of it. "You're working on a plan and if she feels threatened she should come to me?" Great. She was drawing him in.

"You speak Malaysian?"

"A bit of Indonesian." He tucked the note in his pocket. "Why can't you just get her out?"

She played with her pendant, passing it along the silver chain. "The Task Force is putting a case together. If I move too soon, we might not have all the evidence we need."

Fair enough. "Where are you staying?"

"At a bed and breakfast." She wrote something on the pad and handed it to him. "My number."

So now she was willing to give it to him. "You still got mine?"

She nodded, looking down at the ground.

"All right. I'll give you a call tomorrow." He collected her empty mug from the table and put it in the sink. Get her out of his house and then he could think things through. "You want me to give you a lift back to your car?"

Hurriedly she stood. "Yes, please. If it's not too much trouble."

"It's fine." Though he wasn't entirely convinced Zamira wasn't a whole lot of trouble in herself.

Chapter 4

The next morning Jeremy drove over to Henk's place and parked his ute near the remains of the dorm building, not far from all the tents. Henk was already there but the rest of the property was deserted.

"Thanks for coming over," Henk said. "The insurance guys are supposed to be out early this week."

Jeremy's muscles were tight. He wasn't close to his neighbour, but he couldn't let what Zamira had told him cloud his judgement. She could be lying. He'd played football against Henk for years and sometimes built things for him. The man was a bit arrogant, and always keen to blame his problems on someone else, but he always donated money to the volunteer fire and rescue when they did their annual fundraising event.

"Has it been cleared to enter?" Jeremy asked as they walked up the charred wooden steps to the front door.

"Yeah, and the men took out the stuff they could salvage."

Jeremy walked in, scanning the front hall, checking for dangers someone might have missed. Smoke stained the walls and its stench filled his nose, but there were no flame marks here. "Do you know where it started?"

Henk scowled. "The kitchen. Might have been someone smoking inside."

Henk didn't know it was Annisa. That was good. Jeremy raised his eyebrows. "The culprit still work here?"

Henk's laugh was grim. "No one's owned up to it yet."

The hall came to an end. Blackened stairs led to the first floor and a corridor branched out each way with doors leading off it.

"Kitchen is that way." Henk pointed left where the walls were black with curled paint and the stench of smoke was even stronger.

Jeremy headed towards it, watching his step so he didn't trip on the debris and peering into the tiny bedrooms as he went past. Each contained a single bed and a chest of drawers. Kind of like a prison cell.

At the end, the kitchen was far larger, and now had a gaping hole in the ceiling. Above had to be the remains of Annisa's room. The window he'd climbed through was boarded up. Debris from the ceiling and charred remains of what would have been the dining table and cabinets were scattered around the floor. Heavy traces of smoke, chemicals and damp wood. He breathed through his mouth as his eyes watered. It would have to be completely gutted.

He moved back down the corridor, past the stairs and inspected the remaining rooms on the ground floor. A small lounge room and a bathroom. They had smoke damage but weren't in too bad a state. The fire hadn't reached this far.

"You should stay down here," Jeremy said as he returned to the stairs. "The less weight we put on the floor upstairs, the better."

Henk nodded. "You know what's best. I'll meet you

outside."

Jeremy tested each step before he put any weight on it and slowly made his way upstairs. He went through the end furthest from the kitchen first. A couple of doors were closed, so he opened them. Not much damage, though the smell of smoke would linger for months no matter how much they cleaned.

He continued back along the corridor, his steps slowing as he cautiously approached the source of the fire. Only bedrooms up here and aside from some smoke and water damage, they weren't in too bad a state. He reached Annisa's room and peered inside. Most of the floor was gone.

The roof was in pretty good shape, stained with smoke, but still in one piece. It wouldn't be hard to replace it with some new plasterboard. The floor was a whole different kettle of fish. He needed to find the main support beams, figure out the damage. His fingers brushed something metal on the door frame. The loop of a padbolt. Frowning, he reached in and drew the door closed, checking the other side. Yep. The door could be locked from the inside.

Annisa obviously didn't feel safe here.

He needed to get to the bottom of whatever was going on. He couldn't turn a blind eye, not now he knew something wasn't right.

He never would have guessed it. In the past Henk had provided him with workers to help with big jobs he couldn't do on his own. Jeremy had always paid the industry rate, but maybe they hadn't received it.

With a sigh, he headed back outside to where Henk waited.

"How bad is it?" Henk asked.

"The right side of the structure isn't too bad. You'll need some heavy-duty cleaning to get rid of the soot and smoke stains, but you can probably make it liveable fairly quickly if you want to get your guys out of the tents. I can recommend some products to use or a couple of cleaning companies."

Henk nodded. "And the rest?"

"I'd say it will need to be structurally reinforced and rebuilt. Before you do anything you should get a structural engineer in."

"Can you give me a ballpark figure?"

Jeremy shrugged. "Until I know what the engineer says it's difficult to estimate."

Henk scowled. "Hopefully insurance will cover it."

"When you've got the structural report I can come back and do a full measure and quote, give you an exact figure."

"I appreciate it."

They walked back to his ute and Jeremy scanned the tents. "You sure you don't want some of the guys bunking at my place? It's cold."

"Thanks mate, but I don't want to put you out. If those end rooms are structurally sound, I'll get them to move back two to a room for the meantime. They're all pretty shaken up by the fire and they'll be happy to clean up."

Two to a room would be very squeezy, and if they didn't clean them properly, the smoke stench would be unpleasant, but he didn't insist. It was Henk's business. "Is Annisa around?"

"Ah, no. She had a cleaning job this morning."

"On a Sunday?"

"Some people like to be at home when she comes," Henk said. "I'll tell her you stopped by."

He couldn't give her the note. "Can you call me when she gets back?" When Henk frowned at him, he rubbed his beard. "I like to check on people after a fire.

Make sure they're doing OK." He flashed Henk a grin. "Besides, she was kind of cute."

Henk rolled his eyes. "Don't try to pick up one of my best workers." He sighed. "I'll let you know when she gets back."

"Thanks." He returned to his ute and with a wave, he drove away. As he checked his rear-view mirror, he discovered Henk watching him leave.

He couldn't make the man suspicious.

But if he wasn't mistaken, Henk really didn't want him speaking to Annisa.

Which meant Zamira was probably right about him.

Damn it.

***

Zamira checked her phone for the umpteenth time. Almost midday and Jeremy still hadn't called. How long did it take to quote for repairs?

She sat in the back corner of Mai's bakery, pretending to read a comic. But it was hard to concentrate.

Finally her phone rang and she snatched it up, nearly dropping it on the floor in her haste. "Hello?"

"It's Jeremy. I didn't get to see her."

Disappointment flooded her. "Why not?"

"Henk said she was working. I asked him to call me when she got home, said I liked to check on all the people I rescue."

It was a good excuse. "Do you think he will?"

"I don't know." Jeremy sighed. "Something's odd though. No one was there except Henk. They shouldn't all be working."

She agreed. "Can we find out where they're employed?"

"I'll ask around at football this afternoon."

She raised her eyebrows. "You play?" She enjoyed watching Aussie Rules football, the action, the physicality of it, the men in short shorts.

"Yeah. My game's at two if you want to watch a bunch of blokes run around a field."

It would give her something to do aside from fretting and Jeremy would look good in shorts. "Where?"

"The town oval." He gave directions. "Can you remember them this time?"

She rolled her eyes. "Yes. I might see you there." She hung up and sighed. At least she'd found Annisa. Should she let her mother know? Best not until she had more details. Her mother was likely to call the police immediately.

What now? Zamira couldn't exactly door knock on every house in town to find her cousin. But she could explore the town, familiarise herself with it just in case.

She left the bakery and drove around making note of where the hospital, school and police station were and eventually ended up at the tourist centre again. The day was cloudy and cool, but no rain was forecast. Inside, she went over to the racks of tourist brochures and pamphlets. There was a lot to do in Blackbridge from whale watching and deep-sea fishing, to myriad wineries and food places; cheese factory, ice cream factory, olive groves and lavender and berry farms, plus a bunch of artisans and crafts people. It was a creative area.

The Vale winery looked like a quirky place for lunch, its decor classy yet with whimsical touches. Perhaps she could take some photos while she was there. She had planned on practising her photography on her holiday. She plugged the directions into her phone and drove along the winding road, beneath the canopies of huge karri trees. Forest gave way to rolling farmland and then forest took over again. Cows, sheep and alpacas grazed on the green hills and cute farmhouses puffed smoke from their chimneys. Beautiful.

The winery carpark was half full and surrounded by towering gum trees. No one braved the cold to sit at the tables underneath the restaurant which was raised on stilts. To one side the rows of grapevines stretched up the hill. She got her camera out of her bag and shot a couple of photos of the vines. It really was pretty and blue wrens flittered around the grevillea bushes lining the path up to the restaurant. She stopped at a distance, using her zoom lens to capture them when they were still — a difficult task.

Some of the tension fell away as she randomly took photos of birds and flowers and whatever captured her interest. She walked around the restaurant to a small playground for children and a little further away stood a couple of large silver sheds. Probably where they made the wine. She snapped a couple of photos, zooming in to frame the door as some workers came outside. Asian men, possibly Malaysian and dressed in dark blue workmen's gear. She took more photos as they walked into the vineyard.

Could they be some of Henk's workers?

"What are you doing?" The demand had Zamira whirling around to face a woman in her forties, hands on her hips and a deep scowl on her face.

Zamira forced a smile. "Taking a few photos before lunch."

The woman scowled. "No photos allowed."

"Oh, I'm sorry. I didn't realise." She tucked her camera back into her bag, glad she'd got some shots before the woman had appeared. "It's fascinating to see where the wine comes from." She widened her smile, tried for super friendly. "Do you run tours of the winery?"

"No. Tastings are at the restaurant."

Zamira blinked. This woman had a lot to learn about customer service. Though she was dressed in work gear, so perhaps she didn't often deal with the public. She bit her tongue rather than snap back. Her mother had ingrained it into her to be polite and apologetic in the face of conflict. "I'll go inside now."

When Zamira reached the top of the stairs, she glanced back. The woman still watched her.

Zamira frowned, tempted to leave rather than stay for lunch. But the delicious smells wafting from the restaurant changed her mind. She wouldn't let one woman spoil her day.

And at least she had a lead on where Henk's workers could be.

***

Jeremy pulled into the town oval a little before two and scanned the carpark for Zamira's white hire car. Plenty of utes and four-wheel drives but no little white car with a logo on the side. He ignored the twinge of disappointment. Stupid to think she'd want to sit outside on a cold day and watch a small-town football game. Most of their spectators were family members, or teenagers looking for a place to hang out.

"Jeremy, over here." His friend, Kim waved at him from where he was speaking with Jamie and Adam.

He wandered over. "How's things?"

Kim grinned. "Busy. The new delivery service is proving to be a hit. No one wants to go out on a wet winter's night."

"That's great." He glanced at Jamie. "You going to be at the motocross next weekend?"

"Yeah, if I can weld up my frame before then. Kit's

been too busy being a newlywed to help."

"I can do it after work. Give me a call." The more helpful he was, the more likely they'd keep him around.

Jamie grinned. "Thanks, mate."

"What about you?" Kim asked. "I heard you rescued a woman from a burning building."

It felt like a lifetime ago. "Yeah. Thursday night." A waterproof dressing protected the couple of stitches in his hand. It would hurt to mark the ball, but his team needed him to make up the numbers. He'd manage the pain. His attention was caught by the other team walking out on the field in black and white striped jerseys, Henk in the lead. "Any of you know where Henk's migrants are working?"

Jamie shook his head. "Mum and Dad wanted to employ one to help at the cheese factory, but they all had jobs."

"A couple might work at the Vale winery," Kim said. "They need help now Richard is ill."

"Why do you want to know?" Adam asked.

"Got a couple of big jobs coming up," Jeremy lied.

Kim frowned. "You should ask Nicholas. He's looking for construction work now his development has almost wrapped up."

"I will." The umpire blew the whistle to get them onto the oval. "I've gotta put my stuff down." He jogged into the locker rooms and dropped his backpack on one of the benches. If Henk was here, it could mean no one else was at his house. He looked at his phone. No, Zamira out there on her own was asking for trouble.

"Hurry up, Mendelson."

Jeremy turned at the shout, saw Jamie waiting for him at the door. "Coming." He dropped his phone back into his backpack and jogged out to start the game.

***

Zamira parked at the town oval as the game started. She sat inside her car and scanned the players, finding Jeremy out on the oval in a red and white striped singlet. As she watched, he was tackled by a player in a black and white jersey and she gasped. Henk. If he was here, then he wasn't at his property. Annisa might be back from work by now.

It was the perfect opportunity.

She started the engine and drove out of town, her heart beating heavily in her chest. Only Henk had seen her when she'd dropped by yesterday on the pretence of being lost. She shouldn't raise anyone's suspicions, particularly if she bypassed the main house and went straight to the tents.

The way out there was familiar now and she drove confidently down the gravel road, past Jeremy's letterbox to Henk's gate.

His very large, metal *closed* gate that screamed stay away. It was the type that required a passcode to get through. On the top of one of the pillars was a security camera pointing directly at her.

Damn it. She accelerated down the street until she was out of view. What now? Should she try the fire access track again? The electric fence was bound to be on and she didn't feel like getting zapped today. What other options did she have?

Annisa may already be inside the compound or she might still be working. Should Zamira wait inside Jeremy's drive in case she returned?

It might be a fool's errand.

Tomorrow would be better. Annisa would go out to work and Zamira could follow her. Then she'd definitely be able to speak to her.

Satisfied with her plan, she did a U-turn at the end of the road and drove back to town.

***

By half-time Jeremy's team was ahead by a goal. He scanned the crowd as he slugged back water and used his towel to dry the sweat from his body. A lone figure huddled on a bench seat in a dark red jacket, a camera lifted to her face. Zamira.

Pleasure filled him as he wandered over to her. "I didn't think you'd make it." She pointed the camera at him and took a couple of photos.

When she lowered it, her smile was cautious. "I enjoy watching football."

He raised an eyebrow. "Who do you follow?"

"Carlton."

He winced. "My sympathies."

She laughed, the sound light and free. "They're doing better this year than last year."

"They couldn't have been worse."

"True. Your team is playing well."

He shrugged off the compliment and flexed his aching hand. "We have fun." The breeze was cold and he shifted downwind of her in case he stank.

"Is your hand all right?"

He hid it behind his back. "Yeah. Old injury, just a little sore."

"I've got some painkillers in my bag if you want."

"That'd be great." Another half a game with the ball slapping into his hand would be torture.

She handed him the packet and he swallowed two tablets. As he gave them back, she hesitated. "Do you want to get a drink after the game?"

His chest swelled and he smiled. A date.

"There's something I wanted to ask you."

He exhaled. Right. Of course. Her cousin. "Sure. I'll meet you back here after I've showered." He hunched his shoulders, wrapped his arms around his waist as he jogged back to his team members.

Kim grinned at him. "Who are you chatting up?"

"Zamira. She's in town on holiday and we're going for a drink after the game."

Adam shook his head. "I need to watch and learn. I don't know how you pick them up so fast." He rubbed his bare chin. "Maybe I should grow a beard."

Jeremy laughed. Let them think they'd just met. Less questions that way. "It's all about confidence." Normally he didn't care when women turned him down. Long-term relationships weren't for him.

Love lasted only until you did something wrong. His family had proven that.

He rubbed at the pain in his chest as the umpire blew his whistle. "Let's beat these guys. I've got a date to get to." He winked at his friends and jogged out on the field.

Chapter 5

It was a pleasure watching Jeremy play football. His red and white striped singlet exposed his muscled biceps and the short shorts revealed his legs were equally toned. He was also a good player, scoring goals, tackling the opposition and keeping the ball moving. Zamira took photos of the action, playing with her camera settings to get a sharper image, changing lenses to zoom in on the action. Focusing on her technique and trying to get the right shot calmed her, allowed her worries about Annisa to fade a little. A couple of times she caught Jeremy's face screwed up in pain as he marked the ball. His hand was hurting more than he let on.

Despite living in Melbourne, the home of Australian Rules football, she hadn't been to a live game in a long time. Not since her best friend had moved away and their weekly tradition ended. It didn't feel right going with anyone else. This was a different atmosphere. Kids played chasey on the grass and the small crowd yelled encouragement and beeped their car horns when their team scored. It was a community.

She'd witnessed the same thing at the beach after lunch. She'd taken photos of the surf as the waves crashed onto the sand and people walked their dogs, stopping to chat for a good ten minutes or more. It was nice to take the time to soak up the day, observe life.

She shivered as a gust of icy wind hit her. After going out to Henk's, she'd parked at the bed and breakfast and walked down to the oval. Her hire car was too noticeable with the logo on the side door and she didn't want to attract Henk's attention. The hot chocolate from the canteen was all she had to warm her.

When the final siren wailed, Zamira couldn't wait to get out of the cold. Jeremy walked with his team mates into the locker rooms and she stayed where she was. Hopefully his shower wouldn't take long.

The image of Jeremy naked and wet popped into her head and she blinked rapidly to clear it. It was so unlike her to sexualise a man. She barely dated anymore, unless her parents set her up with some new suitor. She'd had too many failures at university. She blamed her parents for sending her to an all-girls high school and discouraging any interaction with boys she wasn't related to. Her uncertainty, part of her longing to widen her experiences and the other part echoing her mother's warnings had led to some awkward hook-ups. She'd had one short-term boyfriend, who after their first dismal attempts in the bedroom had agreed they should just be friends. At least they'd had fun discussing the latest Marvel comic or movie.

She sighed.

But she wasn't ready to give into her parents' pressure to marry someone of their choosing. She wanted to have her career on track before she settled down.

Around her car engines growled as people left. The canteen had rolled its shutters down already so no chance for more hot chocolate. She hugged her rain jacket tighter around her. Maybe she should wait near the locker rooms, out of the wind, but a lot of people mingled over there. They'd wonder who she was.

She rubbed her arms and stayed seated.

Ten minutes later Jeremy came out, his hair damp and a backpack slung over one shoulder. He wore jeans and a dark blue woollen jumper, and he chatted to a couple of his team mates.

Zamira stood and then hesitated. He might be talking privately. She should wait until he approached her.

He waved her over.

She crossed her arms, then uncrossed them again as she approached. The other men studied her.

"Zamira, this is Kim and Jamie," Jeremy said.

"Hi." Kim was of Asian descent, with short dark hair and dark eyes, and around her height, but Jamie was a lot taller and had some kind of Mediterranean ancestry, brown hair, brown eyes and his designer beard trimmed to perfection. Both attractive, but neither stirred her nerves like Jeremy did.

"Nice to meet you." Jamie stuck out his hand and she shook it, his grip firm. He turned to Jeremy. "I'll call you about the bike."

Jeremy nodded and waved as they left. Then he turned his attention to her, and his gaze was all encompassing.

She swallowed. "Ah, where do you suggest we go for a drink?"

"The pub will be packed," he said. "Everyone goes for a drink after the game, so it will be noisy. It might be a good place to talk without being overheard."

Nice and public was good. "If you give me directions, I'll meet you there."

"Follow my car. I know what you're like with directions." He winked.

She deserved that. "I walked down."

"Then I'll give you a lift. It's not far and I'll drop you back when we're done."

Don't get into a car with a strange man. Zamira wished she could shut her mother's voice off in her head. There'd been so many warnings over the years. "I don't want to put you out."

"Don't sweat it." He gestured for her to follow as he walked towards the carpark.

It would be fine. He was being nice.

His ute was very much a work vehicle. Its silver canopy had sides that could fold open and on top was a ladder and other bits of equipment. When she opened the passenger door, chocolate bar wrappers littered the floor and she wrinkled her nose.

"Sorry. Give me a second." Jeremy reached over from the driver's side and picked up the wrappers. "I don't have many passengers."

And he didn't clean up after himself. Strange that the outside of his house had been so neat and tidy.

The pub was on the corner of the main street, across the road from the river. Its burgundy brick walls gave it a rich dignified air, and as Jeremy opened the door, raised voices and the scent of beer wafted out. Some country rock tune thumped over the speakers.

Jeremy bent closer to her and pointed. "Grab the corner booth while it's free. I'll get us drinks. What would you like?"

She fumbled for her purse. She didn't want him to buy her drink. She'd asked him here.

He placed a hand on hers. "My shout. You can get the next round."

His smile melted her concerns. "Ginger ale, please."

He looked surprised but nodded. "Won't be long."

Zamira headed for the corner booth and slid inside, choosing the far side so she had a view of the rest of the pub. She recognised Jamie and Kim with a group of other men. Jeremy had chosen a drink with her over his friends.

She'd be quick, ask him about the winery and what time the workers left Henk's place and then leave. A few older men sat by the bar, chatting and then another group of men walked in, Henk in the lead. She slid further into the booth, not wanting him to see her.

He sat at a long table not far from her, but didn't look in her direction. They spoke about today's game and Henk sounded unhappy they'd lost.

Jeremy chatted to an old man sitting on one of the bar stools. He had their two drinks in front of him, but he didn't look to be in a rush.

That was one of the differences between a big city like Melbourne and this little country town. Everything took longer because everyone knew each other.

"Sorry." Jeremy slid into the booth and placed her pint of ginger ale in front of her. "When Mr Corson gets talking, it's hard to get away."

"It's fine." She sipped her drink. The ginger ale had just the right amount of bite. "Thank you."

"Don't sweat it. Did you enjoy the game?"

She nodded, her thumb tracing the raised lettering on her pendant. She could manage simple conversation. "You've got some good players."

Jeremy grinned. "We do all right for a small town. What did you get up to this morning?"

"I went to the bakery and then out to the Vale winery." Which was a good segue.

"So, you've had plenty of good food then," Jeremy said. "I was going to ask you to share a bowl of chips."

She shook her head. "I've eaten way too much today."

Silence fell between them as Jeremy studied her. The intensity of his gaze made her body flush. No man had ever given her such singular focus before.

"What did you want to ask me?" He sipped his beer.

She blinked and her face heated. Of course. The reason she was here. "When I was at the winery today, I saw some Asian workers," she said. "I wondered whether they might be from Henk's."

Jeremy raised his eyebrows. "Could be. Kim thought a couple worked there."

She would have to go back. "A woman told me off for taking photos. Do you think she knows what Henk is doing?"

He frowned. "Short, curly brown hair, permanent scowl on her face?"

She smiled at his apt description. "Yes."

"That'd be Kay. She's taken over running the place since her father got dementia. She's always like that."

Oh. A parent with dementia couldn't be easy.

"Any other questions?" he asked.

He probably wanted to get back to his friends. "I might go back tomorrow. Find out if their situation is like Annisa's."

He pursed his lips. "You might not be able to talk to them. The Pattons don't let people into the winery area. They had a small fire up there last spring. When we arrived, they told us they had handled it and we weren't needed. Wouldn't even let us ensure they'd put it out properly."

"That's odd."

"Richard — that's Kay's father — has always been slightly paranoid. Believes everyone wants to steal their wine-making secrets."

"I didn't realise there was so much involved."

"Me neither."

A waitress brought over a basket of chips with a few bottles of different sauces. "Thanks, Dee." Jeremy popped a chip into his mouth, hissing a bit at the heat. When he swallowed, he said, "Help yourself."

Zamira took a chip to be polite though she wasn't hungry. "Do you know what time the workers usually leave Henk's place in the morning?"

"I sometimes see the bus go out when I leave for jobs around seven."

She sipped her drink working up the courage to ask her next question. She cleared her throat. "Would you mind if I waited on your driveway in the morning for it to go past?"

He frowned. "What are you going to do?"

"I thought I could follow it and find out where Annisa is working."

"I don't know. It might be safer if I ask around some more. Someone might know."

"But how long will that take?"

Jeremy shrugged. "I'm seeing one of the biggest gossips in town tomorrow."

Maybe that was the most sensible way. If she changed her mind, she could wait on the road near the fire break. "All right. Thank you." The silence dragged out between them. She should have thought of other things to say. "Ah, were you born in Blackbridge?"

"Moved here from Albany about five years ago."

"Why?"

He shrugged. "It's a nice town and the local builder wasn't the best. The guy I worked for kept getting called out here and he preferred to work in Albany and avoid the drive. So I decided to branch out to my own business here."

"Did you build your own house?"

He nodded. "Haven't quite finished the inside the way I want it yet."

"It's really beautiful."

His smile was wide. "Thanks."

She gasped. His eyes sparkled when he smiled like that. Her heart raced and she couldn't look away even though she was staring.

Someone came up to the table and Zamira ripped her gaze from Jeremy and her eyes widened. Henk.

A large man, like a rugby player, he'd been a little too friendly when she'd stopped to ask for directions and had treated her like she was a complete ditz. She'd been partially relieved when Jeremy had arrived.

"Annisa should be home by now," he said to Jeremy. "You can drop by if you want." He smirked at Zamira. "You found the retreat?"

She nodded, her mind whirling. She couldn't miss the opportunity to see Annisa, but how to convince Jeremy to take her? Only one thing came to mind and her mother-sounding alarms shrieked at her not to be stupid. She gritted her teeth. She could do this. She narrowed her eyes, tried to look suspicious. "Who's Annisa?"

Jeremy sat back at her change in tone. "She's a woman I rescued from a fire the other day."

"Oh." She sat straighter. If Henk already believed she was a ditz, she would act like one. She tried for breathless. "How brave!"

"Not really." He bit his lip. "I wanted to see if Annisa was recovering."

She hesitated. Modern women took control of their own wants and desires all the time. Hopefully Jeremy wouldn't get the wrong impression. "You should go." She glanced at Henk and then leaned closer to Jeremy, lowered her voice, her chest tight. Men like Henk would take this at face value. This had to work. "Perhaps we could visit her on our way back to your place?" She fluttered her eyelashes and pictured her mother having a heart attack.

Jeremy's eyebrows raised and he stuttered, "Sure." He winked at Henk. "How about we go now?"

Crap. He realised she was acting, didn't he? Zamira left her half full drink there and forced herself to take the hand Jeremy held out to her. "I'd love to." Her smile felt fake.

Henk scowled. "I didn't mean to interrupt."

"You're not. I was going to suggest we go somewhere quieter." Jeremy grinned at her. "Shall we?"

She nodded, nausea welling in her stomach. All the way out of the pub she felt Henk's gaze on her. Could she trust Jeremy? He had to know she wasn't serious.

She let out a deep breath as the door shut behind her.

Jeremy's low chuckle stirred something in her belly. "That was quick thinking."

Relief filled her, but as she went to pull her hand out of his, his grip tightened. "Just in case Henk follows us."

She nodded. His firm, slightly calloused grip made her feel safe and she missed his touch when they got into his ute.

He didn't start the car immediately. "You switched to breathless airhead in a blink of an eye." He glanced at her. "Should I be worried everything you say is an act?"

She frowned. "Was I that convincing?"

He nodded.

She grinned. "Wow. I nearly failed drama in high school." She clicked her seatbelt into place. Jeremy still waited for an answer. Guilt hit her. She hadn't considered the situation from his point of view. He was trusting her word, like she had to trust his. And at least when this was over, she could go home. He lived here, would need to answer to his community. She touched his hand. "Back there in the pub was an act, but everything else I've told you is the truth. I'm here to help my cousin."

He stared at her a moment longer before he started the car. "All right. Let's get out there before Henk heads home."

He wasn't convinced, but seeing Annisa would prove her story.

The sun sat low in the sky and shadows stretched over the road. It would be dark soon and the kangaroos would be out looking for a meal. Jeremy drove confidently and it wasn't long before they turned down his road.

"Better let me do the talking when we get there," he said. "We don't know who to trust and it will look odd if you talk to her first."

Zamira gripped her pendant, rubbing the raised inscription for calm. This was it. If she could get enough information, she could call Border Force in the morning and report it.

Jeremy drove past the house towards the tents. Men stood around in groups talking, but they watched as Jeremy drove up and got out. Zamira followed him.

"G'day. I'm looking for Annisa," he called to the group.

One of the men pointed to the last tent in the row. Zamira's heart raced and she moved forward, only to be stopped by Jeremy taking her hand. "Me first," he murmured. "You're not supposed to know her."

"Sorry."

They walked over to the tent and Jeremy called, "Annisa, are you there?"

No response.

"Annisa, *saya… ah… bapak api.*"

Zamira swallowed her laugh. "Try *ahli bomba.*"

Annisa stuck her head out of the tent. She looked at Jeremy first and then her mouth dropped open. "Miri?" she whispered.

Tears sprang to Zamira's eyes and she nodded. Annisa leapt out of the tent but before Zamira could hug her, Jeremy stepped in front, hugging Annisa. "People are watching," he hissed.

Annisa was no longer the lanky, awkward child Zamira remembered. Instead she'd matured, grown into her limbs and was tall and elegant, her wide brown eyes drawing attention.

Quickly Zamira explained what was going on. Annisa stepped back from Jeremy, brushing a tear from her eye. "Come into my tent," she said in Malaysian and gestured.

Jeremy shook his head. "Tell her it's too easy for people to listen in. Can we go for a walk?"

Zamira repeated what he said, itching to hug Annisa. She hadn't seen her for six years.

Annisa nodded and led them towards the back of the property, away from the men. It was almost dark and hopefully they wouldn't be able to tell who was talking.

"Are you all right?" Zamira asked quietly.

"I am healthy. This man rescued me." She smiled at Jeremy and switched to English. "Thank you."

"You're welcome."

"How did you get to Australia?" Zamira asked.

"A man came to our village. He said he could get a work visa for me and I didn't have to pay much up front. He said I could pay the rest from my earnings in Australia." Tears glistened in her eyes. "I wanted the same opportunities you had, so I agreed without telling *ibu* and *ayah*. Henk and a woman picked me up from the airport. They drove me here and told me to give them my passport for safe-keeping. I trusted them."

Without her passport she had little other identification. "Then what happened?"

"I started work as a cleaner. Henk told me he would pay me every fortnight, but when the first fortnight arrived, he only gave me twenty dollars." She glanced at Zamira. "I knew it should be more, but when I asked him about it, he said the rest was for food, board and the visa."

It was all too common a story.

"He wouldn't let me call anyone or go into town. When I told him I wanted to leave, he said I would be arrested, that my visa wasn't real and I would be deported." She gripped Zamira's hand. "I didn't think I was doing the wrong thing."

"Don't worry. We'll get you out of here." She squeezed Annisa's hand and released it. "Are you safe?"

Annisa shook her head. "I lit the fire, hoping to escape in the confusion but the doors outside were locked. It wasn't until the fire alarm went off that someone let us out. I hid upstairs waiting for the firemen to arrive, but they took so long and I got confused."

"What about the men? Are they in the same situation?"

Annisa shrugged. "No one will talk about it. One man did tell me women never stayed more than a couple of months, but I don't know why."

Zamira tensed. She needed to call the Task Force. Annisa's statement had to be enough to get them to put a stop to this.

"We need to go." Jeremy's deep voice made her jump. "Henk's car is coming up the drive."

Goosebumps leapt to her skin as she spun around and saw the headlights of a dark four-wheel drive coming towards them. Jeremy moved back towards the tents.

It was too soon.

Annisa clutched her arm. "He's coming. Take me with you."

Zamira's heart clenched. She couldn't take Annisa without a damn good excuse. Not without blowing Border Force's mission. "I will get you out of here," she said. "But I can't take you now."

She clung to Zamira. "Why not?"

"I need to help everyone. If Henk knows why I'm here, he might move the men somewhere else." She shivered in the cold and her eyes widened. "Jeremy, can you suggest to Henk that Annisa stays with you? It's freezing tonight and she shouldn't be in a tent." The light from the four-wheel drive illuminated his face. She was asking a lot of him.

Jeremy moved in front of them to block them from the vehicle and gently separated their hands. He sighed. "I'll try. Tell her where I live and warn her about the electric fence. If this doesn't work, she can come over at any time."

"Thank you." He was truly amazing. Zamira translated and nodded towards Jeremy's property.

"OK, now remember you're totally hot for me," he said.

She nodded. "If this doesn't work, I'll get you out of here as soon as I can," she said quietly to her cousin.

Annisa stepped back from them as Henk wandered over.

"Didn't think you'd still be here."

Jeremy rubbed his beard. "Turns out my dodgy Indonesian is worse than I thought. It's kind of hard to translate what she's saying."

Henk laughed. "Yeah, I get that too."

Zamira tugged on Jeremy's hand, accidentally pressing her breasts into his side. "It's so cold out here. Surely she doesn't have to stay in this little tent."

His sharp intake of breath made her body warm. She went to step away, but he wrapped an arm around her waist, keeping her close. "You're right." He glanced at Henk. "My offer still stands. I'm happy for Annisa to stay at my place until the dorm is fixed. She won't want to share with one of the men."

Henk studied them. "I'd imagine she might cramp your style." His grin was lewd.

Zamira's skin crawled. Think bimbo. "Oh, well, I can be quiet." She giggled, hating herself.

Henk frowned. "No, I can't allow it," he said. "Duty of care. I can't let her stay with a single man. You understand."

They were so close. "I'll be there."

"Sorry, missy. I don't know you from a bar of soap and Annisa shouldn't be exposed to what you two will be getting up to."

She opened her mouth to disagree and Jeremy squeezed her butt, making her jump.

"Yeah, good point." He grinned at Henk. "I'll see you later." With his arm firmly around Zamira, he steered her towards his car, his hand caressing her side. "Sorry," he whispered. "I'll stop when we get into the car, but we have to make this convincing."

She said nothing. His gentle touch on her skin sent her whole body into a tizz, clamouring for attention.

Then as she got into the car, she saw Annisa's

forlorn face. Jeremy's touch had been an act, a way of supporting her, helping her save her cousin. There was nothing sexual in it.

Her only goal was to rescue Annisa. She needed to remember that.

Chapter 6

Jeremy missed Zamira's warmth against his side as he got into his ute. She fit so nicely against him and it wasn't a hardship to pretend they had a thing going on. If only it was true. She smelled like peppermint and when she'd pressed her breasts into his side, he'd forgotten to think for a moment. He was almost glad Henk had refused to let Annisa go with them — it gave him more time alone with Zamira. He rolled his eyes. Talk about selfish.

It had been too long since his last date.

Now with a little distance from her, his brain started working again. He drove towards the road. "We'd better stop at my house, in case Henk's watching."

"That's fine."

He glanced at her, but couldn't read her expression. "What did Annisa say?"

Zamira sighed. "She's trapped here. Henk has her passport, takes most of her pay and she's not allowed to leave."

Jeremy's chest tightened. He hadn't wanted confirmation his neighbour was a bastard. "So what now?"

"I hope she can escape to your place tonight." She wrapped her pendant around her finger. "I'll call work in the morning. See if I can talk to someone from the Task Force." She stared out the window and he squeezed her hand.

Then he frowned. "Aren't you on the Task Force?"

She sucked in a breath and he removed his hand, turning into his own drive. "Of course. I meant I had no phone reception last night out here."

"There's reception at my place." Shouldn't she be keen to call them in?

"I'll wait until tomorrow. There's nothing they can do tonight." She smiled.

Yeah, something like this probably shouldn't be rushed.

What should he do about her? His body couldn't tell she was acting and really wanted to explore the apparent spark between them. But she'd made it clear that it had been an act.

She was so far out of his league anyway. She was educated, had an important job with plenty of travel and probably had her eye on the corporate ladder. The only ladder he climbed was to get onto a roof. She even wore black pants to watch a football game. Did she own a pair of jeans?

Still, maybe she'd be happy to slum it with a blue collar builder for a few days.

He parked outside the shed and Fetch trotted over. Jeremy grinned. He was after his dinner, otherwise he wouldn't have bothered leaving the porch.

He stroked the dog and gestured to Zamira. "Come inside."

He pushed the back door open. "Do you want something to eat?" He was starving, having only had time to eat a few chips before Henk had come to their table.

"A drink would be nice."

He cleared the sketches he'd been working on from the kitchen bench. "Have a seat." He pointed to the bench stools and she slid onto one. Carrying the plans over to his table, he hesitated. No room there, or on the coffee table. He dumped them on his diary and glanced around the room. Paper, half-made models and half-finished projects lay on almost every flat surface. In his defence, he didn't often have people out to his place. He had no one he wanted to impress and no one to worry about disappointing. Still Zamira must think him a total slob.

He shouldn't care what she thought. He opened the fridge. "I've got beer, soft drink, tea, coffee, water."

"Tea, please."

He switched on the kettle and then stared into the fridge. He'd finished the casserole for lunch and that had been the last of his leftovers. He needed to go grocery shopping. Getting out a block of cheese, he then examined the bread in his bread bin. Still good, if a little stale.

Toasted cheese sandwiches would have to do.

Quickly he buttered the bread, slid the cheese on top with some cracked pepper and put them into his sandwich maker. Then he made Zamira a cup of tea.

"I'm sorry I interrupted your dinner at the pub."

He shrugged. "Don't sweat it. This will do."

She reached out, brushed his hand and the softness of her fingers sent a thrill through him. "I appreciate what you're doing, Jeremy."

No way could he resist those deep brown eyes. "I'm happy to help." He checked his sandwiches and his phone rang. Jamie.

"Hey, mate. What can I do for you?"

"Shit, you're probably with that woman. Sorry, it can wait."

Jeremy chuckled. "It's fine. What do you want?"

"Can I come out tomorrow afternoon with the bike?"

He dug out his diary. "I should be home by five."

"Thanks. See you then."

He hung up and then slid his nicely browned sandwiches onto a plate. "Sure you don't want one?"

Zamira smiled. "I'm fine. They smell good. I haven't had a cheese toastie since I was at university."

The thought of her at university, eating standard uni student food made him smile. "What did you study?"

"Commerce and political science."

She had to be pretty brainy.

"What about you?"

She had to be kidding. "No university for me. I didn't even finish high school. Started an apprenticeship with my dad at fifteen." His lungs constricted. Would he ever be able to remember his father without the pain? He was lucky his father's best friend, Pete had agreed to take on his apprenticeship afterwards.

"He's a builder too?"

Jeremy didn't correct her tense. Instead he nodded and took a big bite of his sandwich.

"Do your parents live in Blackbridge?"

Jeremy scowled and swallowed. "Mum's in Albany." Or had been the last time he'd spoken to someone who knew her.

"Any siblings?"

"Two younger sisters." He needed to get the conversation off him and his family. That was a dead-end zone. "What about you?"

"Two sisters as well." She sipped her tea. "They both live in Melbourne with my parents. They won't leave home until they marry."

He had no idea where his sisters lived or if they were married. "Must be a good home then."

Her smile was a little sad. "It is, but there are a lot of expectations. It's nice to visit."

He understood that. "So where do you live?"

"I've got a little apartment in Melbourne, not far from work."

He grimaced. "I couldn't deal with neighbours so close and no backyard."

Zamira smiled. "Well you do have a beautiful home. I can see why you love it here."

Her praise washed over him. He'd worked hard for what he had with little help from others after he'd finished his apprenticeship. "Thanks." He got up and put his empty plate in the dishwasher and switched it on. He turned back to Zamira. "I'd say the house isn't normally this messy, but I'd be lying." He flicked on the kettle.

She moved over to the table. "Are these customer projects?"

"Some are." He stood next to her, inhaling a minty scent, and had a strong temptation to place an arm around her and pull her close. Instead, he handed her a couple of sketches from the table. "I'm doing a couple of granny flats for some clients. That's the floor plan for the first one. It's pretty straightforward, but the other is on a sloping block so I need to make a few adjustments."

"Do you work by yourself?"

"I get help in when I need it." But working alone was far preferable. Then he didn't have to worry about hurting anyone.

"Does your dad still work?"

He flinched, stepped away from her. "No. He's

dead." He strode back to the kitchen, his hand shaking as he poured his cup of tea.

"I'm sorry." Her gentle tone made him squeeze his eyes closed as his chest tightened.

Finally, he shrugged. "It is what it is." He looked up. The compassion in her eyes had him gritting his teeth. "Do you want another cuppa?"

"No, thank you."

He added milk and then carried the mug out of the kitchen and over to his worn couches away from her. She followed. "Did you make your letterbox?"

The change of subject had him blinking. "Yeah." He sat on his couch and her knee brushed his as she sat. He told his body to behave. Something about her ticked all his boxes physically. He wanted to run his hands through her short hair, tug her closer and cover her mouth with his. He shifted away as she spoke.

"It's lovely. It's what made me come down your drive and not Henk's. I figured anyone who cared about their letterbox couldn't be too crazy."

He grunted. "Appearances can be deceiving."

"I know. When I first saw you, I thought you were a cave man."

Her admission surprised a laugh out of him, and he rubbed his beard. "Are you suggesting I need to shave?"

"No! It's just you looked a little scary, a little reclusive, but it turns out you're incredibly nice."

She was right about being a recluse. Although he helped people whenever he could, and socialised at the football or motocross, he preferred being alone. Less ways he could disappoint people or get hurt. "Thanks."

She glanced at the time. "I should probably go. I've taken up too much of your time already."

He ignored the pang in his chest and placed his half

full mug on the coffee table. "I'll get my keys."

"Oh, I forgot you drove me here." She gripped her pendant. "Finish your tea at least. I'm sorry to be an imposition."

He wouldn't use that word to describe her. "I'm enjoying having you here."

She flushed. "I'm enjoying being here too."

Her eyes met his and darkened. Maybe she was attracted to him. Some women thought the cave man look was hot. He smirked.

She blinked and reached for a cardboard model of a birdhouse. "Wh… What's this?" Her voice was a little breathless.

He sipped his tea and relaxed. "It's going to be a bird house. When I'm happy with the concept, I'll make it out of wood."

She turned to him, eyes wide. "You designed this?"

He nodded.

"It's so… quaint. It makes me wish I had a garden I could put it in."

He grinned. "I'll make you one when you do." It wasn't anything special, but it was nice to be appreciated. "What are your plans for tomorrow?"

She shrugged, a delicate lift of her shoulders. "It depends if Annisa gets away and what Border Force say." She tilted her head. "I might be able to show Annisa around Blackbridge. Can you recommend any good places to go?"

He frowned. "There are lookouts all along the coast and some pretty beaches. Green's Pool is a nice spot." He thought about it. "If you want more bush and trees, the Valley of the Giants treetop walk is about an hour's drive from here, and the national park has a few walking trails through it. You could probably pick up a map at the tourist bureau."

She retrieved a notebook from her bag and made some notes. Her fancy looking camera sat inside. "You must be serious about your photos."

"I'm an amateur at best. I'd like to get better, but I don't practise much."

"Can I see what you've taken?"

"Ah… sure." She switched the camera on and showed him how to flick through the shots.

They were pretty good. She'd taken sharp action shots of the football game and also photos of the winery. Her shot selection wasn't what a normal person would take. She zoomed in, focusing on a door, a flower or leaf, looking at the object in a different way. Seeing more than people would if they only glanced at it. Hopefully she wouldn't look too closely at him. She wouldn't like what she saw. "These are great." He handed the camera back to her, his fingers brushing her wrist.

That jolt again. He should take her home before he did something he might regret. "Ready to go?"

"Oh. Of course." She stuffed her camera back in her bag and got to her feet. She hesitated, opened her mouth and then closed it again.

He chuckled. "What do you want to ask?"

She screwed up her face in the cutest way. "I was thinking… I know I'm being such a pain and I hate to ask you for more…"

Jeremy braced himself. "What do you need?"

"Well, it's just I told Annisa to come here when she could."

He nodded. "I'll call you if she arrives."

Zamira sighed. "Thanks." She moved towards the back door. "What are your plans for tomorrow?"

"I'm laying the slab for one of the granny flats." He grabbed his jacket from the laundry. "Then I've got to finish the hen house remodelling I've been working on." He handed over her jacket. "Feel free to hang out here if you want. The back door's always unlocked and Fetch likes visitors."

"Thank you, that's kind of you."

Kind. Nice. Not words he deserved to hear.

He grabbed his keys and led the way out of the house.

***

When Zamira pried her eyes open the next morning it was bright outside. She checked the time and groaned. Already eight o'clock. Though she wasn't particularly surprised. She'd lain in bed tossing and turning after Jeremy had dropped her off. She should have been agonising over Annisa, trying to figure out how to get her out, but instead her mind was full of Jeremy, the way he smiled at her, the sexy way his eyes had widened and deepened when she'd said she enjoyed being at his place, the shivers running through her when he'd accidentally brushed her wrist.

She'd never been so worked up about a man.

It was foolish.

Her mother would be horrified she was considering a holiday fling. Good girls didn't sleep around, especially not with ruggedly handsome men.

No, good girls waited until they met a nice man with good prospects and dated extensively before even seeing the inside of his place. Judging from her dating failures at university her mother was probably right.

But none of the men she'd dated had given her tingles the way Jeremy had. She didn't imagine he'd be bad in bed. No, he was too masculine, too confident.

Zamira rolled her eyes. Her fantasies had to stop.

She'd go home any day — as soon as Annisa was

safe. Her heart leapt and she sat up, grabbed her phone. No missed calls. No messages. Hadn't Annisa gone to Jeremy's last night?

He'd promised to call her if she did.

She gritted her teeth and then texted him. Calling would be too needy and she didn't want to disturb him at work. She'd been enough of a hassle.

Then to stop herself from staring at the phone waiting for a reply, she showered, dressed and when he still hadn't responded, headed into town for breakfast.

She parked outside the bakery. Before she called Border Force she needed a strong coffee and fortification. As she walked in, Mai waved to her. "You're becoming a regular. What would you like today?"

She should have something savoury. She spotted something on the menu that made her smile. "A cheese toastie and a flat white please." The sandwiches Jeremy had made last night had looked good. She paid and then took a seat.

The bakery was quieter today with only a couple of grandparents and grandchildren too young to be at school, and a group of middle-aged women dressed in exercise gear. The sky was clear which would be good for Jeremy. She imagined pouring concrete in the rain wouldn't be great. She huffed out a breath. And she was right back to him again.

He'd be home by five to meet whoever he'd invited over. She hadn't been brave enough to ask and it wasn't any of her business. Though he had also invited her to hang at his place, so it probably wasn't a girlfriend.

The bell above the door jingled and her heart skipped a beat. Jeremy.

He wore workman's gear today, dark blue cargo pants, steel-capped boots and a high-visibility shirt.

Smudges of grey lined his shirt, probably from the concrete he'd been pouring. He greeted Mai cheerfully and ordered a large coffee to go.

Should she go over and say hi?

He was probably sick of her.

Mai asked him about the fire and Zamira remembered she was also a fire-fighter. Jeremy glanced around the bakery and his eyes met hers. She waved, feeling like a fool.

The smile that spread across his face made her body flush.

He strode over. "Morning."

"Good morning." Focus on why she was here. "Did you see Annisa?"

His smile faltered. "No. She didn't come over."

Zamira's spirits fell. Hadn't Annisa been able to leave? Maybe she should go back to Henk's. No, she should call Border Force. She confined her panic. "Did you get the slab laid?"

"Yeah, went perfectly."

Mai brought over her coffee and toastie. "Here you go. How do you two know each other?"

Zamira glanced at him.

"Met her at the football yesterday," he said easily. "Mind if I take a seat?"

"Go ahead."

His knees brushed hers as he sat and Mai said, "I'll bring your coffee over when it's ready."

"Thanks, Mai." When she'd left, he asked, "What have you been up to?"

She winced. "Actually I've only just got up."

"You don't have to check in with work?"

"No." Telling him she was on holidays might complicate matters. "Are you between jobs?"

He nodded. "I'm about to head over to Shirley's

place to finish remodelling her hen house. She had some chickens stolen last year and since then she's been buying more and needs more space. She also wants to increase the security, so no one can simply walk in there and take them. It's part upgrade, part extension."

His mind was elsewhere, already thinking through what to do. It was fascinating.

He blinked and then added, "I'll ask her about Annisa. She knows most of what's going on in town."

"Thank you." There had to be some way she could repay him for all his help. "Can I buy you dinner?" The words popped out of her mouth.

He smiled. "I'd like that."

Her heart raced. Hell. Maybe this wasn't such a good idea. "Ah, tonight? Do you have somewhere you can recommend?" Great, now she was asking him to do the work.

He swore. "I promised Jamie I'd weld his motocross bike tonight."

"How long will it take?"

"Probably an hour or so. Jamie likes a good chat."

"How about afterwards then? I could cook you dinner at your place." What on earth was she saying? That wasn't a sensible idea. She'd be alone with him, trying her hardest to ignore the pull of attraction. No. Annisa would be with them. It would be a simple thank you dinner. Providing sustenance for someone was the perfect way of showing gratitude.

She wasn't fooling herself. She liked him.

This time his smile was slow and warm. "That could be fun. I need to go grocery shopping though. I don't have a lot in the fridge."

"I'll bring what I need with me, say about six?"

"Make it six-thirty so I have a chance to clean up."

She nodded. "All right."

Mai came over with Jeremy's take-away coffee. "Here you go."

"Thanks." He got to his feet. "I'd better keep moving. I'll see you tonight." He walked out.

Zamira slumped in her chair. What had she done?

"Are you all right?"

She'd forgotten Mai was still there. "Um, yes?"

Mai laughed and sat in Jeremy's chair. "You look a little flustered."

"I offered to cook dinner for Jeremy." She played with her pendant. "What was I thinking? I barely know him."

"Let me ease your mind. Jeremy is about the best guy you could find," Mai said. "He's genuinely nice, always lends a hand and I honestly don't know why someone hasn't snapped him up long ago."

Zamira glanced at her. "Why didn't you?"

Mai screwed up her nose. "There was never the spark. We went from strangers to friends after our first fire call-out together and there was never anything else. But I know he'd be there if I needed a hand and I trust him with my life. When you fight fires, you've got to trust your crew."

It did make Zamira feel better. "Thanks."

"So what will you cook for him?"

She groaned. "No idea. I didn't even ask if he was allergic to anything."

"He's not — we often eat together at the station." She got her phone out of her pocket. "Give me a second." She spoke briefly to someone and hung up. "OK, Kim tells me he orders stir-fries and pho from the restaurant."

Zamira frowned. "Kim?"

"My brother. He works at the local Vietnamese restaurant and Jeremy often gets take-away. He likes it spicy."

"Does Kim play football?"

Mai nodded.

"I think I met him yesterday at the game." A stir-fry wouldn't be hard. "Thank you."

Mai grinned. "No problem." She stretched. "I'd better get back to it. Drop by tomorrow and tell me how it went." She winked.

Zamira waved. Seriously, Mai just saved her life. Thank goodness for small towns.

With one issue sorted, she needed to address the other.

It was time to call Border Force.

Chapter 7

Zamira drove down the street to the park next to the river. She sat on a bench under a big Moreton Bay fig tree and stared at her phone. If she called Vince, he might fire her for getting involved. No, better if she called the hotline and remained anonymous. She dialled the number she had memorised. She followed the prompts, her heart beating heavily in her chest.

"Australian Border Force, what would you like to report?" The female voice was perky.

Zamira swallowed. "An employer sponsor breach."

Keys clacked in the background. "All right. In which state and town?"

"Blackbridge, Western Australia."

"Name of employer?"

"Henk Jennings."

"And what is the nature of the breach?"

Zamira described the situation and explained she worked for Border Force but preferred to remain anonymous. The woman occasionally asked for clarification and all the while keys clattered in the background.

Finally the woman said, "Thank you for the

information. Please be assured every report is taken seriously and read by one of our officers. Is there anything else I can help you with today?"

"Yes, this is urgent. Annisa is scared. We need to get her out as soon as possible. The Task Force is building a case at the moment. They need this information."

"I understand your concern," the woman said. "But I can't guarantee anything, unless you're willing to give me your employment details. I will flag this as a high priority but it's up to the Task Force to follow up."

Zamira clenched her jaw. Either way someone got hurt, but at least if she did something, Annisa would be safe. Zamira could find another job. She gave the woman her details. "Tell them if they don't call me today, I'll go and get her myself."

"Ma'am I really can't recommend that. It could be dangerous. Border Force are trained for this."

"And Annisa's my cousin. I won't leave her in danger." Tired of the conversation, she hung up and blew out a breath.

No. She wouldn't feel guilty about her threat. She'd done the right thing, she'd reported it to the authorities, but if they were too slow to react, it wasn't her fault.

Frustration swirled through her and she stood and shook out her arms. Calm down. "Aarrgh." She didn't want calm, she wanted to talk to someone who could actually help.

"Everything all right, miss?"

She whirled around. An older man in his mid-sixties sat on a park bench on the opposite side of the fig tree. Had he heard her conversation? She should have been more careful, but there'd been no one there when she'd sat down. "Fine. Thank you." She couldn't stay here.

She strode back to her car. She would drive past Henk's place, check whether she could see Annisa, make sure she was all right. And maybe, if she could get Henk's number, she could call pretending to need a cleaner. No, that wouldn't work. Henk would want an address and probably knew most of the people in town.

She pursed her lips. And if Jeremy asked, Henk would get suspicious about his sudden interest in Annisa. But maybe one of his friends could ring.

Which would involve way too many people, one of whom might tip Henk off.

Her mind still whirling with ideas, she drove out of the carpark, along the river towards the beach. What was she doing? This was the wrong way.

She checked her rear-view mirror. Not a good idea to do a U-turn in the middle of the street, especially with a big four-wheel drive behind her. There was bound to be another carpark ahead she could pull into.

The ocean appeared through the trees, dark blue and wavy this morning, a few whitecaps from the wind. The swell crashed against the granite rocks and sprayed into the air. A great photo opportunity. She'd come back later after she'd checked on Annisa. The road curved away from the ocean and then dipped, causing her to brake sharply, her pulse racing. Pay attention to the road, not the ocean.

Her car slowed as it climbed the hill and she pressed the accelerator to give it more speed. A brown sign told her a lookout was five hundred metres ahead. Perfect. She'd turn around there.

The road curved again and she slowed, a movement in her rear-view mirror causing her to check it. The four-wheel drive was so close behind her that it would ram her if she braked hard. She frowned. She crested a rise and the lookout carpark sat about halfway down the hill surrounded by bush. A wooden platform jutted out over the cliff. The bitumen ended as if they'd run out of supplies and the last half was gravel. She braked to slow her descent and was jolted forward as something crashed into her.

Her heart leapt as she glanced in her mirror. The 'roo bar of the four-wheel drive was hard against her boot. What the hell? She braked harder, but it had no effect, the car behind accelerating and pushing her towards the edge. Her skin prickled. If she couldn't stop, she'd fly off the lookout and into the ocean.

The driver was crazy.

Her fingers clenched the steering wheel as the edge got closer.

She'd take her chance with the thick trees and shrubs on the sides of the road rather than plummeting to the ocean below.

She jerked the steering wheel right, heading straight towards the bush.

Please let this work.

The four-wheel drive's engine roared behind her like an animal as her car spun, hit the road shoulder and crashed into the low beach scrub on the side of the road. Her airbags deployed with a bang. The screech and thud of broken branches made her wince, then suddenly the car hit something hard and was still.

Zamira's head spun and she gasped for breath, checking her mirror.

The car was driving away.

Her heart rate slowed and her other senses returned, pain thudding in her chest. She shoved the door hard but it didn't budge. Her ears strained for any hint the car had stopped, or was coming back, but the engine rumble faded.

Straining, her fingers brushed the strap of her bag which had fallen to the floor. Another reach and she grabbed it, pulling it towards her and frantically dug out her phone. The car still might come back.

She dialled triple zero and as the call connected, her breath huffed out of her.

She kept glancing in the rear-view mirror in case the four-wheel drive returned as she reported what had happened.

She was alive.

***

Jeremy's phone beeped as he finished packing up. The remodelling of Shirley Jameson's hen house was complete. He grabbed the invoice off the front seat and got his phone out as he went to find Shirley.

Traffic accident. All available respond.

He winced, even as his pulse rate spiked. They hadn't had a crash in a while. His next job could wait. He texted his response as he walked into the house. "Shirley, I'm done."

The older woman came out from the kitchen. "Want to stay for a coffee?" She winked.

He grinned back, used to her flirty ways. "Can't." He held up his phone. "Just got called in. Traffic accident."

"Oh, I hope no one is hurt."

"Me too." He handed her the invoice. "If you decide you want to stain the wood, call me." After checking that he had everything stowed properly, he waved goodbye and drove to the fire station, his muscles tight. For the crash to need Fire and Rescue to attend, it couldn't be good. He'd seen a lot of blood and trauma over the years and it never got any easier. Nausea swirled in his belly. Much better if he didn't think about it.

Lawrence was already there, prepping the vehicles when Jeremy walked in.

"What have we got?" Jeremy asked, heading for his spare set of gear.

"Car went off the road at the lookout by the inlet. Driver is trapped."

He dressed quickly. "Anyone hurt?"

"She was able to call for help."

Good. "Who else is coming?"

"Nicholas. Can you hitch up the trailer?"

They worked in sync and as the vehicle was ready, Nicholas arrived, already dressed in his gear.

Lawrence drove, sirens on as they raced through the town towards the beach. On the scenic road they were forced to slow as the road twisted and turned.

The police had set up a road block and Adam moved it out of the way as they approached. The road dipped and at the bottom of the carpark the white car was some distance in the bush, its bonnet bent against one of the only large trees in the area and the boot dented.

He frowned. That was odd.

As the truck pulled up, he noticed the hire car logo on the side door. The breath left Jeremy's lungs. No. It couldn't be. He jumped out and strode through the bush to where Sergeant Lincoln Zanetti stood at the window of the car.

Lincoln nodded a greeting. "The firies are here, Zamira. They'll get you out."

He pushed Lincoln aside and glanced in the window. "Zamira?" Her face was covered in blood and the steering wheel pressed up close to her chest.

"Jeremy." His name was a sob and she clutched his hand, her hand trembling.

"What happened?"

"A four-wheel drive rammed me, pushed me towards the edge. I had to swerve into the bush or else…" Tears welled in her eyes.

Or else she'd be at the bottom of the ocean right now. His skin prickled and he squeezed her hand. "Yeah. Good choice."

She snorted a laugh.

Her laugh dissipated his fears. He'd worry about which bastard had done this later. First he had to get Zamira out. "Are you hurt? Any broken bones?"

"A screaming headache and squashed legs, but nothing broken."

He sighed. "OK. I can hear the ambulance, but we've got to get you out." He examined the car as Lawrence strode over.

"Jaws of Life?" he asked.

"Get the spreader." They might be able to force the door open.

Lawrence raised his eyebrows at the way he held Zamira's hand. "You know her?"

"Yeah."

"Stay there then. Lincoln, can I get a hand with some equipment?"

Lincoln nodded and they walked back to the truck. Nicholas was already setting up the generator.

Jeremy stroked Zamira's hand. "The paramedics will examine you and then we'll have you out."

She checked her rear-view mirror and then said, "It was a dark four-wheel drive."

He made the connection. "You think it was Henk?"

She shrugged and then winced. "I can't think of anyone else who'd want to push me off a cliff."

"Did you see him today?"

"No, but I sat in the park while I called Border Force. Someone could have overheard me and yesterday I drove past his place while you were playing football. Henk's got a camera on the gate."

That wasn't great.

Back at the road, the paramedics spoke with Lawrence and Lincoln, then Guy walked over to them. Jeremy stepped back to give him room.

"Hey, I'm Guy and I'll be your friendly neighbourhood paramedic today." He smiled.

"Zamira."

"OK. I'm going to ask you a few questions before we get you out."

She nodded.

Jeremy examined the car while Guy talked to her. It wasn't as bad as he'd first thought. The low-lying scrub must have slowed the car before it hit the tree at an angle.

Lawrence walked over with the spreaders. He waved Jeremy over. "You want to sit this one out?"

Jeremy shook his head. "I'm not leaving."

"Figured as much. Doesn't look like it's too bad. Once Guy gives the OK and we get her out, Nicholas and I will be fine to pack up if you want to ride with her to the hospital."

Relief swept through him. "Thanks, mate."

"No worries. 'Course you'll have to tell us who she is at training Thursday night." Lawrence was straight-faced but he was only partially kidding.

Jeremy grinned. "Yeah, fair enough."

It didn't take Guy long to give the all clear. He placed a neck brace on Zamira and then Lawrence used the spreader to open the door. Jeremy helped her out. Her hands shook a little and he resisted the urge to sweep her into his arms and carry her. She might have other injuries.

Guy made her lie on the bright yellow stretcher and she looked so small on it. Jeremy helped Guy carry her down to the ambulance. As Guy and Cynthia got her ready to travel, Lincoln tapped Jeremy's shoulder.

"How do you know Ms Musa?"

Great, Lincoln was in cop mode. "She's a friend. I met her the other day."

"Know why someone would want to push her off the road?"

He hated to lie to Lincoln, but it wasn't his place to tell. "Maybe a bad driver?"

Lincoln raised his eyebrows. "I need Zamira's statement for the incident report. I'll meet you at the hospital."

Jeremy grimaced. Hospitals had no privacy. "How about I bring her by the station when she's discharged? It's more private."

The sergeant stared at him for a long moment. "All right. Straight after, no detours."

Jeremy nodded. "What about the car?"

"We'll get it towed to Morgan's place."

"Jeremy, are you riding with us?" Guy called.

"Be right there." He glanced at Lincoln. "Are we done here?"

Lincoln smiled. "Not nearly, but we'll talk when you come to the station."

He nodded. Yeah, Lincoln was a good cop. They'd dealt with each other a lot in the past and had a level of trust. "See you then." He climbed into the ambulance, sitting across from Zamira's stretcher. She smiled and his heart skipped a beat.

Not good.

He couldn't pretend to be simply a concerned citizen, the only person Zamira knew in Blackbridge.

He was already way too involved. But she didn't feel the same about him.

He didn't need more heartache.

Chapter 8

Zamira felt shaky from her legs to her soul, like she might burst out crying at any minute, but she kept it together while the emergency department nurse, Fleur, asked her a bunch of questions. She was safe in the hospital, mostly uninjured and Jeremy stood by her side.

It had been a long wait between calling triple zero and the police arriving.

The police sergeant had been suspicious, but she'd been unable to focus on his questions. When Jeremy had arrived, she'd instantly felt safer, her relief so great she burst into tears.

"We'll take you to be x-rayed now," Fleur said. "Then the doctor will see you."

Jeremy got to his feet.

"You can stay here," Fleur told him.

His scowl made Zamira smile. "I'll be fine."

"I'll wait right here."

As Fleur pushed her towards the x-ray room, she asked, "How did the crash happen?"

Zamira hesitated. She couldn't tell her the truth, not without a whole bunch more questions following. "I lost control on the gravel."

"It's lucky your car didn't roll," Fleur said. "I've seen some nasty roll-overs from people going too fast on a gravel road." She helped the radiologist position Zamira and then said, "I'll see you out there."

It didn't take long to get the scans and she was wheeled back to the emergency department where Jeremy and a female doctor were waiting.

"Any damage?" Jeremy asked.

"Nothing," the radiologist answered. "She's fine from my point of view."

The doctor nodded and did her own examination. Finally, she said, "You're lucky. You'll probably ache for a few days, but the bruises will fade. Take some painkillers if you need to but follow the instructions on the packet. If anything changes, dizziness or sharp pains, come back here." She glanced at Jeremy and then back to Zamira. "Do you have someone who could stay with you tonight?"

"She can stay with me," Jeremy said.

Her cheeks warmed. She didn't want to be alone, particularly if someone wanted to hurt her. Jeremy would shelter her. "All right."

The doctor turned to Jeremy. "She doesn't appear to have a concussion, but if she complains of nausea, or anything else, bring her back."

"I will."

"Great. You're free to go."

"Thank you." Zamira winced as she sat up. Every muscle in her body ached and her chest was tender from where the seatbelt had tightened. Fleur handed her discharge paperwork and then Jeremy slipped his arm around her waist and walked her out. She leaned against him, needing his comforting presence. Being in his arms felt right.

Outside, a light rain fell and she inhaled the fresh, cool air. She was alive.

"Stay here and I'll get the car." He brushed a kiss on her forehead and jogged out into the rain before she could protest.

Her heart jolted. He'd kissed her.

It was a friendly glad-you're-OK kiss, but it was a kiss nonetheless. Did it mean he cared for her? He was so incredibly sweet, staying by her side when he had work to do.

When the ute pulled up, she got in and her bag was on the floor. She'd forgotten all about it. Quickly she opened it and checked her camera. It looked fine. "How did your car get to the hospital?"

"Nicholas dropped it off for me."

More examples of what a nice town Blackbridge was. She stretched her legs out, feeling the pull of her muscles.

"Are you all right?" He turned right into town, rather than left towards his house.

"Just stretching," she said. "Where are we going?"

"The police station. I promised Lincoln I'd bring you by so he can get your statement." Jeremy glanced at her. "You should tell him why you're here."

He was right. This was more than she could handle on her own, but the information Vince had told her was highly confidential.

She got out of the car and walked up the steps to the police station. Jeremy opened the door for her and she stepped into a little reception area.

"Hey, Adam," Jeremy greeted the policeman who came to the desk. He had been at the football yesterday. "Lincoln wanted to see us. Zamira was rescued from the crash this morning."

"Come through. He's been waiting for you."

Zamira's stomach clenched as Adam opened a side door and gestured them through. The back of the station contained three desks and an office. The sergeant stood in the office doorway. "I'm glad you're all right, Ms Musa."

"Thank you. Call me Zamira." She shook his hand and followed him into the bland, grey office. He closed the door behind them.

"Can you tell me what happened?"

She took a breath to calm her rapidly beating heart. "I took a wrong turn in town and ended up on the road along the beach. There was a dark four-wheel drive close behind me, so I continued until I got to the lookout where I was going to turn around. When I got to the top of the hill before the carpark, the four-wheel-drive hit me and pushed me towards the edge. I steered into the bush to stop going off into the ocean."

"Why would someone want to push you over a cliff?" His stare was piercing.

She hesitated. Another six hours before the deadline she had given Border Force. She couldn't tell him before then.

Jeremy squeezed her hand. "You can trust him, Zamira."

She sucked in a breath. Damn him.

Lincoln continued to watch her, his expression unchanging.

She had to say something. "It's need to know."

He raised an eyebrow. "Who do you work for?"

Inwardly she winced. He could easily find out if he made some phone calls. That would get her in real trouble. "Border Force."

"Customs or immigration?"

"Immigration." No need for him to know she worked for the support side rather than operations.

Lincoln tapped his fingers on his desk. "Got anything to do with the Task Force?"

She hesitated. "I can't say."

"Could the incident today have to do with this work?"

"Potentially." She had to give him something to stop him snooping further. "I'm not at liberty to discuss details currently, but I hope to be able to by tomorrow."

Lincoln sighed. "All right. Where are you staying?"

"My place," Jeremy said.

Her skin flushed. "For tonight."

"How did you two meet?"

"I got lost," Zamira said. "Ended up at his place."

Lincoln nodded as if satisfied and made some notes. "I've got everything I need. I'll print you a copy of the incident report for the hire company. The car is being towed to the local mechanic's place. Jeremy can give you directions."

"Thank you." She let out a sigh of relief. He was dropping the matter. She opened the office door and Lincoln called, "Adam, can you get Ms Musa the incident report please?"

Zamira followed the constable across to the other side of the room to the printer. He handed her the document and studied her, his expression suspicious. "Here you go."

She forced a smile. "Thanks." She turned to find Jeremy still speaking with Lincoln. "Jeremy?" she called.

"Coming."

She waited until they left the station before she asked, "What did you say to the sergeant?"

"I told him not to worry and that I'd keep an eye on you."

Maybe staying at Jeremy's wasn't the smartest idea,

considering she'd be right next door to Henk. She glanced at him and he smiled. Her chest swelled. She'd feel safer with him than she would alone.

She settled into the passenger seat and closed her eyes.

"Do you want to pick up some clothes before we go to my place?" Jeremy asked.

She hadn't thought that far ahead. "Yes, please."

Jeremy drove them to the bed and breakfast and greeted the owner with a grin. "How are you, Enid?"

The older woman smiled. "Jeremy, your ears must be burning. I was just saying I needed you to quote on building a pergola out the back."

He glanced at Zamira.

"Why don't you go with her while I get my things?" she said. He didn't need to see her underwear.

"Oh, I don't want to interrupt," Enid said.

"You're not." Jeremy gestured to the back door. "This way?"

Zamira waited until they'd gone outside before climbing the stairs to her room. Her muscles pulled but it wasn't too uncomfortable.

She packed her things, checking she had everything from the little en suite.

It felt weird to pack a full suitcase for a single night, but she didn't have a smaller bag. She glanced out the window, down into the lovely garden where Jeremy and the owner were talking. He'd found a tape measure and notebook and was taking measurements.

From their movements she could guess the conversation. Jeremy was asking what the woman wanted and she was gesturing, showing him, smiling so brightly it was a wonder she didn't burn him. Zamira smiled. Jeremy definitely had a way with women, even those old enough to be his grandmother.

As they returned inside, Zamira wheeled her suitcase to the door. It wasn't too heavy but it had been awkward carrying it up even before she'd been injured. She stood at the top of the stairs as Jeremy entered the foyer.

He glanced up. "Let me help." He climbed the steps two at a time and lifted her suitcase as if it weighed nothing.

"Are you checking out?" Enid asked.

Jeremy placed a hand on Zamira's arm before she could respond and lowered his voice. "Why don't you stay at my house while you're here? You'll be there when Annisa arrives and it might be safer for you."

How incredibly generous. Although she'd already been a real hassle, she wanted to say yes. "Are you sure?"

"Yeah." He smiled. "I haven't had company in a while."

Though she liked the idea of spending more time with him, she didn't want him to have certain expectations. "Have you got a spare bed?"

He hesitated. "I've got a camp bed I can use and you can have my bed."

She shook her head. "I'm not kicking you out of your bedroom."

"But you will stay?"

The idea had merit. She didn't want to be alone, and while she'd be closer to Henk's property, Jeremy and Fetch would be there. "Yes, all right. Thank you." She moved down the stairs and then clarified, "On the camp bed."

He nodded.

She walked down to the owner and handed her the key. "I will check out."

"Let me get you a refund then."

"Oh no, don't worry about it." She didn't want the woman out of pocket because she'd changed her mind. "Put it towards your pergola."

Enid smiled. "Thank you, that's very kind."

"I'll have the quote to you by tomorrow," Jeremy told her.

They walked out and he put her suitcase in the back of the ute. It was a squeeze with all his equipment.

Zamira settled into the passenger seat, wincing at her aches. "Thank you, Jeremy."

"Don't sweat it."

She closed her eyes and smiled.

***

Zamira's phone rang not long after they arrived back at Jeremy's house. She lay on the couch, while Jeremy made them a late lunch. She couldn't remember the last time someone had taken care of her, and she'd never had a man cook for her. She could get used to it. Especially when Jeremy whistled such a happy tune as he worked.

She sat up as Jeremy called, "Don't get up." He handed her the phone and she winced. Vince. Only one reason why he'd be calling her. "Hello?"

"Do you want to explain why I've just been talking to a police sergeant in Blackbridge, Western Australia?"

She cringed. Damn Lincoln.

"Or why the hell you're even in Blackbridge?"

She stood up and walked away from Jeremy, heading outside. "I'm on holidays."

"You were going to Cairns," he growled. "Tell me this isn't anything to do with your cousin."

She was silent. It was none of his business.

"I told you to leave it alone. The Task Force has it under control."

She wrapped one arm around herself and moved around the verandah out of the cold wind. Through the window Jeremy smiled at her at it gave her strength. Enough of keeping her head down. "No, they don't," she snapped. "Annisa is scared and trapped there. She was supposed to come to me last night and she didn't."

"That proves nothing. There are rules for what we do. We can't arrest anyone without evidence."

Zamira scowled. As if she didn't know that.

"Now I have to call the Task Force and explain what's going on."

"Maybe you'll have better luck with them than I did." The words shot out and she pressed her lips together, her heart thumping.

"You called them?"

"I reported what Annisa told me."

"Wait. When did you speak to her?"

Zamira swallowed hard. "I saw her last night."

He sighed. "I told you to stay away. If you've ruined the investigation…"

"Women have been disappearing from there, Vince. You know what that means."

He swore, then sighed. "This sergeant mentioned you were in an accident."

The less Vince knew the better. He'd be furious if he thought Henk was suspicious. Guilt hit her. She could have ruined the investigation. "I'm fine."

"I'll call my contact on the Task Force. She isn't going to be happy."

Zamira flinched. "If the Task Force needs my help, I'll be here until Sunday." Maybe she could make it up to them somehow.

Vince grunted. "I doubt it." He hung up.

She sighed and ran a hand through her hair. Work wasn't going to be fun when she went back next week.

Perhaps it was time she looked for a new job. She wasn't advancing anyway. Maybe she could transfer to a different office.

"I thought you were on the Task Force." Jeremy's voice made her jump. He held two steaming mugs of tea and had a deep frown on his face.

Guilt squeezed her chest. He'd been so helpful and she'd fudged the truth... OK, she'd lied. Time to come clean and hope he understood. She tucked her phone into her pocket and took the mug of tea from him. "Not exactly."

"Then what?" The steel in his voice made her wince.

"Can we go inside?"

He nodded and followed her into the living area. "Who do you work for, Zamira?" he asked as he sat.

She clutched her pendant. "I work for Border Force in Melbourne. I'm a policy officer."

He scowled. "What do you do?"

"I deal with legislation, international policy matters and other things."

"So not bastard neighbours who exploit vulnerable migrants?"

She couldn't read his expression. She sighed. "No. I reported Annisa's status to my boss, who told the Task Force and they told me I couldn't do anything because it might blow their whole operation." His expression grew darker. She had to make him understand. "I couldn't leave her here alone and I was going on leave anyway."

He leaned back into the couch, crossed his arms. "Why didn't you tell me the truth?"

"Because I didn't know you and it sounds crazy. I figured if it appeared like I had a whole team behind me, I'd be safer."

His scowl lessened.

She wanted him to understand, to forgive her. "No one knew I was here."

He shook his head. "That takes guts and some stupidity. You could have got into real trouble if Henk had caught you."

"Yeah." She gave him a half smile. "I'm sorry for not telling you the whole truth."

He sipped his tea and then chuckled. "I wondered why a kangaroo freaked out a hardened Task Force officer."

Her muscles relaxed. "Yeah, going to Henk's property in the middle of the night was the scariest thing I've ever done."

He smiled. "So what happens now? Are you in trouble?"

"Yes." She wasn't looking forward to Monday.

"Your boss will come around."

Jeremy didn't know Vince. But she'd worry about it when she got back to Melbourne. She could breathe a little easier now Jeremy wasn't mad at her.

She stood up. "Shall we have lunch?"

***

Jeremy watched Zamira as they ate. How much did he know about her really? She'd flicked personalities in an instant when Henk had come to their table at the pub. He only had her word she worked for Border Force and it had been her boss on the phone.

Though Annisa had recognised her, hadn't been scared of her so that had to count for something.

His phone ringing broke through his thoughts. "Mendelson Construction, Jeremy speaking."

"It's Lincoln. Is Zamira with you?"

"Yeah."

"Good. Can you put me on speaker?"

"Just a second." He covered the microphone and said to Zamira, "Lincoln wants to talk to us both." He hit the speaker button. "Go for it."

"Kay Patton brought her father, Richard by the station this afternoon to hand in his driver's licence. Turns out he brought their black four-wheel drive back with a couple of scratches, but he can't remember how they got there."

Jeremy raised his eyebrows. "You think he hit Zamira?"

"Kay said aside from his memory lapses, he occasionally checks out altogether, like he's not there, so it's possible that's what happened."

"Why wouldn't he stop after the crash?" Zamira asked.

"He doesn't remember a thing," Lincoln said. "Apparently the lookout has been a favourite of his for decades and he often goes there. I've asked Kay to bring the car in so we can examine it."

Jeremy let out a breath. So it really had been an accident. "What will happen to him?"

"We can charge him for failing to report an accident and leaving the scene, but it's difficult because he doesn't remember anything. Kay's offered to pay any damages the insurance doesn't cover."

He glanced at Zamira.

"Don't charge him with anything on my account," she said. "Can I get Kay's number in case there's an issue with the hire company?"

Lincoln rattled it off.

"Thanks."

Lincoln cleared his throat. "I've spoken with Border Force."

"I know," Zamira said.

"And?" Jeremy's muscles tensed. Lincoln would

mention if Zamira had lied.

"I asked them to contact you today. It's clear you're worried about your cousin, but neither of you is qualified for this kind of thing. You're a policy officer, Ms Musa."

Relief filled him. She'd told the truth.

"Sergeant, Annisa's in trouble," she said.

"I can't say any more than I have." Lincoln sighed. "Please don't do anything until you hear from them."

"All right. Thanks, mate." Jeremy hung up.

Zamira frowned at him. "I can't promise that."

"That's why I hung up. Hopefully Border Force will call soon." He gathered their lunch dishes and put them in the dishwasher.

She stretched, wincing a little.

"Why don't you take a nap? You can use my bedroom and I'll set up the camp bed in the spare room in the meantime."

"The couch is fine." She hesitated. "Since the crash was an accident, you should go back to work. I'll be fine after a rest and then I can go into town and buy something for dinner like I promised."

"We can get take-away."

"I'd like to cook for you." Her smile brushed his heart.

"The doctor didn't want you alone." And he didn't want to leave. He'd promised to take care of her and she could get worse. What if she died because he wasn't there?

She played with her pendant. "How about I call you in an hour when I wake up?"

With his history, she was probably safer if he wasn't around. He hesitated. Staying and watching her sleep was creepy. He could be back at the house in ten minutes if she didn't call him. "All right, but call me every hour until I get home," he said. "I'll get you some blankets." He couldn't shake the urge to take care of her. He dragged the rug off his bed and grabbed a spare pillow. He lay them on the couch. "Are you sure you'll be OK?"

She ran a hand through her hair. "Yes. I feel so much better knowing Henk isn't trying to kill me."

So did he.

They stood only a metre apart and he wanted to hug her. But it might freak her out. Instead he stepped away, picked his keys off the table. "I'll take the truck and leave the ute here for you." He took the key off his keyring. "If you go out, leave the house unlocked, and put Fetch outside."

She followed him. "I will."

Too close.

He brushed her fringe off her face, unable to resist her soft skin. Her eyes widened.

He shifted closer, his hand still cupping her cheek. "I'm really glad you're OK."

She didn't blink. "Me too."

All he needed to do was bend down and kiss her.

His brain kicked in and he stepped back letting out a breath. Back off, buddy. She's vulnerable, injured and relying on you to give her somewhere safe to stay. Now is not the time to get fresh.

"I'll see you when I get home." He walked out without looking back.

Chapter 9

Zamira let out a deep breath as Jeremy walked out. For a second, she thought he was going to kiss her – and she'd wanted him to.

She'd never been so attracted to someone that she'd wanted to throw caution out the window.

But she did with Jeremy — even with everything that was going on.

A nap would help her think clearly. She sighed again. At least she had one less worry. Henk wasn't coming after her. Kay's behaviour at the winery the other day was a little more understandable now Zamira knew what she was dealing with. She had to be under a lot of stress.

Fetch lay in the dog bed next to the couch snoring his head off. He had the right idea. She settled on the couch and set her phone alarm for an hour, then she snuggled down.

The rug and pillow smelled like Jeremy, cocooning her in its warmth. She closed her eyes, pretended Jeremy's arms were around her and fell asleep.

When her alarm went off an hour later, she groaned as

she moved. A few more aches had moved in while she'd slept. Switching off the alarm she sat up, brushing her hair off her face. Time to scope out Henk's place, see how much was visible from Jeremy's fence line, then she'd go into town and buy something for dinner.

Her phone rang and she smiled when Jeremy's name came up. "Hello?"

"You're OK." He sighed.

"Sorry, I just woke up." And she'd forgotten her promise to call him every hour.

"How are you feeling?"

"A little sore, but much better, thank you."

"Good. Don't forget to call me in an hour." He hung up.

Warmth spread through her. He was looking after her, even though they barely knew each other.

The best way to repay him would be to cook him a lovely dinner. She'd write a list now, before she headed outside.

The fridge's shelves were as barren as a wasteland. A few essentials were in order on top of the ingredients for the stir-fry.

Her list got longer and longer as she checked his pantry. She might as well get herself some food she liked to eat if she was staying a few days.

She'd ask Jeremy what he wanted when she called him in an hour.

Shoving the list into her pocket, she grabbed her bag off the table. Fetch could come with her while she checked out Henk's property.

She glanced towards his dog bed but he wasn't in it. "Fetch?"

No response.

Slowly she scanned the rest of the living area. Every flat surface was covered in paper or projects. Jeremy needed to learn how to organise. A single photo stood on the entrance table revealing a teenaged Jeremy and an older man who must be his father. No photos of his mother or sisters which was kind of odd.

She walked around the couches, but the dog wasn't there. "Fetch, come here." She headed towards the hallway, her muscles tense. Jeremy hadn't shown her through the house yet, but he had invited her to stay, so he shouldn't be annoyed. She couldn't leave Fetch inside.

The first two doors were closed so she continued down the hallway. A bathroom on the right with towels haphazardly hung over the towel rail and at the end of the corridor was a huge bedroom. The pitched roof had exposed rafters and a sky light to let in the sunlight or starlight. A huge king-sized bed sat directly beneath it, the sheets half on the ground and a brown bulldog curled up next to the pillows.

"Fetch!"

The dog opened one eye, glanced at her and then closed it. She stalked over to him, stepping over clothes Jeremy had left on the floor. "Get down." She pointed at the ground which did nothing considering the dog's eyes were shut.

How could she get him off?

Cautiously she wrapped her fingers around his collar and gave a gentle tug. Fetch opened his eyes and groaned.

"Off." She made the command as authoritative as she could.

He snorted and closed his eyes again.

"No!" She knelt on the bed, the softness of the mattress sinking around her knees. Jeremy slept here every night. She flushed, blocking the thought and pushed Fetch, hoping to slide him towards the edge, but he barely budged. The dog was heavy.

She pushed him again and this time he slid a little way. He yawned and watched her.

Stubborn creature.

She brushed her hair back and shoved him again, getting him to the edge. Now what? She couldn't push him off. The mattress was a long way off the ground. Bulldogs weren't like cats, always landing on their feet. She climbed off the bed and stared at Fetch, her hands on her hips.

She bent over, patted her lap. "Come on, Fetch. Come here."

His tail thumped on the bed, but he didn't move.

She walked further away, towards the window and tripped over Jeremy's football boots. She landed with a thud on her butt. "Ow."

Jeremy was definitely a slob. Clothes were left where they landed when he took them off… and that wasn't an image she should have in her head. She glanced towards the bed. Did he sleep naked?

No, don't go there.

She shouldn't be in here at all. Determined, she got to her feet and tugged on Fetch's collar again. This time he snorted. She snatched her hand away. He might not bite, but she had little experience with dogs.

She huffed. She wasn't willing to force him down which left her two options; leave him here or call Jeremy and ask him what to do.

Well he was expecting her to call. She got her phone out of her pocket and dialled.

"What's up?"

She pulled a face. "Ah, well, I've got a bit of a problem."

"Do you feel nauseous? Do you need me to take you to the hospital?"

His concern touched her. "No. I want to get some groceries, but Fetch is on your bed and he won't get off." The words came out in a rush.

He chuckled. "Slow down. You're in my bedroom?" She couldn't read his tone.

She winced. "Yeah. Fetch must have gone in while I slept. He's ignoring my attempts to get him outside." She tilted her head. "He looks pretty happy." To be honest, she would have ignored her too. The bed would be far more comfortable than the cold outside.

"Don't sweat it. He always goes in there if I don't close the door. He'll follow you anywhere if you get him a treat. They're in the laundry cupboard."

Right. She hurried along the corridor back to the laundry. "Where exactly?"

"Good question." He laughed. "I think I put them in the top cupboard above the sink."

She opened the cupboard, which was surprisingly bare, and found a red packet of dog treats. "Found them." The packaging crunched as she got the treat out and a fast, clicking sound came towards her. Fetch hurried into the room, his tongue hanging out and drool starting to form. "Huh."

"What's wrong?" Jeremy asked.

"Fetch is here."

"He must have heard the packaging. I swear that dog has excellent hearing for treats, but is deaf when I need him to go outside." His affection was clear.

She smiled. "Well thanks for your help. I've got it sorted now." She led Fetch outside, closing the door behind her and then gave him the treat.

"All right. I'll see you tonight." He hung up.

Zamira inhaled deeply, the eucalyptus scent tickling her nose. It was so peaceful out here. In the little garden beds below the verandah, green shoots peeked out of the ground. Plants weren't her forte, but they didn't look like weeds. Down the path, his vegetable patches were much greener with beans hanging off one of the bushes. Maybe his fridge was bare because he grew a lot of his food.

She itched to take photos, but if she started now, she'd forget everything else.

She hung her camera around her neck in case she happened to see Henk, and then wandered towards the bush on Jeremy's side of the fence. The fence wasn't visible from here, but it couldn't be too far away. Fetch trotted by her side, looking up at her every so often as if she might conjure another treat out of thin air.

The low grasses and shrubs were heavy with raindrops and the bottom of her pants was soon soaked through. She reached the fence with large signs on it proclaiming it was electrified. The ground a metre either side of it was cleared so no plants grew against it.

First she wandered down towards the road, checking if there were any breaks in it. Not likely, but she had to check.

The gate was still firmly closed and the gravel driveway veered away from the fence and disappeared behind the bush. Turning, she returned the way she came, taking random photos of trees and shrubs in case there were other security cameras she hadn't noticed.

Through the trees she could just make out the main house, and she used her zoom lens to try and get a better look, but it was too far away.

She continued walking as a few spots of rain hit her. She increased her pace and Fetch left her, trotting back towards the house.

Wimp.

Not that she could easily explain why she was taking photographs in the rain. She'd have to be quick.

Towards the back of the property were a mass of grevilleas, planted almost like a hedge. It was impossible to see through them and would be difficult for anyone to force their way through. Natural security.

The rain was coming heavier now and she tucked her camera back in her bag and jogged back to the house. Maybe by the time she got back from town, Henk's gate would be open.

She checked Fetch was happy on the verandah and retrieved Jeremy's ute key from her pocket.

Now she just needed to remember how to drive a manual car.

***

An hour later Zamira was back at Jeremy's and she had checked in with him. Henk's gate was still shut. If the migrants worked a typical nine to five shift, Annisa should be home soon. The Task Force was yet to call, but she'd been clear on what she planned to do.

With a sigh, she put away the groceries and stretched, her muscles pulling in response. Some yoga would help to gently stretch the aches from the crash. The rain had stopped so she changed and went outside.

Breathing deeply, she worked through a simple yoga routine and her muscles sang. Fetch wandered over while she was doing downward dog and shoved his face in hers. She laughed and pushed him away. "Sit."

He plonked his butt in front of her, his head tilted to the side.

When she finished her session, the cloudy sky made the light perfect for photos. She retrieved her camera and walked outside, Fetch following her. The neat garden beds contrasted with the wild bush on the edges of his property — tamed and untamed, tidy and natural. Did it reflect Jeremy's personality? His house was a mess but he was calm and organised with work.

She framed her first shot and then hesitated. Was taking photos of his house an invasion of his privacy? He seemed pretty relaxed about everything, but she'd ask when she called him next. She could always delete them.

Starting at the front of the house, she took photos of the garden, the flowers, the leaves, even the path. She walked back down the driveway and took long shots of the house and shed, and then came closer, picking up the detail around the windows and doors. The beautiful workmanship with the joints fitting snugly together — such attention to detail.

How could a man who was so careful with his work be such a mess with the rest of his things?

She paused outside the entrance of the huge shed. The doors were closed and wood shavings were scattered along the ground on the outside. Peeking inside would be an invasion of his privacy. Instead, she wandered towards the tree line to take some shots.

She followed the trees around the block until she reached the electric fence between Jeremy's and Henk's properties.

Still no call from the Task Force.

Zamira sighed and turned back towards Jeremy's house. Her stomach rumbled. It must be almost time to check in.

Fetch watched her from the back step as she approached, and she snapped a photo of him. His jowls were so droopy she wanted to rumple his face. He might be a little grubby, but he was cute in a boofhead kind of way. Why had her mother warned her against dogs? Walking closer, she took a dozen photos and then squatted down to his eye level. He wagged his tail and trotted over, pressing his head into her lap with such enthusiasm he knocked her off balance and she sprawled on the ground.

Fetch followed, his tail wagging faster and tongue licking her face. Ugh. She held up one hand to fend him off while the other held her camera off the ground. He was too heavy to push out of the way.

The growl of a car engine and the crunch of tyres on the gravel had her turning away from Fetch as Jeremy's truck drove up.

Fetch lost interest and ran to greet Jeremy. Great. Jeremy had seen her sprawled on the ground in an undignified heap.

Not her best moment.

Zamira sat up, running a hand over her face and pushed her hair out of the way. Carefully she got to her feet, brushing the dirt off her pants as Jeremy jogged over, concern on his face. "Are you all right?"

She grimaced. "I'm fine. Fetch got a little enthusiastic and you drove up at exactly the right moment to see me at my worst."

He huffed. "I'm glad. I was worried you'd been lying there since you last called."

"Seconds only. I've been taking a few photos." She held up her camera. "I hope you don't mind."

"I'd love to see them." He walked towards the verandah and she fell into step beside him.

"Have you finished for the day?"

He shook his head. "I need to make a few calls, write a couple of quotes and work out the design for the granny flat."

The business of being a builder. She stepped back. "I'll get out of your way. I can take some more photos." A drop of rain hit her hand. She glanced up, saw the clouds had lowered. "Or read a book."

"You won't disturb me. Come inside, have a cuppa.

I bought some biscuits."

She followed him into the house. "I know I'm being an imposition. Tell me what you need from me and I'll do it."

He turned, his eyebrows raised, eyes dark and a small smile on his face.

Her face flushed. That came out the wrong way. "Ah, what I meant was, if you want privacy while you work, I can sit outside or in the ute or whatever."

His smile grew. "Take the couch, or if you want to go through your photos, I'll clear some space at the table for you."

Her heart fluttered. "Yeah, space would be good." She played with her pendant, her whole body hot. Was he interested, or just teasing her?

She stayed where she was as he cleared one end of the table and then gestured to a seat. "Go for it. I'll make us a drink."

He was back to the familiar easy-going man, but she couldn't shut off her body's response to him.

She wanted to be brave and express her interest.

But risk taking wasn't in her DNA — not until this holiday at least. So maybe she could change.

She smiled, placed her camera on the table and went to get her laptop out of her suitcase.

Chapter 10

Jamie arrived as Jeremy finished his design for Gladys's granny flat. Jeremy had completely forgotten about him coming around, but it was perfect timing. He'd been struggling to ignore Zamira next to him for the past half an hour. He should have cleared the whole table and told her to sit at the other end. Then he wouldn't have occasionally brushed her knee with his under the table and he wouldn't be close enough to hear her little sighs as she worked on her photos. Each sigh of satisfaction tightened his groin, made him picture her on his bed beneath him.

So Jamie's arrival had stopped him from doing something he might regret. He had offered her shelter and sanctuary, and making any moves on her was not appropriate. He stood up as Jamie called out at the back door, "You home?"

"Come in." He glanced at Zamira. "I promised Jamie I'd fix his bike."

She smiled. "Go for it. I'm happy here."

Jamie's eyes widened as he walked in. He grinned. "Hi, Zamira, right?"

"Yes." She reached for her pendant. "How are you,

Jamie?"

"Great. The kids were well behaved today."

She frowned and Jeremy explained. "He's a high school English teacher."

Jamie nodded. "Teacher by day, SES volunteer by night."

"Does everyone here volunteer?" she asked.

Jeremy grinned. "Not everyone. Kim's with marine rescue, but Adam helps enough people as a cop." He turned back to Jamie. "Let's go to the shed."

Jamie waited for the back door to close behind them before he whistled. "I'm impressed, mate. Is she staying with you?"

"Yeah." He debated briefly whether to let his friend jump to conclusions, but it wasn't fair to Zamira. "She was in a car crash this afternoon. The doctor wanted someone to keep an eye on her overnight."

"Shit, is she all right?"

"A few bruises and aches." He helped get the motorbike off the trailer and wheeled it into his shed. "What needs to be welded?" He crouched down by the bike as Jamie pointed out the issues, and put Zamira into the back of his mind.

***

Zamira watched Jeremy walk out and then let out a sigh of relief. Being so close to him, feeling the warmth of his knee brush hers was sweet torture.

Time to get control of herself.

Her phone rang, the shrill sound in the silence making her jump. Her heart leapt. Could it be the Task Force?

She grabbed it and answered, "Zamira Musa speaking."

"Ms Musa this is Agent Tara Franklin from the Task

Force."

Zamira swallowed hard. "Thank you for calling me."

"I'm in charge of the Blackbridge operation. I understand your cousin is one of the migrants staying at Henk Jennings' place and you've spoken with her."

"That's right."

"Can you tell me exactly what she said about how she got there and what her situation is like?"

"Of course." Zamira's pulse raced as she told the agent everything she knew.

Franklin asked questions, wanting her to expand where she could and then she said, "This information is a great help. Thank you."

"When are you going to get Annisa out of there?"

"You do realise Annisa will be sent home afterwards?" Franklin asked. "She's here illegally."

"Yes, I do. But she thought she was doing the right thing."

"Hmm." She didn't sound convinced. "I realise you work for Border Force, but I can't give you the details of our operation."

Zamira narrowed her eyes. This was stupid. "My cousin may be in danger and I'm not going to stand around while you get the correct paperwork together."

"Your actions might hurt the other migrants who are there."

Guilt pinched her. "Then give me some kind of guarantee, otherwise I'm going over right now to get her."

Agent Franklin growled. "I don't like to be threatened." Keys clacked in the background and then a sound of surprise. "You've got high security clearance."

"That's right."

A long pause. "We should get the warrant tomorrow and we'll be ready to raid his property by Wednesday at the latest."

A full day and a half, maybe two. Would Annisa be safe until then?

"I understand your concern, Zamira, but please let us help everyone there. Our information indicates it's not just Annisa who is being treated badly."

She gritted her teeth.

"Could you perhaps slip Annisa a phone so she can call if she needs to?"

Zamira should have thought of that yesterday. But if she followed the bus in the morning and found out where Annisa was working, she could give her a phone. She sighed. "All right. Thank you."

"I'll be in touch." Agent Franklin hung up.

Zamira stared at the phone. Annisa should be fine. Henk wasn't suspicious, and Annisa hadn't been able to come over because the property was like Fort Knox with the gate closed. She was trapped inside at night.

It would be OK.

But tomorrow she'd buy a phone and get it to Annisa somehow.

She couldn't be too careful.

***

Jeremy checked the time. He'd finished welding Jamie's bike twenty minutes ago and Jamie was still chatting about his SES training. Usually he'd be happy to spend time with his friend, but normally he didn't have an attractive woman inside waiting for him.

He tugged on his beard. "Listen, mate. I hate to interrupt, but you need to go."

"Oh, sorry." Jamie stepped back. "You've got plans?"

"Ah, well, Zamira's inside and she'll probably want dinner soon." His face heated.

"And you'd prefer her company to mine." Jamie grinned. "I get it. Go. I'll load the bike on my own."

"Thanks." Relief filled him as he moved towards the shed door.

"Hey, Jeremy!" Jamie called.

He turned.

"If you want to get some, you might want to tidy your house. It's a tip." He winked.

Jeremy gave him the finger and continued walking. He was right though. Not that he expected anything to happen, but it was time he did more than move things from one surface to another.

He whistled to Fetch as he entered the house and stopped in the laundry to fill Fetch's bowl with food. Fetch raced over to him, his toenails clicking on the wooden floor. Jeremy smiled. "Hungry are you?" He continued into the living area where Zamira was still sitting at the table. She concentrated on her computer screen, a cute little furrow in her brow as she clicked the mouse.

She glanced up. "Are you finished?"

"Yeah." He caught sight of her suitcase still by the couch. "I'll set up the camp bed in the spare room before I have a shower."

"I'll start cooking."

Was he being a chauvinist letting Zamira cook for him? She *had* offered... "If you can wait twenty minutes, I'll help."

She smiled. "I can manage, just point me to a cutting board and knife."

The kitchen was in a slightly better state than the living room. The sink was clear and he'd remembered to turn the dishwasher on before he left this morning, but several notebooks and his unopened mail were scattered on the bench top. He gathered them into a pile and looked for somewhere to put it. In the end, he shoved a few things aside and put them on the sideboard.

"Don't you have an office?" Zamira asked, getting the vegetables out of the fridge.

His face heated. "Not yet. It's one of the rooms I haven't finished. I'm in the middle of making a desk."

"What's it like?"

"It's pretty basic at this stage. Just a table really." He rubbed his beard. "What are we having?"

"Stir fry."

He took his wok out of the cupboard and put it on the stove.

She grinned at him. "That will make it easier."

"Need anything else?"

"No, I'll be fine." She was already chopping carrots, looking so at home in his kitchen his heart pinched.

Get a grip.

"I won't be long." He headed down the hallway and opened his junk room. He carried the camp bed and sleeping bag across the hallway to the empty spare bedroom. A nice sized room though there weren't even curtains on the windows. He paused. If it bothered Zamira, she could take his room.

He set up the camp bed, adding a pillow and blankets. Not fancy, but she'd be warm. Did she sleep naked? He squeezed his eyes shut. Don't think about it.

He headed for the bathroom and stripped off, dumping his clothes on the floor. No, he had a guest. He threw his clothes in the laundry basket and the soap scum on his sink caught his attention. Damn it. Why had he let it get so bad? Zamira wouldn't be impressed having to shower in a bathroom this dirty.

He threw his pants back on and hurried to the laundry to get some cleaning products.

Zamira's mouth dropped open, and she looked him up and down, her face flushing, but definite interest in her eyes.

Nice. His body stirred and he flashed her a grin. "Sorry, I realised the bathroom needs cleaning." He got the products he needed, and a fresh set of sheets for his own bed in case Zamira wasn't comfortable in the spare room without curtains.

Or if the attraction went anywhere.

He scrubbed the bathroom quickly and then showered, mindful of the time. After he cleaned the toilet, he headed for his bedroom.

A pile of dog hair on his sheets reminded him Zamira had already been in here. Would she think it creepy he'd made his bed after she'd already seen it dishevelled? No, Fetch's hair was a good excuse.

Not that he expected her to be in here again.

But damn he wanted her.

He groaned. Don't think about it.

Moving fast, he threw on a clean pair of jeans and the Thor T-shirt Mai had given him for Christmas and then made the bed. The rooms looked better, but he needed to do some washing tomorrow.

The living room was still a mess, but he wouldn't kid himself. That needed far more than a quick tidy.

Zamira stood at the stove, stirring the wok, her back to him. She had changed into a red knitted long-sleeved dress with black leggings underneath and red, white and blue Captain America socks. The fun socks were such a contrast to the proper, dignified clothing she wore. Did they represent the true Zamira? The whole look was more casual, but she still looked stunningly beautiful. He swallowed. "How's it going?"

She turned, her gaze intense. "Good timing. It's ready."

He walked quickly into the kitchen. "Can I get you a drink?"

"Water would be great."

He breathed deeply as he poured her a glass and the spicy stir-fry scent made his stomach rumble. It reminded him of the noisy dinners with his family; his youngest sister Moira always with some new absolutely thrilling thing that happened at school to tell them about and his other sister, Heather always more dignified, telling her not to gossip, so like their mother.

"Are you hungry?"

He pushed away the thought of his family. "A little. It smells delicious."

No one had cooked for him since he'd moved into his own place and even when he'd lived with Pete, he'd been expected to cook a few days a week for the family. He owed them that much for taking him in. His chest ached with longing. Stupid. He was fully capable of cooking for himself.

He hadn't relied on anyone to take care of him.

The table was still half covered in papers, but he had nowhere to move them. There hadn't been any point finishing his office when he lived alone. He hadn't imagined anyone wanting to move in with him. That was asking for trouble.

He never saw the rejection coming.

He gathered up the bills and invoices. They could go on the office floor.

Zamira was dishing up as he came back. She put both bowls on the table and he took a seat. "*Selamat makan.*"

"*Terima kasih.*" He bit into the noodles and stir-fry and his eyes rolled back into his head. Spice and flavour, salt and sour. "So good," he said when he swallowed.

"It's my grandmother's recipe," Zamira said. "I'll write it down for you if you like."

A reminder she wasn't staying. "That would be great."

Zamira sipped her water. "So how do you know Indonesian?"

"I spent a month in Bali last year helping to build an orphanage. I learnt a bit before I went."

She stared at him. "That's a wonderful thing to do."

He shrugged. "It's what I could do to help." Someone in town had been raising funds and while he hadn't had a lot of money to give, he figured his skills might be valuable.

"The orphanage must be amazing." She glanced around. "How long did it take you to build this place?"

Her praise washed through him. "About a year. I lived in the shed for a while and worked on it in between my other jobs."

"How many rooms haven't you finished?"

"Just the office." The others were simply empty. He had no family who'd want to stay over. He gritted his teeth. Stop feeling sorry for yourself. "Did you get any good photos today?"

She sipped her water. "Yeah. I'm pleased with them."

Not much at his place worth photographing, but maybe it was practice. Which reminded him. "Did Border Force call?"

She nodded. "Agent Tara Franklin called me."

He waited but when she didn't continue, he asked, "And?"

Zamira screwed up her face. "I can't tell you. It's confidential."

He sat back, hurt hitting him. Right. She didn't trust him even though he'd been helping her. He shoved more food into his mouth rather than comment.

She hesitated and sighed. "I should be out of your hair in two days."

The flush of disappointment was unwanted. He frowned. Zamira wouldn't leave without Annisa. That meant Border Force had to be acting within the next two days.

He smiled. "There's no rush. How long are you on leave for?"

"I fly back on Sunday."

"You can stay until then. You might as well make full use of your holiday." Having a finite time together meant he wouldn't get attached, but they could still have some fun together. Although Annisa would be around, so maybe not. He picked up her bowl. "Do you want any more?"

"No, thank you."

He carried the dishes to the sink and put them in the dishwasher. "I've got ice cream if you want dessert."

She shook her head. "I'm full."

He put on the kettle, more for something to do than any real desire for a cup of tea. Zamira brought their glasses into the kitchen, brushing up against him as she placed them in the sink. He stepped closer to her soft body. He hadn't dated in a while and his hormones were taking over.

"Do you want a cuppa?"

"That would be nice." She stepped back, a tiny frown on her face.

Maybe he was reading her wrong. He distanced himself from her as he made the tea.

Handing her one of the mugs, he said, "I didn't get a chance to light the fire earlier. Are you cold?" He walked into the living area and moved a model off the coffee table so they could put their mugs down. The office was moving higher on his priority list every day.

"No. It's cosy in here."

He smiled. "I'm glad you like it." He sipped his tea. He needed some innocuous conversation. "So what do you do for fun?"

She blinked at him and then turned towards him, bringing one knee up on the couch, brushing his, while she blew on her drink. "I like reading comic books and going to the movies."

He raised his eyebrows. "Which comics?"

"I'm a Marvel girl. Thor's my favourite." She nodded at his T-shirt, a smile on her lips and he glanced down. He'd forgotten what he was wearing.

Hope flared in him. "What about the movies — love them or hate them?"

"Love them." She grinned. "I've got the whole collection on DVD."

She didn't strike him as the comic-reading type. He would have flagged her as literary or classics. "I've only seen the movies. Mum banned comics in our house."

"Why?"

"She was an English teacher, only had time for the literary stuff, and Dad wasn't a reader." His stomach clenched at the thought of his father.

"The odd couple."

"I suppose. They made it work." Until he'd ruined it all. "I tend to listen to audiobooks these days. Keeps me entertained when I'm working."

"What a great idea."

Fetch snuffled up looking for a biscuit. Jeremy rubbed his ears. "There's nothing for you, mate. You've had your treat today."

Zamira winced. "I'm sorry about that."

"Don't sweat it. Fetch has the run of the house. The only reason he doesn't sleep in my room is he snores too loudly."

Her laugh was light and full of delight. "Really?"

"Like a freight train. I can still hear him faintly when he's sleeping in here."

"I've never had any pets," she said. "I didn't know what to do with him when he ignored me."

"Not even a goldfish?"

"No. It never occurred to me to get one when I moved out, because the apartment's so small."

He'd always had animals. His dad's kelpie used to go to work with them and even after his mother had kicked him out, Pete's family had had dogs and cats. Pete had been his lifeline, taking on his apprenticeship and giving him a place to stay. "They're good company."

"I can see."

Fetch leaned against his leg, eyes closed, drool leaking out of his mouth as Jeremy rubbed the spot behind his ears. He chuckled. "We do have a bit of a drool problem though." He grabbed a tissue from the table and wiped Fetch's mouth, then threw his favourite chew toy into his bed. Fetch ambled after it.

He collected both their empty mugs and took them to the kitchen, washing the dirt from his dog off his hands. Another downside.

He settled back on the couch next to her. "Which is your favourite Thor movie?"

"Ragnarok of course."

"Glad we agree." He shifted to face her and ran his hand along the back of the couch so it rested near her shoulder. He wanted to forget about the outside world and get back to the attraction pulling him in.

"What's your favourite movie?" She leaned into the back rest of the couch so her silky soft hair just brushed his fingers.

He itched to run his fingers through it, pull her head back and kiss her.

"Jeremy?"

Crap. "Sorry, what?"

"Which film is your favourite?"

"Right…" His desire to touch her was driving him crazy. Get it together. "I'm a fan of thrillers."

She winced. "Too suspenseful for me."

"You could always close your eyes at the suspenseful bits."

She laughed. "Then I'd miss half the movie."

Her laugh lit up her whole face, her eyes sparkling and the sound tickling him. He couldn't take it anymore. He had to risk it. He circled his thumb over the back of her hand and her eyes widened. "I've got to be honest." He moved a little closer and her lips parted. "I'm finding it difficult to concentrate on our conversation, because all I can think about is how much I'd like to kiss you."

She stared at him.

He'd stuffed up. Inwardly he cringed. "Sorry, I've read it wrong, haven't I?" He ran a hand through his hair. Awkward. "Don't worry, I'll still help you with Annisa and you can stay here." He shrugged and smiled. "I'll ignore my attraction to you."

After only a brief hesitation, she launched herself forward, into his arms and her lips met his.

***

Some other being had taken over Zamira's body, but she was happy to let it. She'd been hot and bothered since Jeremy had come out half naked. Zamira kissed him hard, all the pent-up attraction pouring out of her. He tasted spicy and warm and his tongue teased her as his arms wrapped around her.

This hot, bearded builder with a heart of gold pressed all her buttons. Even the fact he'd taken the time to assure her he would still help no matter what made her weak at the knees. Being cautious had got her nowhere. In was time she went after what she wanted.

He gripped her hips, dragging her closer and she dug her hands into his hair, her lips on his mouth, his beard brushing her face. She ran her tongue between his lips and they parted on a groan. His hardness pressed into her and her body heated. She wanted him, more than she'd ever wanted anyone before. With him she felt sexy, desired and safe.

The knowledge that he wanted her too was heady and while some thought deep at the back of her mind told her she should slow down, it was easy to ignore. She'd never been this eager, this rash and she wanted to be with him. She had limited time here and would use all the moments she had.

Her hands slid down his side, under his T-shirt and over his smooth, warm, tight muscles. Time to see it, to kiss it and taste it. Shoving his T-shirt upwards, she brought her hands around to his firm chest and he drew a sharp breath in.

"Jesus, Miri. You're driving me crazy," he growled.

Power shot through her at his restrained desperation. "Take it off."

He stripped the T-shirt off and threw it on the floor and then pulled her closer as he kissed her again. She teased his nipples with her fingertips, circling them, wanting to taste them. With other men she'd always been uncertain, but not with Jeremy. He wanted her as much as she wanted him.

She pushed him back and bent to suck one of his nipples.

His head tilted backwards, his eyes closed as he

surrendered to her. It wasn't enough. She wanted to be naked with him. She leaned back and his eyes flashed open, dark and deep.

"My turn."

Pleasure shot to her core as he pressed against her, his lips ravishing hers. He fumbled for the bottom of her knee-length dress and swore under his breath. The desperation in it made her laugh. "Let me."

She drew her dress over her head and dropped it on the floor. If the evening was cool, she didn't notice.

He sucked in a breath. "Does it hurt?" His fingers softly traced the light purple bruising on her chest.

"No." It was impossible to feel pain when each brush of his fingertips sent a warm thrill through her.

"Good." His eyes darkened and he cupped her breasts, his thumbs gently circling them the same way as they'd done the back of her hand. Every nerve ending celebrated and demanded more.

"You're so fucking perfect." With deft hands, he flicked her bra open and slid it off. Before she had a chance to consider being half naked, his mouth was on her breast, kissing and sucking.

"Oh, my."

His chuckle tickled her skin as he continued to taste her as if she was a dessert to be savoured.

Her body throbbed, heat pooling between her legs. She wanted more. So much more. "Jeremy," she gasped.

He lifted his head, his gaze wicked. "Yes?"

"Bedroom."

He picked her up and she shrieked, wrapping her legs around his waist as he carried her down the hall. She kissed his neck, nibbled below his ear and his hands squeezed her butt, pulling her even closer, rubbing his length against her.

Yes, please.

He kicked the door shut behind them and lowered them both to the bed. She squeezed his butt, loving the lush hardness of it, but his jeans were too thick. She reached between them to find the button as his teeth grazed her neck and she forgot what she was doing.

"You taste so sweet," he murmured.

The slight ache of her muscles was nothing compared with the aching need inside her and she resumed her attempts to get rid of his jeans. With another kiss he rolled away and shucked his jeans off and he was gloriously naked and erect.

Wow.

He moved, getting something out of the drawer next to his bed and when he turned back, she slid down his body and took him into her mouth.

"Fu…" His words died as she sucked him harder and he gripped the sheets, the muscles in his arms tight.

She teased him, licking and sucking before he sat up and dragged her up his body, rolling her so quickly she barely had time to register it. He kissed her hard, and she could taste his desperation.

Then he was gone, sliding down her body and tearing down her leggings. She gasped as his tongue touched her core and every thought left her brain. He teased her, caressing and tasting, using his fingers, his tongue. She writhed. "Jeremy, please. Now."

She needed him inside of her.

His gaze didn't leave hers as he reached for the condom and slid it on.

Then he lowered his body to hers, kissing her again, his cock nudging her entrance. "Ready?"

The care in his expression made her heart sing. This man was special.

"Yes." She widened her legs and as he kissed her

deeply, he slid in and she moaned.

Finally.

She wrapped her legs around his waist, urging him deeper and he complied, thrusting into her.

Every nerve ending sang as he moved, building the pleasure as he went. She couldn't take any more. She arched her back as her climax hit her. "Jeremy!"

***

Jeremy's legs were unsteady as he rolled off the bed to clean up. Not even in his wildest dreams had he expected Zamira to be a wildcat in bed.

He disposed of the condom and hurried back, finding her still lying on her back, her eyes closed, her short hair thoroughly messed, and a satisfied smirk on her face.

Aphrodite.

As he joined her on the bed, she opened her eyes and smiled at him. "Wow."

He grinned, the one word causing more pleasure to course through his body. "I'll say." He pulled her closer to him, needing to touch her soft skin.

She shivered and moved in.

"Are you cold?" They were lying on top of the sheets, but he shifted, pushing the bedspread down under him so he could pull it back up.

"You made the bed." She lifted her head to confirm and then raised an eyebrow at him.

Heat flushed his cheeks. "Ah, it was due." He covered them both with the bedspread and she kissed him.

"Thank you."

Her lips were addictive. When she pulled back, he cupped the back of her head and drew her closer, deepening the kiss. He couldn't get enough of her.

She moaned. "You're insatiable."

"With you." He didn't want her to leave.

Her fingers played with the silver pendant around her neck.

He plucked the pendant from her hands and examined it. Arabic letters were engraved on the front. "What does it say?"

"It translates as praise the God. It was a gift from my grandmother."

"After what just happened, I'll amen that." He grinned. "Is it Islamic?"

She nodded.

"Is that your faith?" He'd never dated anyone religious before.

"Yes." She screwed up her nose. "Though I'm not as strict as my father would like."

"How strict is that?"

"Well I don't wear a headscarf and I have had pre-marital sex." She winked.

He grinned. "I can't remember the last time I was in a church... maybe my aunt's wedding when I was about twelve." Religion wasn't a sexy topic and if what Zamira said was true, they had only two nights together.

He would make the most of them. He peppered soft kisses over her face. "Since we're friends, I have to tell you the camp bed is really uncomfortable." He slid his hand down the curve of her waist, across to her butt. "But you know, there's plenty of room in my bed."

She grinned. "I can see."

He fondled her breast, enjoying the way her nipple puckered. "It makes sense to share, don't you think? That way both of us are comfortable."

"You're a generous man, Jeremy." She squeezed his butt and desire stirred again. It had definitely been too long between drinks. "I'd love to share with you."

"Good." He rolled them so he was on top. "Now, where were we?"

Chapter 11

Jeremy lay awake in bed long after Zamira was fast asleep. He couldn't stop looking at her, which would be completely creepy if she woke and caught him. But something about her had captured his attention so thoroughly he couldn't help it.

He wanted to take care of her, protect her, help her any way he could.

And that was bad. She'd be gone in a few days. It didn't matter that for the first time since he'd moved in, his house felt full and warm, more like a home than a roof over his head.

He couldn't trust this kind of happiness. It could be too easily ripped from him.

He ran a hand over his beard. He wasn't getting any sleep at this rate. He got up and took clothes out of his drawer. Then he closed the bedroom door behind him so he didn't disturb Zamira and dressed in the living room. Fetch snored in his bed, the light and Jeremy's presence not enough to wake him.

He needed something to keep his mind busy.

He flicked through some of his paperwork. No, it wouldn't occupy his mind enough.

Grabbing his jacket and shoving his feet into his boots, he headed outside. The cold stung, drawing the heat from him. The clear sky revealed stars and the crescent moon. He jogged over to the shed, pulled back the doors and switched on the light. He inhaled the fresh timber and immediately his muscles relaxed. A bunch of cut pieces lying on his large work bench represented his office desk. He wandered over to his design, reviewed the shape. He hadn't cared how it looked when he'd first designed it. He planned to spend as little time as possible at it, but now, having Zamira here made him rethink. If one day someone moved in permanently, then his office needed to be a place for him to store all his paperwork, designs and models. His current desk design was little more than a table.

Jeremy dragged a chair over to his work bench and sat down with the design, sketching in some drawers and a desktop paperwork sorter. He'd need shelving to store his models, so he drew a rough plan of what he wanted. He'd take exact measurements later.

Now he had a complete office plan. He huffed. Too optimistic as usual, thinking he'd need an actual office, but it would give him something to do now. The bits he'd already cut for the desk were still usable, he just needed to tweak bits to incorporate the drawers.

He got to work, finding the wood he needed and cutting it to size, the buzz of his table saw whining in the night.

The joy of being so far from his neighbours was no one complained when he worked all hours of the night as he often did.

He cut the sides of the two drawers. He'd dovetail these and cut a groove for the base to go in. He'd need to go to the hardware store to get the right sized ply. The pressure in his chest eased as he worked, replaced by the satisfaction of making something.

"Jeremy?"

He jumped and found Zamira standing at the door, her black hair sticking up at all sorts of angles. She was wearing her blue slacks and one of his woollen jumpers. So beautiful. His.

His heart leapt. "Sorry, was I making too much noise?"

She shook her head. "I woke and you weren't there." She rubbed her eyes and walked in, glancing at the wood stacked on the sides, the sawdust on the floor and his workbench. "What are you doing?"

"Working on my desk."

"It's midnight." She gasped. "Is this what you should have been doing today rather than rescuing me?"

"No, I couldn't sleep." He walked over to her, secretly pleased she was concerned about his job. "Go back to bed. I won't be long."

She hesitated. "Can I see what you're making?"

He clasped her hand and led her to his work table. "It's a desk for my office, but I've made a few adjustments to it." Actually, the desktop would be a little nicer if it was slightly curved. He found a pencil and made the change.

"These bits of wood will become that?"

He smiled at her disbelief. "Eventually."

"Wow." She wandered over to his shelves which contained myriad stains, polishes and varnishes as well as different bits of equipment and projects he'd made and not known what to do with. "Did you make all of this?"

"Yeah."

She picked up a wooden clock and ran her fingers over it. "It's lovely. What are you going to do with it all?"

He shrugged. "Give it away, I guess."

She frowned. "You're not going to sell it?"

"It's just stuff I was playing with. What I made in my spare time."

"It's fantastic, Jeremy. You could sell this in one of the shops in town."

Her praise warmed him. "That's extra paperwork." No one wanted his insomnia driven projects. "Why don't we both go back to bed?"

"I don't want to interrupt."

"Nah, I've done what I can tonight and it's cold." He never noticed the temperature when he worked, but now he'd stopped, the cold seeped into his bones. He wrapped his arm around her waist, tossed his safety glasses on the bench and led her over to the door. "Let's go."

He wanted to make the most of the few days they had.

He wanted to be with her.

***

The next morning Jeremy woke to find Zamira snuggled into his side. He inhaled deeply, her hair tickling his nose and her minty scent making him smile. She snored softly. After the day she'd had yesterday, he wanted to let her sleep. His lungs constricted painfully at the thought of the crash. He could have lost her.

Christ, he needed to get his head read. He was latching onto Zamira already. Too many years alone had made him needy. Annoyed, he sneaked out of bed, taking one last look at Zamira, and then closed the door behind him.

His first stop today was to show Barbara the granny flat he'd designed. He'd cancelled yesterday and he couldn't disappoint her two days in a row.

Fetch trotted to the corridor to greet him, already up and waiting for his breakfast. Jeremy opened the back door and then added food to Fetch's bowl. He flicked on the kettle and studied his fridge. It was a bacon and eggs morning. Should he make enough for Zamira or let her sleep? He reached for the packet and then hesitated. He'd once read something about Muslims not eating certain meats.

Taking his tablet from where it was charging on the bench he did a quick search. Pork was forbidden.

If Zamira wasn't a strict Muslim, did that mean she ate bacon? Better not risk it. The scent would permeate the kitchen and he didn't want to put her off.

With a sigh he reached for the cereal packet instead.

"Morning." Zamira's words were sleepy and he turned to find her stretching, her T-shirt rising up and flashing her bare stomach.

Hot damn.

She yawned, placing a hand over her mouth and her hair was all dishevelled — definite sex hair. He grinned.

"Hey." He pulled her close and kissed her. "How are you feeling this morning?"

"Sore." She stretched again and groaned, touching her chest.

Gently he pushed up her top, and discovered the bruises had darkened overnight. He winced. Had he made things worse? "Do you want some painkillers?"

"I'll eat first." She plucked the cereal packet out of his hand with a smile and grabbed a bowl.

"Cuppa?" He took down two mugs and the coffee.

"It depends. Do you have any decent coffee?"

He frowned. "How do you define decent?"

"Not instant swill."

He held up the instant coffee jar. "So not this?"

She grimaced. "No. I'm from Melbourne, the coffee capital and instant is only one step up from dirty dishwater. Trust me."

He'd never got into the coffee culture, made a thermos of coffee before he left home if he was going to be at a job site all day. He placed a tea bag in her cup. "So what constitutes good coffee?"

"Proper coffee beans for a start." She got the milk out. "I'll take plunger coffee if there's nothing else on offer, but a good espresso is hard to beat."

"I'll keep it in mind." They took their bowls and mugs to the table. "What are you doing today?"

Zamira checked the time. "I want to follow the bus that takes the migrants to work, see if I can talk to Annisa again. What time do they normally leave?"

"In about half an hour." He frowned. "Do you think that's wise?"

"Agent Franklin suggested I buy Annisa a phone so she can call me if she has any problems. If I can find out where Annisa is working, I should be able to give it to her."

He didn't like the idea of her spying by herself.

"Where's the best place I can buy a phone?"

"The supermarket." Maybe he should take another day off work and go with her.

"What have you got planned?"

He rubbed his beard. "Well, I could come with you."

She raised her eyebrows. "I don't need baby-sitting, Jeremy. All I'm going to do is see which house Annisa gets dropped off at and then get her a phone. You've got better things to do. Didn't you do that granny flat design yesterday?"

He nodded. She was right. "I've got a client meeting and I need to head into Albany for some supplies." He squeezed her hand. "Be careful, all right? Text me after you've seen Annisa. I might be able to tell you who lives at the address."

"I will."

Checking the time, he got up, eating the rest of his cereal as he walked back to the kitchen. "I've got to get a move on. Call me if you need anything." He put his bowl in the dishwasher. "I'll take the truck today, so you can take the ute again." He handed her some painkillers.

She kissed him. "Thanks."

He smiled, resisting the urge to deepen the kiss and take her back to bed. He headed towards the hallway and then stopped and turned back to her. "Want to share a shower?"

She grinned. "Of course. I'm very environmentally responsible." She joined him as he walked to the bathroom.

He could afford to be a little late this morning.

*****

Zamira waved to Jeremy as he drove down the drive. Their shower together had been quick but energising, and now she had to focus. She'd parked the ute next to some peppermints so it couldn't be seen from the road. Then she crept closer to watch Henk's gate.

Her breath fogged in the cool morning and the thick clouds smothered most of the sun's early morning rays. She hugged her jacket closer to her body.

Hopefully she wouldn't have long to wait.

In the distance the growl of an engine started. That could be it. She waited, staring at the gate and as the engine grew louder, the gate slid open. It was still too dark to see who was inside the small bus, so she jogged back to the ute and waited until it had passed before she started the engine.

The advantage of it being such a dark morning was that she needed to use her headlights, so the bus driver shouldn't be able to get a good look at the ute. He might not realise he was being followed.

The bus drove towards Blackbridge and then turned in the direction of the Vale winery.

Damn. She hadn't thought this through. She couldn't possibly follow the bus into the winery to see who disembarked. It was far too early to pretend to be a tourist going for a wine tasting and the driver might recognise Jeremy's ute.

Though if Annisa was working as a cleaner, she might not be working there.

When the bus turned into the winery, she continued driving past. The road was narrow and winding without an easy place to turn around. She accelerated, hoping to find another driveway she could pull into.

The bus would have reached the sheds by now. It wouldn't take long for the workers to get off.

Jaw tight, she scanned for somewhere to do a U-turn.

There! A slight widening in the road. She slammed on the brakes, glad no one was behind her and did an awkward three-point turn.

Accelerating again, it wasn't far until the vines appeared on the left-hand side of the road. In the distance, the sheds and restaurant were silhouetted against the glow of the clouds.

Where was the bus?

Headlights moved down the driveway.

She was going too fast. She slowed, but it was too late. She was going to pass the driveway before the bus exited.

Damn.

Checking her speed, she slowed to just under the

speed limit and glanced in her rear-view mirror. The bus had turned towards her.

Thankfully.

When she reached the main highway, she turned towards Blackbridge and kept glancing in her rear-view mirror until she confirmed the bus was following her.

Now what?

She decreased her speed until the bus caught up, but there weren't many places for it to pass. She kept at the speed limit until she drove into town and then she turned down the street that ran past the river. The bus continued straight on so she quickly looped around the block and back to the main highway.

The bus was gone.

No! She turned left, scanning the nearby streets. She slowed as she passed each road and spotted the white bus parked in the carpark of what looked to be a mechanic and wreckers' yard.

That had to be where her hire car had been towed. A good excuse for her to drop by later and check what had happened to it, and also see who was working there.

She pulled into the tourist bureau and parked, the engine still running, and grabbed her camera from the seat next to her. She zoomed in and took a couple of photos of the bus and the people getting off, but the light wasn't great. If she was lucky, she'd be able to see more detail when she enlarged the shots on her laptop.

The bus made two more stops in town and while the day was now bright enough for her to see who got off, it was never Annisa.

The bus drove past her and it had only two occupants in it – both male.

Annisa had to have disembarked at the winery or the mechanics'.

Zamira headed for the supermarket and bought a cheap phone. When she got back into the ute she unpackaged it and inserted the sim card. Her shoulders slumped. The battery showed a low charge. Of course.

Putting the car into gear, she headed for the bakery.

***

"Jeremy Mendelson, you're a genius!" Gladys's shrill delight made him smile as relief swept through him.

"You like the design?" She had strong opinions and wasn't afraid to air them, but it wasn't just her decision. The granny flat was going on her daughter's property.

Barbara nodded. "It's perfect. How long will it take?"

"I can start work next month, if the council approves it," he said. "Assuming we run into no issues when we dig the upright supports, it'll take about two months." He looked out their window. "You'll need to remove a couple of trees in the meantime."

"Can't you build around them?" Gladys asked.

"It would add a significant cost and they'll be a fire hazard." The garden was already covered in piles of leaf litter, which wasn't a big deal at this time of year but would be come summer. He directed his next comment to Barbara. "I can do a fire safety assessment for you if you'd like. It's lovely to be amongst the trees, but your block will be hard to defend if a fire comes this way." He shouldn't say anything, knew people didn't like to be preached to, but he wouldn't be doing right by them if he didn't at least mention it.

"Yeah, that would be great. I've been meaning to do it for a while now."

He packed up his things. "If you're happy to go ahead with the construction I'll put together a detailed job plan and get it to you by the end of the week."

"Perfect."

Jeremy checked his watch. "Do you want me to do the fire assessment for you now?"

"Yes, please."

Gladys hugged him. "I can't wait to move in."

He smiled at her enthusiasm. "I'm glad. Now let me get my checklist."

A few minutes later he wandered around Barbara's yard making notes. She walked next to him, occasionally pulling out a weed.

"Hey, Barbara, do you know where Henk's migrants are working?" He wrote down that one of the eucalypts needed trimming.

"Some work at the Vale and Morgan hired a couple," she said. "I think another few work for the local fishermen. Why do you ask?"

"You heard about the fire at his place the other day?"

She nodded.

"I rescued a woman from the building and I realised I'd never seen her before." He shrugged. "I wondered where she was working."

Barbara pursed her lips. "I think the ag school might have hired one," she said. "Though I heard Bec Simons complain they don't last long. Apparently they always get homesick and go home and she has to train a new one."

Jeremy's heart jumped. "Thanks." He pointed to the branch above them. "Those are going to need trimming."

Maybe Jamie could get them in to see Annisa.

An hour later he whistled as he drove his truck towards Albany. He'd sent Jamie a text asking him to call, but it would probably be a couple of hours before he'd have a break between classes. Jeremy slowed at the turn off to his place. Stopping to check on Zamira wouldn't be productive and she might not be there. She'd messaged him to say she hadn't found Annisa but needed to check on her hire car.

After he heard back from Jamie, he'd call her and if he got his work done he could go home early. The idea of someone to go home to made him all warm inside.

He drove directly to the large hardware store and parked near the trade entrance. Aside from varnish, he needed to buy the ply for his desk drawers and then he'd pick up his order.

The massive warehouse had the ceiling arching high above and the shelving in long rows. He found a trolley, headed for the varnish aisle.

As he examined the different options a voice said, "Jeremy?"

He turned and then stumbled back like he'd been punched in the gut. "Moira." He only recognised his baby sister because a mutual friend had pointed her out at an Australia Day celebration a couple of years ago. His fingers tightened on the can he held. She looked well. Her long blonde hair was styled in layers around her face and her cheeks were flushed from the cold. She was waiting for him to say something. "How's it going?"

"Really good." Her smile was cautious. "I just got engaged." She gestured to the man next to her. "This is Ollie."

His chest squeezed. Christ. His little sister was old enough to be engaged. Of course she was. It had been thirteen years since he'd been part of her life. Jeremy shook Ollie's hand summing him up. His handshake was firm and he smiled, his eyes kind. That was good. Not that he had any say in his sister's life. Hadn't been a part of it since he was fifteen. "Congratulations."

"Nice to finally meet you. You should come to dinner one night."

Jeremy glanced at his sister. Didn't this bloke know what had happened?

"Great idea," Moira said. "I'd really like to catch up." She touched his arm, her eyes uncertain.

His throat closed over. She'd been only ten when their father had died, when their mother had kicked him out. He remembered her as a sweet girl, playing with her dolls and obsessed with dancing and singing. She'd always begged him to play with her and he could never refuse. He'd even let her put makeup on him and they'd put on a show for their parents and Heather. He closed his eyes, trying to block the pain. How much of that girl was still there? He doubted she played with dolls anymore. Who was he kidding? This young woman was a stranger. "Where do you live?"

"We've got our own place in Lockyer," she said.

So no longer living with their mother.

No, he couldn't get his hopes up, couldn't stand here making small talk with her. It was too painful. "I've gotta go."

She grabbed his arm. "Wait. Can I get your number?" she asked. "We can arrange a time for dinner, or coffee?" Her expression was so hopeful, the same as it had been all those years ago when she'd asked him to play Barbies with her.

His throat ached. "Um, sure." He rattled it off and she put it in her phone.

"It's really great to see you, Jeremy." She hesitated and then hugged him.

He hugged her back automatically, tears glistening in his eyes. He blinked them back and cleared his throat. "Yeah, well, see you." He walked blindly away, not caring what varnish he held in his hand or where he went.

When he reached the back of the store, he stopped, took a deep breath to stop his hands from shaking. His baby sister was all grown up, getting married and wanted to see him.

He gritted his teeth and pressed his tongue to the roof of his mouth to stop the tears from forming.

Why now?

It had been thirteen years since he'd had contact with any of his family. Thirteen years since his mother had ordered him out of the house. Thirteen years since he'd forgotten to flick the power off.

Thirteen years since he had killed his father.

Chapter 12

Mai had let Zamira charge the phone at the bakery while she filled up on coffee, pastries and planned her next step. When she was done, she went to the mechanics' first.

A middle-aged man with dark hair looked up as she walked into the workshop. He wiped his hands on a rag. "Hi, how can I help?" The name tag on his overalls said Morgan.

She smiled at him. "My name's Zamira. My hire car was towed here yesterday."

"Oh sure. Do you want to take a look?"

She nodded and followed him out of the workshop and around the side to the wrecker's yard. Two Malaysian men worked across the yard, stripping parts out of cars and her white hire car sat close to the entrance, a mass of scratches and dents.

"The insurance assessors are due later today," Morgan said. "I think Nicholas cleared out all the possessions, but you can check."

"Thanks." She hadn't left anything in there, but she went through the motions of checking, opening the passenger side door. "What will happen to it after the assessors have been?"

"Depends. I'd guess they'll consider it a write-off, so I might buy it and strip it for parts."

She raised her eyebrows. "Is that what they're doing?" She pointed to the migrants.

"Yeah. Lots of things can be recycled."

Zamira couldn't think of any reasonable excuse for her to go over and talk to them, but it was clear Annisa wasn't here.

"Thanks for your help."

She drove out to the Vale winery. The restaurant had just opened. She didn't dare get her camera out as she spotted Kay and the migrant workers over by the shed, loading wine barrels on to the back of a truck. But at least she now had an excuse to go over there.

She walked quickly past the playground to the fence that divided the restaurant from the sheds. Kay spotted her and strode over, a scowl on her face.

"There aren't any tours of the sheds."

Zamira smiled. "You're Kay, aren't you?"

The woman nodded once.

"I'm Zamira. Your father crashed into me yesterday, and I wanted to check he was all right." Behind Kay one of the migrants stopped to look at her, a frown on his face. Then another man called to him and he moved back into the shed.

Kay's scowl deepened and she placed her hand on the wooden post. "He's fine." She sighed. "I'm really sorry about that. How are you?"

"A little bruised, but not too bad." She rested a hand on Kay's. "I can't imagine how hard it is for you to deal with his dementia."

Kay snatched her hand back, ran it through her hair. "It's no picnic. At least now he can't hurt others… if he remembers he doesn't have a licence."

Of course. Zamira nodded. "I can see you're busy, so I'll let you get back to it. Take care."

Kay's nod was curt and she spun on her heel and returned to supervise the men. Zamira stood there a moment longer, scanning the people, hoping to see a glimpse of Annisa, but aside from Kay, they were all men.

Maybe she was still at Henk's place.

Zamira returned to the ute and drove back to Jeremy's. Henk's gate was shut again.

She must have been lucky on Saturday to find it open. Or maybe it was only open when Henk was home. Annisa might be inside at the moment, waiting for her next job. She needed to check.

Fetch trotted out to greet her and she patted his head as she inhaled deeply, some of her worries fading at the peace of the place.

Jeremy was lucky to live here.

She smiled at the thought of him. The sex had been amazing, and afterwards she'd fallen asleep in his arms. But both times she'd woken, he hadn't been there. Maybe he wasn't as comfortable having her in his bed as he'd said.

She stretched to ease her aches and pains, her bag bumping against her side, the camera safe inside. She would do more yoga later, but first she needed to see if Annisa was next door. Fetch would give her the perfect excuse.

She opened the back door, checking the laundry cupboard for a lead, but couldn't find one. Jeremy left him outside to roam when he wasn't home which had to mean Fetch didn't wander far. "You want to go for a walk?"

His ears pricked and he thumped his tail.

She grinned. "Come on then."

The cold hovered around her. She tucked her hands under her armpits and walked down the back steps, taking a deep breath in. Wet grass, wet eucalypts, fresh air. Nothing like Melbourne. Her boots were damp in seconds but the leather would be fine. Fetch trotted next to her, occasionally dashing off when a scent caught his attention and then coming back to her.

She retrieved her camera and took a few photos. If only this was really a holiday, if only Annisa was safe, if only she could truly enjoy her time here.

A kookaburra laughed, its cackle loud and lingering in the air before fading. A couple of galahs sat in nearby trees, nibbling on leaves and nuts. A silver-eye hopped over the grass searching for insects.

She'd never noticed much bird life in the city. Her journey to work consisted of walking to the bus stop outside her apartment and then changing to a tram to take her into the city. It was concrete and traffic all the way. Stress and aggravation from her fellow passengers as they all tried to squeeze into a carriage so they weren't late for work.

She didn't miss it.

She hadn't been happy in her job for a long time, but had stuck with it, toeing the line in the hope eventually she could move into the area where she really wanted to work.

But now who knew what was going to happen? She'd made demands when she had no right to do so. What would she do if she didn't work for Border Force?

She didn't have a backup plan.

She sighed and walked through the bush at the back of Jeremy's property. There might not be as much vegetation along the fire break and she'd get a better look at Henk's place.

Her footsteps slowed as a thought occurred to her. Perhaps the bus did a second work run. Annisa might have been on that. The dormitory building would have housed more people than the bus carried. She should have thought of that.

She sighed.

Perhaps she should be patient. Border Force might be raiding Henk's property at any minute – and by tomorrow it should all be over. Annisa would be safe, even though she would be in trouble for being here without a visa.

Zamira would help her however she could, and then return to Melbourne.

Aside from the coffee, she didn't miss the place. Her best friend lived in the Northern Territory and Zamira had no other close friends. She associated her apartment, her work and even her family at times with stress and aggravation. Too many parental expectations she hadn't lived up to.

She'd never considered going to the country on the weekend, or taking long walks through the bush. Curling up on the couch with a comic or a movie was her ideal way to spend the day. So why did Blackbridge give her such a sense of peace?

She reached the fire break and headed towards Henk's property. It was a lot less scary walking in daylight when she could see all the trees and bushes, and birds flitting from branch to branch. She scanned the area, keeping one eye on Fetch who trotted along next to her and one towards Henk's place. She spotted the fence through the bush as soon as it came within view. Those poor people were trapped, unable to run away.

Border Force couldn't act fast enough for her.

Her footsteps slowed. The bush had been squashed

in two places, running parallel towards Henk's place. Tyre tracks.

On a whim she walked along them and came to another big metal gate at the corner of the property. Signs declared 'Danger, electric fence', and the bush both sides of the gate was flat enough to suggest it was used semi-regularly. Through the gap in the trees she could see a couple of people walking near the tents. Her skin tingled. Was that Annisa? It was definitely a woman, slim, with long dark hair. The person ducked into Annisa's tent. Yes. It had to be.

Now to get to her. Should she yell to get her attention?

She scanned the gate for signs it was electrified as well and her gaze caught the security camera pointing directly at her.

Damn.

She forced herself to smile as Fetch snuffled closer to the gate. "Come here, Fetch." She whistled and turned back towards the fire break as if there was nothing interesting to see here.

Hope filled her. She hadn't missed Annisa at all.

A rustle in the bush had her spinning around, heart racing and skin hot. Nothing there.

Beside her, Fetch pricked his ears and then bounded into the bush with a bark.

"Fetch!" She hadn't known he could move so fast. If she lost him, Jeremy would be devastated. And what if it was a snake? One bite would kill Fetch. Damn it. She should have left him behind.

She ran after the crashing noises ahead of her, her steps large and clumsy as she avoided bushes and tried not to trip over dead branches on the ground. At least he raced away from Henk's place and wouldn't get himself electrocuted.

"Fetch!" Every muscle in her body ached as she moved as fast as she could.

She burst out of the trees and stopped. Row upon row of beehives stretched out in front of her. She scanned the area and yelled, "Fetch?"

A person stood up at the end of one of the rows, her long red hair drawing attention.

Zamira winced and waved. The woman walked towards her. Would she get into trouble for trespassing? She moved forward and as she stepped into the row, she saw Fetch trotting happily by the person's side. "There you are!"

Fetch wagged his tail but didn't run to greet her.

As the woman in her mid-twenties reached her, Zamira said, "I'm so sorry. Fetch heard something in the bush and he ran away from me."

The woman frowned. "This is Jeremy's dog. Who are you?"

"Zamira." With a smile, she held out a hand. "I'm staying with Jeremy for a few days."

The woman's handshake was gentle, a little uncertain and Zamira noticed faded bruising under one of her eyes. "Alyse."

"I'm sorry to bother you." She glanced at the beehives, her curiosity stirring, and beyond them she could make out the burnt structure on Henk's property. "You've got a lot of hives."

Alyse smiled. "I harvest honey commercially."

"Is it hard?"

"The bees do all the work."

"Oh, right. I don't know anything about beekeeping."

"Why don't you come over to the shed and taste some of the honey?"

That country friendliness again. Zamira grinned. "I'd

love to, but I don't want to impose."

Alyse glanced over her shoulder to the buildings in the distance. "No trouble. I just finished here. Besides it's always good to get someone else hooked."

Zamira laughed. "All right." She looked towards Henk's place. "Were you worried the fire next door the other night was going to spread?"

Alyse frowned then shook her head. "The fire brigade arrived pretty quickly, and it had been raining all week."

They walked through the beehives towards a large silver shed. "I don't suppose the hives would be easy to move."

"No, but I have more in other parts of the forest."

Zamira glanced at her. "Have you been doing this long?"

"All my life. I grew up here."

In the distance stood a small house and at the border of the property towards the bush stood a similar building to the one that had burnt down at Henk's. Zamira's muscles tightened. Could Alyse be involved too? "You've got a lot of buildings."

Concern flittered over Alyse's face, her laugh a bit forced. "That's my partner's man cave," she said. "He was envious of my shed, so he had to go big too."

An understatement. The dorm-like property was almost as big as the commercial shed. "Does he have a lot of toys?"

Alyse rolled her eyes. "Everything imaginable."

As they reached the shed, a dark four-wheel drive pulled into the driveway towing a large silver dinghy and approached the man cave.

"Come on." Alyse grabbed Zamira's arm, pulling her towards the honey shed, her hand shaking.

Zamira went with her, goosebumps on her skin.

Alyse was worried about something. She should get out of here.

Her fear faded a little as the sweet scent of honey drifted towards her and Alyse led her into a small room with jars of honey as well as beeswax candles and a bunch of beauty products. "You make more than honey?"

"I try to use all the components." Alyse smiled as she lifted a small pot of honey from the shelves, her whole demeanour relaxing. "Recently I've been experimenting with creams and balms, but they're not ready for market yet."

"Do you do all of this?"

"I hire help when I need it and sometimes my partner helps. The winter is always slow for honey production so I experiment on other things."

"I'm impressed."

She shrugged. "We do what we need to survive." The sadness in her voice made Zamira pause.

"Alyse! Where are you?" a male voice bellowed.

Alyse flinched, glanced around as if looking for a place to hide. "You'd better go." She hurried out of the store room. "I'm here, Mark. I was just chatting to a friend of Jeremy's."

Mark's head almost reached the top of the doorway and he wore a baseball cap over his dark hair. His whole bulk and posture threatened in a way Jeremy's never had. Zamira stepped back. The only other exit was a large roller door across the other side, but it was closed.

Mark's deep scowl changed into a leer when he saw Zamira. "G'day, sweetheart."

Zamira smiled even though the hairs on her arms stood on end. "Hi." She didn't want to leave Alyse here with this man, so she turned and asked, "Would you like to come over for coffee?"

Alyse hesitated.

"Not today," Mark answered. "I need her for something."

Alyse shrunk into herself and nodded. "Take the road back to Jeremy's. It'll be a little shorter and there are less things to distract Fetch. Follow the driveway and turn right." She walked Zamira to the door.

"I'm staying until Sunday," Zamira said. "Drop by whenever you want. I'd love to hear more about your bees." Conscious of Mark still staring at her, she let out a breath. "Thanks for the honey." She hurried away, Fetch by her side. When she reached the house, she turned back but Alyse and Mark had disappeared.

Was Alyse in trouble?

She'd have to ask Jeremy about her when he got back.

***

Jeremy threw himself into installing new shop fittings after he left the hardware store. Anything to keep his mind off his sister and what had happened. But it didn't work. Being on a work site reminded him of his father, of the beginning of his apprenticeship when everything had been so damned good. He'd no longer been trapped in school, spent his days outside working with his father and sometimes if they finished a job early, they'd go fishing for an hour or so before they went home.

His mother hadn't approved of him leaving school before he graduated, but that was one argument his father had won. And Jeremy had been so thankful for it.

Rote learning and text books did his head in. School had only been good for socialising, and summer days had been a particular hell when there had been far better things he could be doing.

His mother had constantly berated him, trying to make him pay attention when she lectured about the importance of getting an education. He'd been so sure he knew better — life was an education, and he not only learnt how to build, but also about customer service and project management from his dad and it had really lit him up.

All he'd ever wanted was to be like his dad. His father had known everything about anything important and was successful. Plus he let Jeremy experiment and then they'd both analyse an idea if it didn't work.

He'd been challenged far more working with his dad than he ever had at school.

Until the day he'd been distracted and made the biggest mistake of his life. Jeremy hadn't just lost his father that day, but his whole family — his mother rightly blaming him for his father's death.

Jeremy turned the last screw into the shelving and stood back. It was done. He packed away his tools and cleaned up the area. As he dated the invoice, his pen paused. His mother's birthday was today.

Moira hadn't mentioned it. Did they still go to his mother's favourite restaurant for dinner? Would Moira mention she'd seen him today?

Jeremy had always hated the restaurant because his mother had made him wear dress pants and a shirt and tie which strangled him. They'd always sit at the same table in the corner of the room, his mother tapping the menu impatiently waiting to be served, Heather sitting straight, her hands in her lap, the perfect lady, Moira fidgeting or whispering to him about school, and his father... well he'd always seemed perfectly content, complimenting his wife on how beautiful she looked.

That last birthday he'd complained to his dad about the clothes and it was one of the only times he remembered his father getting stroppy. "Little things like appearances are important to your mother," he had said. "This is one night when she wants something special. It's not a hardship to be uncomfortable for one night to make her happy."

Jeremy had been surprised by the depth of emotion from his father and had immediately stopped complaining. At least the food had been good.

He shook away the thought and went next door to the bakery where the owner said she'd be waiting. She sat at a window seat with a coffee, and he gave her the invoice and then headed for the counter. The scent of coffee reminded him about what Zamira had said this morning.

"What can I get you, Jeremy?" Jodie asked.

If he asked Jodie about where to get the makings for proper coffee it would be around town in seconds. He scanned the goodies in the cabinet. All women liked chocolate, didn't they? "A couple of chocolate brownies, please."

"These both for you?" she asked as she boxed them up.

He smiled. "No." He paid and then left. Mai would know about coffee, but she might still be sleeping. He wandered down the street back to where he'd parked his truck and walked past a homewares store. On a whim, he ducked inside.

Zamira had mentioned plunger coffee.

He scanned the shop until he saw teapots and headed over.

"Can I help you?" an older woman asked.

"I'm after a coffee plunger."

"What size?"

"Ahh…" He had no idea.

"I've got a one cup plunger, or four or eight."

"Four." Seemed like the best option.

She showed him the relevant one and he nodded, following her over to the cash register to pay. "Where can I get the coffee?"

"It's a gift?" she guessed.

"Yeah."

"The coffee aisle in the supermarket is a good start. If you don't have a coffee grinder, then look for the pre-ground coffee packets. On the side they usually say if they can be used in plungers or espresso machines." She handed him his receipt and the bag.

"Thanks."

He drove to the supermarket and after agonising over different coffee options he chose one and headed back to his car. They could have afternoon tea together and then he'd finish off the components for the reception desk he was installing tomorrow.

His phone rang. Jamie. After seeing Moira, he'd forgotten all about Annisa. "Hey, mate."

"What can I help you with?"

Jeremy checked to make sure no one was standing nearby and got into his car. "I wanted to ask about a cleaner who works for the ag school."

"Sure. Who?"

"I heard Annisa might work there. I rescued her in the building fire last week."

Jamie was silent a minute. "She's one of Henk's Asian migrants, right?"

"Yeah."

"I haven't seen her, but she might work over at the dormitories. Want me to check?"

"If you could." He hesitated. "Just don't mention I was asking."

"Do I want to know what this is about?" Jamie asked.

"I'll tell you when I can."

"All right. I'll head over there after class and call you back."

"Thanks." He hung up. Hopefully Jamie could give him some good news to tell Zamira.

As he drove into his property, Zamira and Fetch were walking along the drive towards the house. He smiled as they both turned and Fetch danced on the spot in excitement. He wound down his window. "Hey, been for a walk?"

Her smile warmed his insides. "Yes. Though Fetch decided to visit your neighbour a couple of blocks down."

He frowned. "Alyse?"

She nodded, a wry expression on her face.

"Let me park and you can tell me about it." He drove up to his shed and got his purchases out. Zamira and Fetch met him and they walked over to the house. Jeremy asked, "So what happened?"

"I took Fetch for a walk along the fire break and he heard something and dashed off. I found him in the middle of Alyse's beehives."

He chuckled. "I should have warned you. Occasionally something gets him excited enough to get out of first gear." It was sweet she'd taken him for a walk though.

Zamira held the back door open for him and he went through and put his purchases on the bench. "Do you want a cuppa? I bought you decent coffee." He unpacked the plunger and coffee and glanced at her. "I hope it's right."

She stared at him, her mouth open a little, and then

she beamed. "Thank you. You didn't have to do that." She wrapped her arms around him and kissed him soundly on the mouth.

Hell yes. He pulled her closer, deepened the kiss and slid his hands gently down to her butt. Stopping for afternoon tea had definitely been a good idea.

Her moan of approval shot heat straight to his groin and he backed her up against the fridge.

She gasped and pulled away, flinching. "Ow."

Guilt swept through him. "Sorry. I forgot about your bruises. You OK?" He caressed her arm.

Her eyes were dark. "I'd forgotten about them too."

With a look like that he would forget again. He turned back to the bench and washed the plunger in the sink. "You'll need to tell me how much coffee to use."

"A spoon for every cup."

He filled the kettle and dried the plunger. "I bought us something to eat too." He gestured towards the bakery box.

She opened it. "Yum. I've discovered anything from Mai's bakery is delicious."

"Yeah, it is."

A few minutes later they sat in the lounge room, the coffee sitting or stewing or whatever it did in the plunger before it was time to pour, and the brownies on a plate.

"How's your day been?" Zamira asked.

His sister flashed into his mind. The urge to confide in Zamira was strong, but how would she look at him after she knew his dirty secret?

"Jeremy?" Her soft hand touched his.

Why ruin the short time they had together? "Fine." He picked up the plate and handed it to her. "Brownie?"

She took one, but frowned at him.

Best keep her distracted. "Any more news on Annisa?"

"I thought I saw her at Henk's place today."

"You went over there?"

She shook her head. "When I took Fetch for a walk, I noticed tyre tracks and they led to a gate at the back of his property. I could see the tents from there and a couple of people walking around."

"That's great. I asked Barbara if she knew where Annisa could be working and she suggested the ag school. Jamie's checking it out for me."

She beamed at him. "Thank you." She pushed the plunger down and poured the coffees. "I really appreciate it."

He took the coffee she handed him. "I want her to be safe too." If his friends were in danger, he wouldn't wait for the authorities to get their shit together. He sipped his drink and the richer, fuller flavour warmed him. "You're right. This is better than instant."

"Told you." She played with her pendant.

"What's wrong?"

"Nothing."

He covered her hand with his and stilled the movement. "You only play with your pendant when you're worried about something."

She sighed. "How well do you know Alyse?"

He sat back. "My neighbour?"

She nodded and then sipped her coffee.

"I don't see her much. She occasionally works in the football canteen or I run into her when I take Fetch for a walk."

"What about Mark?"

He screwed up his face. "He's loud, opinionated and thinks he's always right. I don't know what Alyse sees in him."

Zamira hesitated and then said, "Would he beat her?"

Jeremy winced. "There have been rumours. Why?"

"Alyse had the remnants of a black eye today and when Mark arrived she seemed scared of him."

He sighed. "We can't do anything if she doesn't charge him."

"It's her place, isn't it? She said she'd grown up there."

He shrugged. "Like I said, I don't know her that well." He placed a hand on her arm. "It's lovely you're concerned, but we should focus on one thing at a time. We can chat to Alyse after Annisa is safe."

"Mark's man-cave building is a lot like the dorm that burned down at Henk's place."

He blinked at the change of subject. "Really? I haven't been over there in a couple of years, not since they stopped selling honey from the shed. Do you think it's a coincidence?"

She shrugged. "Maybe he was envious."

"Wouldn't surprise me. Mark wants whatever anyone else has. Growing up wealthy didn't teach him any better."

Zamira's ring tone pierced the room. She got up to answer and as she checked the screen, her eyes widened. "It's Border Force."

Chapter 13

Zamira's hand trembled as she answered. "Hello?"

"Is this Zamira Musa?" a female voice asked.

"Yes."

"This is Agent Tara Franklin from Border Force, we spoke yesterday. "Did you speak to your cousin today?"

"No. She didn't leave the property."

A pause. "That's a shame. Could you answer some questions for me about Henk Jennings' compound?"

"Of course."

"Where are you staying?"

She glanced at Jeremy. "At a friend's place."

"Can I meet you there?"

"Sure. Let me get you the address." She lowered the phone and Jeremy told her. She repeated it to the agent.

"That's next door to the Jennings place."

"Yes."

Franklin made a considering sound in her throat. "All right. I'll be there within half an hour." She hung up.

"Who was that?" Jeremy asked.

"Agent Franklin with Border Force. She's coming out here to talk to me."

He stood, gathered their mugs from the coffee table. "That's good, right? They must be ready to act."

She hoped so. Either way, she should change so she was presentable. She wanted to make a good impression.

She hurried into the bathroom and checked her reflection in the mirror. Her hair looked like she'd been dragged through the bush backwards, the short strands sticking up in myriad directions. Combing it didn't help. She'd been too sore to lift her arms above her head to blow dry it this morning and the wind had played with it on her walk.

"Everything all right?" Jeremy leaned against the bathroom door frame.

"I look a mess."

He walked in, stood behind her and wrapped his arms around her waist. "You look beautiful."

Her heart expanded and she smiled briefly. No, she couldn't get caught up in the intensity in his eyes. She shook her head. "I need to look professional. My job might depend on it." She sighed. "Ever since my grandmother told me how she was treated like a slave when she migrated here, I've wanted to be an agent with the Task Force. I keep getting knocked back. If I can impress Agent Franklin it might help."

"All right. What can I do?" He stepped back, tilted his head to the side. "I guess you've got another fancy outfit in your suitcase, so what does that leave — hair, makeup?"

Fancy outfit? None of her clothes were particularly fancy. "My hair's the big problem. I can't blow dry it without hurting."

He frowned. "I can give it a shot if you've got a hair dryer."

So incredibly sweet. He was her only hope. "That

would be great. Let me take a quick shower. Can you keep an eye out for the car?"

"Sure." He left her in the bathroom and she stripped, quickly washing and drying herself. Then with the towel wrapped around her body, she hurried down the hallway to Jeremy's room. Her grey pants were the only ones she hadn't worn yet, and she had a nice blue blouse that would work. She dressed and retrieved her makeup kit, checking the time as she went. Fifteen minutes.

Hair first. "Jeremy!" She was being ridiculous, they wouldn't care what she looked like, but she couldn't stop now.

He appeared at the door. "What do I need to do?"

She plugged in the hair dryer and took out her curling brush. Lifting her arm she winced as her muscles pulled and she demonstrated how to dry her hair. She handed the brush and dryer to Jeremy and he looked a bit dubious.

"All right." He emulated what she'd shown him, pulling her hair. "Sorry."

His whole focus was on the task, his tongue just sticking out between his lips as he curled and dried.

He did a good job. When it was dry, she kissed him. "Thank you."

A knock on the front door had her jumping. "Can you stall her? I haven't done my makeup."

He nodded. "For what it's worth, you don't need any makeup." He brushed a kiss over her lips and went to answer the door.

She pressed a hand to her chest. Comments like those could really get to a girl. If she wasn't careful, she'd fall in love with him. Shaking her head, she then quickly applied the basics and in the living room, Jeremy offered Franklin a drink. With a deep breath,

Zamira joined them.

The table was completely clear as were the coffee table and bench top. Jeremy must have tidied while she showered. How sweet.

The woman standing in the kitchen was tall, with long brown hair tied back in a braid, and wore plain clothes — black pants and an emerald green shirt rather than the Border Force uniform. She turned as Zamira walked into the room.

"Sorry to keep you waiting." Zamira held out her hand. "I'm Zamira Musa."

"Agent Tara Franklin." Her handshake was firm, no nonsense. "Jeremy was just making me a coffee."

He had the coffee plunger out and had measured several spoons into it. "Why don't you two sit down while I make it?"

Zamira gestured to the kitchen table and they both sat.

"First I want to check my facts," Agent Franklin said. "Your cousin is working for Henk Jennings?"

"Yes. Annisa came to Australia on what she thought was a legitimate work visa, but Vince — my manager at Border Force — couldn't find any reference to it. No one had heard from her since."

"How did you discover she was here?"

Was Franklin questioning her again to ensure she said the same thing? Didn't she trust her? "There was a fire at Henk's place. She was trapped inside and Jeremy rescued her. They were both taken to the hospital."

Jeremy placed the coffee and mugs on the table. "She was confused by the time I got to her."

Zamira nodded. "She called me from the hospital and since I was going on holidays anyway, I changed my flight to come here."

Franklin raised her eyebrows. "I understand you

went to your boss first."

Zamira winced. "Yes, but he couldn't tell me anything more than that someone in Blackbridge had been identified as a person of interest by the Task Force. I didn't know if Annisa was there, so I came to find out."

"How did you find her?"

Zamira sipped her coffee and told the agent how she'd worked out where Annisa was and about talking to her the other night. "I didn't want to blow the Task Force's operation by taking her with me at that stage."

Franklin nodded. "I appreciate it. What can you tell me about the property and the other workers?"

Jeremy described Henk's place. "Some of the men are working at the winery, and at the local mechanic's."

"How do you know all this?"

He shrugged. "I asked around. Said I had a couple of big jobs coming up and could do with some help."

The agent studied him. "You don't seem upset your neighbour could be involved."

"No point getting upset. If it's true, he needs to be stopped."

"Do you think it's true?"

"Annisa was scared of him, so something's not right." He sighed. "Look, we've had some weird shit happening in Blackbridge this year; stalkers, arsonists, drug-related crime, murder. Several of my good mates were involved and I had no idea. I want to get this sorted before it escalates into something worse." His voice was rough and Zamira squeezed his hand.

"Is there anything else you can tell me which might be of use?"

Zamira glanced at Jeremy and he shook his head. "No."

Franklin studied her. "I'm impressed by your

initiative. You speak Malaysian, don't you?"

"Yes."

"Could you translate for us if required tomorrow?"

Shock speared through her. "Of course. Any time."

"Great." She stood and walked to the front door. "I'll be in touch."

Zamira smiled. This could be her big chance.

When Jeremy opened the door for her, Franklin pointed. "Henk's property is over there, isn't it?"

Zamira nodded.

"How far through those trees is the fence line?"

"About fifty metres," Jeremy answered.

"Can you see anything from there?"

Jeremy shook his head. "Just more bush and his fence is electrified."

Franklin raised her eyebrows. "He got any livestock on the property?"

"No. I always figured it was because he was from South Africa. They're a little more security conscious than us."

She nodded. "Thank you for your time."

She got into an unmarked white sedan and drove away.

Jeremy turned to Zamira. "That went well."

"It did." Her insides squirmed at the idea of helping the Task Force with translation.

"She has a good handle on things." He wrapped his arm around her waist and drew her back inside.

Zamira leaned into him. "Yeah." Tomorrow this would all be over. Annisa would be safe. Jeremy kissed her head and let go. She missed his warmth.

After tomorrow she'd have no reason to stay in Blackbridge.

Where would that leave them?

***

Jeremy needed to put some distance between himself and Zamira. Things with Henk would be going down tomorrow which meant she could be gone within twenty-four hours. He didn't like how his chest ached. Would she be willing to try a long-distance relationship? He cleaned up the coffee mugs. Who was he kidding? They'd known each other a couple of days. "I need to do a bit of work in the shed. Will you be all right in here?"

She smiled. "Yes. I'll make something for dinner. Is there anything you want?"

His chest squeezed. He couldn't get used to this. "You don't have to keep cooking for me."

"I'd like to."

"Why don't you make a salad and then I'll barbecue a couple of steaks when I'm done?"

"Sounds good."

He found the notebook he needed, put his boots on and headed outside. He had some prep work to do before his job tomorrow. One of the local caravan parks had recently extended their office and had ordered a new reception desk.

He opened the shed, inhaling the sawdust smell and slowly his shoulders relaxed. The whole situation with Henk and Annisa was getting to him.

Blackbridge used to be a safe, peaceful town. People used to be able to be trusted.

But first there'd been the drug ring and now this…

He sighed. He couldn't do anything to change it.

He opened his notebook and checked the dimensions of the reception desk. The assembly would happen on site, but he wanted to cut all the pieces to size so he'd have less mess to clean up, and be on site for less time, which would keep his client happy.

He shut all thoughts of Henk, Annisa and Zamira

from his head and got to work.

"How's it going?" Zamira's voice made him jump and he looked up from where he was marking out his next cut. She stood in the doorway, rugged up in a woollen jumper and grey pants, looking as delicious as ever, and behind her the yard was dark. He frowned. He hadn't been out here that long.

He glanced at his phone. Nearly seven. "Shit. I lost track of time." He wasn't used to anyone waiting for him. Jamie had called earlier to say he hadn't been able to find any information about Annisa and that he'd try again tomorrow. After Jeremy had finished the reception desk, he'd continued working on his own desk, making two drawers. He'd completely forgotten about dinner and Zamira. What a waste of time. He could have been with her instead. Putting down his pencil, he walked over to her.

"Don't stop if you've still got things to do."

"It can wait." He'd much prefer to be with her. He wiped his dusty hands on his pants and then flicked off the light. "You must be hungry."

"A little. I've been grazing on nuts."

As they walked inside his phone rang. It wasn't a number he recognised. "Mendelson Construction, Jeremy speaking."

"Jeremy, it's Moira."

His footsteps faltered. She'd actually called him. He hadn't thought she would.

"Jeremy, are you still there?"

"Yeah." He cleared his throat and continued to the kitchen.

"Listen, I was thinking, if you're not too busy, maybe we could meet for coffee tomorrow."

He sat heavily on one of the stools. Coffee, with his

baby sister. His chest squeezed so tight it was hard to breathe. "Just the two of us?"

"Yes." She paused. "Where do you live?"

"Blackbridge." He reviewed his plans for tomorrow. He could take time for a coffee, but did he want to open himself up for that kind of heartache?

"That's perfect," she declared. "I've got to visit some clients there tomorrow. We could meet at the bakery. It's reopened hasn't it?"

"Yeah. What do you do?"

"I'm a physio. I do some home visits."

So much he didn't know about her, about any of his family.

"Would eight o'clock suit you?"

Indecision made his head spin. Zamira's hand covered his and he flinched. He'd forgotten about her. She mouthed, *Are you OK?*

He shook his head and blew out a breath. "All right. Eight o'clock at *On The Way* bakery."

"Great. I'll see you then." She hung up.

He stared at the phone, his heart thudding in his chest.

"Who was that?" Zamira wrapped her arms around his waist, her head resting on his shoulder and her scent slowed his heart rate. He had someone to hold him, even if it was just for tonight.

"My sister."

She shifted so she could look at him. "Don't you get along?"

The desire to confess flooded him and he fought for control. It would completely change how she looked at him. He huffed. "Before today, I hadn't seen her in thirteen years. I ran into her at the hardware store."

Zamira frowned. "Thirteen years? You would have still been a child."

"Teenager." He gritted his teeth. Would she walk out if he told her? She was likely leaving tomorrow anyway. And finally talking to someone about what had happened would be good practice for meeting Moira tomorrow. "My mother kicked me out of home when I was fifteen," he said. "Moira was ten. I haven't heard from any of them since."

Her mouth dropped open. "But why? What happened?"

He stood, and paced away from her, his muscles tight, jaw clenched.

"Jeremy, you can tell me." Zamira stood by the bench, her eyes concerned.

His lungs constricted, making breathing difficult and the words stuck in his throat. The photo of him and his father caught his eye and he picked it up, staring down at it. They'd taken it a week before it had happened.

"Jeremy."

He replaced the photo, turned to face her. Swallowing hard, he then forced the words out. "I killed my father."

Her mouth dropped open and she gaped at him before she shook her head. "What?"

He tugged his hair, and the pain centred him. "I was his apprentice and we were working on a job," he said. "I got distracted by a message on my phone. He called out to me and I fobbed him off, agreed without really hearing what he asked me." He closed his eyes. "Next thing I knew he fell off the roof and landed next to me." The sick thud still visited his dreams regularly. "He was still breathing and I called the ambulance, but by the time they arrived it was too late." He swallowed hard.

Horror and sympathy filled Zamira's eyes as she walked towards him. He held up a hand. He had to get it all out.

"They did a post-mortem. He'd been electrocuted before he fell off the roof. He must have been asking me if I'd switched off the power."

"I'm so sorry, Jeremy." She stepped forward.

He walked over to the window. He didn't deserve her sympathy or her condolences. "When Mum found out, she told me to leave, said she couldn't bear to look at me. My sister Heather called me a murderer." He flinched as her hand touched his shoulder.

"People say things they don't mean when they're grieving."

He shook his head. "No. They're brutally honest. They say things they might not say otherwise, but it's still the truth."

"You're not a murderer." She gripped his shoulder, turned him towards her, her expression fierce. "It was a tragic accident. You were a kid. We all make mistakes."

Her words ripped through his defences. No one had ever said that to him. Everyone had blamed him from his mother, his sisters, his grandparents, even his father's best friend who'd taken him in, taken over his apprenticeship. He'd never been allowed to forget it — he never could forget it. From then on he'd always double checked his work, and then triple checked it when Pete had made him. "The mistake killed my father." Tears welled in his eyes. "He was my best friend and always there for me. And I failed him." And proved his mother right. He should have stayed in school. Then none of this would have happened.

She tugged him over to the couch and pulled him down with her. His mind replayed the day, the movement in his peripheral vision, the sick thud as the body hit the ground. Zamira's arms wrapped around him, and her caresses cut through the loop, bringing him back to the now. She curled up on the couch next to him. "It was a mistake," she repeated. "A horrible, tragic mistake."

His throat burned and fat tears rolled down his cheeks. Thirteen years of pain and guilt battered through him and his body spasmed as they finally overwhelmed him and he sobbed.

Zamira's fingers brushed his fringe, stroking his forehead as he finally cried himself dry. His head thumped and his whole body was heavy, drained. Nausea swirled in his stomach and his instinct was to run, to get away from her and her kind words. But her arms held him gently, comforting him, soothing him and he wanted it too badly. Not even when his father died had anyone comforted him like this. He craved it, craved her.

She must think him crazy to break down over something that happened so long ago. He sat up, moved away from her. "Sorry." He moved to stand and she placed a hand on his leg, stopping him.

"Don't apologise. You needed it." She drew his head towards her and kissed him gently.

She tasted so sweet, like comfort and home and everything right in the world. "Thank you."

She smiled. "Let me get you some water." She went into the kitchen.

He ran a hand over his face, his damp beard, and let out a deep breath. She wasn't judging him.

Zamira handed him a glass and a packet of painkillers. "Thought you might need these too."

His heart squeezed. If he wasn't careful he was going to fall for this beautiful, thoughtful, passionate woman. That would only end in more pain.

"Do you feel like eating?"

Dinner. She was probably starving. "I can cook the steaks." He headed for the kitchen though the thought of food made him nauseous. It was too cold outside to fire up the barbecue so he'd make do with the frying pan.

The sizzle of the steaks cooking and the meaty smell stimulated his stomach, set it rumbling. Maybe he would eat something.

Zamira set the table, placing the salad on it and it wasn't long before they sat down to eat. She cleared her throat. "So what did your sister want?"

His chest tightened at the mention of her. "She wants to meet for coffee tomorrow."

"Do you want me to come with you?"

Yes. The thought of her there with him, gave him strength. But relying on people gave them the power to hurt. "You don't have to."

"I'd like to if it will help. I could get a table nearby in case you need me."

Her gentle smile cut through his good intentions. He'd never had someone stand by him. "All right. We're meeting at eight at the bakery."

"I'll be there."

He covered her hand with his. "Thanks."

"It's the least I can do. You've helped me so much."

Hurt made him lean back, pull his hand away. Was she simply repaying a debt?

He hoped it was more than that.

Chapter 14

Jeremy stared up at the stars shining through his skylight. He'd gone to bed with Zamira, but had been listening to her heavy breathing for the past hour and imagining every possible way the meeting with Moira could go wrong. This was ridiculous. He wasn't getting any sleep so he might as well finish his desk. He went out to the shed, slipped his safety glasses on and got to work, putting the sides together, shaping the top, and then varnishing the cedar wood with a clear gloss that showed off the beautiful grain to its full extent. It was something he could make in his sleep and didn't occupy his mind enough.

His thoughts raced from the day of the accident, to the expression on his mother's face when she'd kicked him out, to Moira's hopeful expression when she'd suggested coffee. Then Zamira invaded, sometimes screwing up her face in disgust and other times being sweet and comforting. She was leaving him soon.

His heart ached.

With the desk complete, he was still too wired to sleep. He couldn't do any more cutting or sanding without risking dust sticking to the wet varnish so he needed something else to keep him busy. He should make Fetch a dog house. He was getting older and the cold affected him more. If he made a collapsible house, he could tuck it into the back of his ute with some pillows so Fetch would be comfortable on the odd times when he came to work with him.

But how to make it easy to break down and set up, yet still waterproof and wind resistant?

He found a spare sketch book and drew, scribbling out ideas that wouldn't work, making adjustments. He worked until his eyes grew heavy and his mind slowed down. When he found himself doodling, he put the pad aside and walked back into the house, stripping off his dirty clothes in the laundry and walking naked through to his bedroom. The luminous clock on his bedside table showed three in the morning. At least he'd get a couple of hours' sleep before he had to get up.

His head hit the pillow and he stared up at the clouds through his skylight until sleep dragged him under.

When his alarm chimed a few hours later, Jeremy groaned, fumbling for the button to switch it off. It was still dark outside.

"Morning," Zamira mumbled.

He reached out to pull her close, wanting to run his hands along her body and find comfort, but paused mid reach. She could leave today. He climbed out of bed. "Go back to sleep. It's early." The caravan park office opened at seven for the few guests who liked to leave at dawn, but it meant he could start too. He'd get some work done before he had coffee with his sister.

Goosebumps leapt to his skin and he rubbed his arms. It would be fine.

"I'll see you later," Zamira said, her voice sleepy.

Should he remind her about the meeting with his sister? No. She'd remember if it was important to her. He dressed in the bathroom and left Fetch sleeping in his bed.

The caravan park owner, Mr Walter, greeted him with a firm handshake. "I appreciate you starting early."

"Suits me too. I need to duck off at eight for a meeting, but I'll be back afterwards."

"I'll leave you to it."

Jeremy set an alarm on his phone to remind him when he needed to leave and then threw himself into the work. Fatigue made it harder to concentrate so he shut out all other thought and focused on what he was doing. All too soon though, his alarm beeped. His chest squeezed. Would Moira even turn up?

He gritted his teeth. He wasn't a chicken.

Wiping his hands on a rag, he went into the temporary office. Lynette manned the desk. She smiled at him. "How's it going?"

"Good. I need to duck out for a meeting, but I'll be back in an hour."

"Oh, are you going anywhere near Mai's bakery?"

"Yeah. Do you want something?"

She reached for her purse. "Could you buy me a pork banh mi? I left my lunch in the fridge this morning."

"Sure." He waved away the money. "I've got it."

He walked out and drove the short distance to the bakery. Parking the truck was a little more difficult, but he found a spot one street over and walked back. He should have washed his hands before he left, should have checked his hair or something. Nerves rained down in his stomach like sawdust flying from a table saw.

Mai might let him wash up out the back.

Taking a deep breath, he pushed the door of the bakery open, the tinkle of the bell announcing his presence to all inside. He scanned the room, but neither Moira nor Zamira was there. Just like he'd figured. He huffed out a breath. Give them a chance. He was a little early.

Jodie grinned at him. "Hey, Jeremy. What can I get you?"

"Can I have a quick word with Mai?"

"Come on back." She gestured and he walked through into the stainless steel kitchen. Mai was mixing some kind of dough. She glanced up.

"Hi. What are you doing here?"

"I've got a meeting and I forgot to wash up. Can I use your sink?"

She grinned at him. "Go for it. I've got a comb in my office."

He grimaced. "Is my hair that bad?"

"It's typical you, but if you want to impress… Who are you meeting?"

He hesitated. No one in Blackbridge knew his history. "A client." He washed his hands and arms and when he turned, Mai handed him a hand towel and a comb.

He dried and then combed his hair. "Any better?"

"Yeah. Go knock their socks off."

Her smile gave him some confidence. "Thanks." As he walked out of the kitchen, he turned back. "Could you make me a pork banh mi to go? I'm working over at Blackbridge Holiday Park and Lynette forgot her lunch."

"Sure."

"Thanks." He went back into the cafe.

Zamira was standing at the counter and her eyes widened. "Hey."

She'd remembered. Some of the nerves in his stomach settled. "Hey." He kissed her and then checked the cafe. Still no sign of Moira.

He ordered a black coffee and an apple pie and paid for both their orders.

"Take a seat. I'll bring it out," Jodie said.

A couple of tables by the window were free.

"She's not here yet?" Zamira asked.

He shook his head and went over to the window. Zamira followed him, hesitating by the table. "Do you want me to keep you company until she arrives?"

The door chimed and Jeremy glanced over, his belly tight. Gladys and Barbara. He didn't need to be caught in a conversation with either of them today. "Yes, please."

She slid into the seat opposite him and he tugged on his beard. "What have you been up to this morning?"

"Waiting for Franklin to call," she said. "And hanging out with Fetch."

Jeremy smiled. "I'm sure he appreciated it."

She chuckled. "From the amount of drool that came out of his mouth, I'd say he did. Though maybe you should ask the vet if that's normal."

He laughed and a little bit of tension left his shoulders. The bell above the door tinkled again, but this time it was Kim and he waved to Jodie, heading straight out the back to see his sister.

Jeremy let out a breath.

Zamira covered his hand with hers. "She'll be here soon."

He didn't tell her about the one thought he'd had where this was all an elaborate joke and his mother and sisters were sitting in a car somewhere, watching him getting more tense and laughing at his expense.

"Where are you working this morning?" Zamira

asked.

"Blackbridge Holiday Park. They need a new reception desk."

"Were you making it last night?"

"Yeah, it was one of the things."

Jodie brought over their coffees. "Here you go. I'll get your food."

Jeremy sipped his coffee, almost scalding his tongue. Damn. He checked the time. Ten past. Some people were always late, though Moira shouldn't be. Their mother had always drilled into them that being late was the height of rudeness, it implied you didn't value the other person or their time.

Jodie put their food on the table. "Enjoy!"

"I should go," he said when Jodie left.

Zamira's smile was sympathetic. "Eat your pie. If nothing else, we get to spend some extra time together today."

He wasn't certain it was a good thing. Being with her made him happy. She would break his heart. He stuffed the apple pie into his mouth, but barely tasted it.

"What would you like for dinner tonight?"

He blinked. "Won't you be busy with Franklin?"

She shrugged. "I don't know, but I can prepare something in case."

Food was the last thing on his mind. "Whatever."

The doorbell jingled again as people left. Moira wasn't coming.

He should have known.

He drank the rest of his coffee and pushed back his chair. "I've got to get back to work."

"Jeremy, give her a few more minutes.

He shook his head as his phone beeped. He glanced at the screen and his skin tingled. Call-out. Another traffic accident. Saved by the text. "I have to go.

There's been another crash." He got to his feet as Mai hurried towards him.

"You going?" she asked.

"Yeah." He had value to some people.

"I'll take Lynette her food and text Lawrence."

"Thanks." He turned back to Zamira. "I'll call you later."

Her eyes were worried. "Be safe."

He nodded and hurried out the door.

***

The sirens wailed as Jeremy drove the fast attack vehicle, following the fire tanker to the crash. He slowed as the tanker braked and he got his first view of the accident. He whistled.

The black sedan had T-boned a little white hatchback and ploughed it into a tree on the opposite side of the road. Bonnets crumpled and glass everywhere. The drivers in both vehicles were slumped against the steering wheels, but the back door of the sedan was open. Had someone managed to escape?

"You ready?" he asked Nicholas.

"As I'll ever be."

A good response. No matter how many times Jeremy had attended a crash, he was never totally prepared. He braced himself and strode over to where Lawrence assessed the situation with the paramedics.

"What have we got?"

"Driver in the sedan is deceased," Guy said, his voice low. "Looks like there was someone in the passenger seat, but they're gone, probably managed to get out the back door. We'll need to search for them in case they're disoriented and hurt. Twenty-three-year-old female in the hatchback, suspected broken pelvis."

"We'll need to move the sedan before we can get to

the hatchback driver," Lawrence said.

Jeremy nodded. "I'll get the tow set up."

"No, you go talk to the driver. You're good at calming them down." Lawrence waved to Lincoln as the police arrived.

Jeremy gritted his teeth as scenes of past crashes flooded him, the blood and fear. At least the fear proved the victims were still alive, unlike the stillness of his father's accident. He braced himself as he pushed his way through the bush, around the tree until he reached the driver's side window. The woman's sobs tore at his heart. "Hey, I'm Jeremy. We'll get you out of there," he said. "You'll be all right."

He managed to squeeze close enough to see the driver and his heart stopped. "Moira?" His little sister's face was covered in blood and she still gripped the steering wheel.

"Jeremy?" she sobbed. "Oh my God, I'm so glad you're here. How did you know? The car, it came out of nowhere. I couldn't swerve." Her voice raised in pitch, getting hysterical.

He carefully removed the remaining glass in the window and then took off his glove, placing a hand on her arm. "It's OK, Moi-Moi. I'm here. I need you to stay calm for me. Take a couple of deep breaths, ready? In… and out…"

She gasped, tears flowing down her face but she tried to do as he said. He assessed the situation. The door was crumpled, dented inwards from the impact of the tree and the steering wheel was hard against her chest. No massive amounts of blood though, no immediate danger to her. "That's it. Just like you used to do with dancing, steady breathing."

"You remember that?" Her disbelief was far better than her panic.

"Of course. You made me learn the steps and you always said breathing was the most important thing."

Her laugh turned into a cough and when she removed her hand from her mouth, there was blood on it.

Not good.

He glanced over the roof to where Nicholas and Lawrence hitched a tow rope to the sedan. "Coming?" he called. It was code for hurry the fuck up and Guy strode over to them, a neck brace in his hand.

Jeremy moved out of the way, but Moira grabbed his arm. "Don't leave me."

"I'm not going anywhere," he assured her with a smile. Inside his stomach tied in knots but he couldn't let her see it. "I need to make room for Guy so he can put that annoying neck brace on you. I'll be the other side of the tree." He kept talking as he removed her hand from his arm and shifted out of the way. "Remember when we were kids, you used to love the peek-a-boo game. I played it with you for hours." His chest squeezed at the memory and he moved around the tree. Then he stuck his head around the side of it. "Peek-a-boo."

She groaned, but it was playful.

"You two know each other?" Guy asked as he put the brace in place.

"Moira's my baby sister."

Guy's mouth dropped open.

A screech of metal and tinkle of glass as the tanker dragged the black sedan away from the hatchback. Jeremy winced.

"You should call your parents, get them to meet us at Albany Hospital." Guy's words were far too casual. Jeremy recognised his tone. It meant things were worse than they appeared. He met Guy's concerned gaze.

Shit.

Moira could have internal bleeding. He had to get her out. He wouldn't be responsible for another death in his family.

With the sedan out of the way, Nicholas set up the line to move the hatchback. Over at the sedan, one of the other fire-fighters used the Jaws of Life to pry open the driver's door.

"Moi, do you have your phone on you?"

She coughed up more blood. "In my bag."

He moved around the car, glancing in the windows until he found her handbag on the floor of the passenger side. The window was already smashed, so he reached in and pulled her bag out. "What's the code?"

"Six, eight, five, two."

He entered it and scrolled through her contacts. His finger hesitated on the call button to his mother. This wasn't about him, this was about Moira. Gritting his teeth, he called.

"Moira, you know better than to call me during the day." The uptight proper tone of her voice hadn't changed at all. His chest squeezed and he said, "Mum, it's Jeremy. Moira's been in an accident."

The sharp gasp was painful. "What? Is this some kind of joke? How did you get Moira's phone?"

Of course she didn't believe him. Stick to the facts. "I work with fire and rescue. There's been a two-car crash and Moira was driving one of the cars. We're working on extracting her from the vehicle and then she'll be taken to Albany Hospital."

"Is she all right?"

He closed his eyes at the fear in her voice. "She's conscious and responding well to questions," he said. "The paramedics suspect she's broken her pelvis."

"I'll be there as soon as I can."

Before Jeremy could ask her to call Moira's fiancé, she hung up.

He walked back to the car. "Mum will meet you at the hospital," he said. "What's your fiancé's name again?"

"Ollie."

He flicked through the contacts until he found the right one and dialled, walking away from the car so Lawrence could shift it away from the tree.

A man answered. "Hey, baby. How did the meeting with your brother go?"

Jeremy winced. "Ollie, it's Jeremy. Moira didn't make it to the meeting. She's been in a car crash." He kept talking as Ollie gasped. "She's conscious and will be taken to Albany Hospital as soon as we get her out of the car."

"She's stuck? Why are you there?"

"I work for fire and rescue," he said. "I've called Mum and she's going to meet us at the hospital. You should go there too."

"Is she going to be all right?"

He gritted his teeth. He couldn't make promises. "I'm not a doctor, but she's talking to us."

A sigh of relief. But Jeremy had been to far too many crashes to know it was no indication of survival. "I've got to go. I'll see you there."

He hung up before Ollie could ask any other questions and placed Moira's bag in the back of the ambulance. Then he went back to Moira's window. Nicholas was there with the spreader to pry the door apart.

"Be quick," Guy murmured.

Jeremy's throat closed over and he moved to the front so Moira could see him. "Mum and Ollie will meet you at the hospital," he told her. "Right now,

Nicholas is going to force the door open and then Guy and Cynthia will help you out, OK?"

She nodded, her face paler than it had been.

"Jeremy, can you come here for a second?" Lincoln called.

He glanced back at his sister. "I'll be right back, Moi-Moi." He strode over. "What's up?"

"We found these in the back seat of the sedan." He held up a bunch of passports. "Is this Zamira's cousin?" He showed Jeremy one of the passports.

"Yeah." He glanced back at the sedan. The driver had already been extracted and lay on a stretcher, covered with a cloth. Another ambulance arrived to take it away. "Did Border Force raid this morning?"

Lincoln frowned at him. "Yeah. Henk got away."

"Think he was in the passenger seat?"

"Possibly. I want to set up a search."

The crunch of metal made Jeremy turn around. Nicholas had the door open. "I've got to help." He didn't wait for Lincoln's permission.

"We'll lift you out," Guy told Moira. "I've given you some pain medication, but tell me if anything hurts."

"Jeremy." She reached for his hand and he squeezed it.

"We've got you. You're in safe hands."

"Nicholas, get her legs," Guy said. He glanced at Jeremy. "Best if you stand back."

He nodded. Having family involved was asking for trouble.

Moira groaned as they lifted her out and placed her on the stretcher. Guy examined her and then said to Nicholas, "Let's get her into the ambulance."

"I'm going with you," Jeremy said, shooting a look at Lawrence.

He nodded. "Get in."

Within moments, the sirens wailed and the ambulance sped towards Albany. Guy checked Moira's vitals and Jeremy sat in the spare seat, his hand on Moira's shoulder. Her eyes fluttered closed.

Guy swore. "Open your eyes, Moira."

They stayed closed.

He checked her pulse and Jeremy's heart clenched. "She's still with us."

Guy didn't need to say anything else. It was touch and go.

Jeremy prayed.

Chapter 15

Zamira paced Jeremy's living room. She'd stayed at the bakery for another half an hour in case Moira arrived, but no twenty-something woman had come in. She ached for Jeremy. And now he was out there, having been stood up by his sister, dealing with a car crash.

How was he?

She wanted to call his sister and give her a piece of her mind. She wanted to call Jeremy or send him a message, but he didn't need the distraction. She could wait, even if she hated it.

Would he go straight back to work afterwards? He must be devastated his sister hadn't come. How could Moira be so callous?

Anger filled her as she thought of all the things she wanted to say to Jeremy's family. To abandon him when he was so young, when it had been an accident, when he'd been grieving too.

It was inexcusable.

Fetch watched her warily and she unclenched her fists, took a few deep breaths.

Why did she care so much? She'd only known him a few days.

But she liked him — a lot. It was impossible not to. She'd really miss him when she left.

She sighed.

She checked the time. Border Force were supposed to be raiding Henk's property today and so far she'd heard nothing from them. Surely Agent Franklin would call her to let her know Annisa was safe.

Her pacing took her down the hallway to the bedroom. The bed was still unmade. She'd barely stirred when Jeremy got up, but she'd missed him when she'd woken properly. It was far nicer starting the day in conversation with a sexy man than alone. She smoothed out the sheets, remaking the bed, her muscles still twinging today. Then she picked up the clothes on the floor, folding hers and putting them back in her case and throwing Jeremy's into the laundry basket which was almost full.

On a whim, she carried it into the laundry, went through the cupboards until she found laundry detergent and put a load on to wash. The first drop of rain hit the tin roof and then another.

Great. Where could she hang the washing when it was done?

A hunt through the cupboards found some pegs and a clothes horse which she put in front of the fire. Inspired now, she returned to the laundry, cleaned the bench top and took more cleaning products from the cupboard.

If nothing else, she could be useful while she waited.

As Zamira got the vacuum out a little while later, her phone rang. Border Force. Finally. "Hello?"

"Ms Musa, this is Agent Franklin. Were you home earlier this morning?" Her tone was direct, authoritative.

"No. I went into Blackbridge to meet Jeremy." She sat at the table.

"Where was he?"

"At work. The Blackbridge Holiday Park. What's this about?"

"We raided Henk Jennings' property this morning and Henk escaped. We hoped you might have seen something."

That wasn't good. The man deserved to be locked up for what he'd done. She shook her head, her heart racing. "No, I didn't see or hear anything. Is Annisa all right?"

Agent Franklin was silent for a moment. "Annisa was not with the group of migrants we found."

"What?" Zamira leaned back. "Is she at work?"

"We're interviewing people now." Franklin hesitated. "We could use your help translating."

She got to her feet. "Sure. Do you want me to go to Henk's?"

"I'll send someone to pick you up." Franklin hung up.

Zamira hurried to the bathroom and washed her hands. Please let Annisa be at work. One of the other workers would know where.

Henk wouldn't do anything to her when he knew she was on Jeremy's radar.

She sent Jeremy a text. *Going to Henk's to help Agent Franklin. If you need me, call me.* How would he cope after the crash? Would he need her support? She might not be able to get away.

She sighed. She'd finally got the opportunity she wanted and she was more worried about Jeremy and Annisa.

Rain battered the roof. Fetch was curled up on his bed near the fire. She didn't have the heart to put him out in the cold.

Instead she grabbed her coat and went outside to wait for her ride.

***

Zamira's heart thudded as she got into the Border Force car and was driven next door to Henk's place. Several cars were parked by the main house including the mini bus full of migrants staring out the window. It must have been stopped before leaving for work. Had they been told what was going on?

People in Border Force uniform were going in and out of the main house, and a temporary gazebo had been set up in the front yard, three of its sides down against the rain.

This was what she wanted to be involved in.

She put her rain jacket hood up as she got out of the car, following the driver over to the temporary gazebo. Franklin was inside with a man.

"Thanks for coming." Franklin shook her hand. "This is Adnan. He's going to question the migrants."

"Take a seat," Adnan said. "Hopefully you can help me sort out who is who." He called out to a man on the house porch. "Can you bring over the first person?"

"I'll leave you to it." Franklin went inside.

Zamira sat. "What do you need me to do?"

"Translate what I ask and what they answer."

It was easy enough. The first man was brought over, his expression worried. "What is happening?" he asked in Malaysian.

"He wants to know what is happening," she said.

"Tell him to sit and ask him his name."

Zamira repeated this and the man answered. Adnan scanned through his paperwork. "I've got him here. He's got a legitimate visa. Ask him what work he's been doing and how much he's being paid."

She translated and waited for his answer. "He's been working full-time at the Vale winery, doing odd jobs. He gets a hundred dollars a week." Outrageous.

"Is he free to leave?"

The man shook his head when she asked him. "Henk has my passport and we must stay here when we're not working." He paused. "Am I in trouble? Will they send me home? My family needs the little money I send them."

"You're not in trouble, Henk is," she told him. "He should have been paying you more and letting you leave the property."

The man scowled and swore. "I knew something was wrong."

"What's he saying?" Adnan asked.

She repeated the information.

"Ask him if all the workers are in the bus."

The man nodded.

Zamira frowned. "What about Annisa?"

His eyes widened. "You're the lady who came with the fireman. You spoke to Annisa."

"Yes."

"I'm sorry. She and the other lady were taken away yesterday."

No. "Other lady? Taken where? By whom?"

"Another woman stayed at the house. Henk and one of his men drove them away."

"What's wrong?" Adnan asked. "What's he saying?"

"My cousin Annisa was here," Zamira told him. "Henk took her and another lady away yesterday."

He scanned his list. "I don't have any Annisa here."

"She doesn't have a legitimate visa. It must have been forged."

Adnan frowned. "Ask him if he'd recognise the

other man if he saw him."

Zamira repeated the question and the man nodded.

"We'll get a sketch artist down here."

Agent Franklin ran out of the house, heading for her car.

"What's the rush?" Adnan called.

"We might have found our escaped perpetrators," she yelled. "There's a crash just out of town."

Zamira tensed. The crash Jeremy had attended. Had Annisa been involved? "I need to make a phone call."

She rang Jeremy and this time he picked up. "Miri." He whispered her name. In the background sirens wailed.

"Are you OK?"

"No." His voice wavered. "Moira was in the crash. We're taking her to hospital."

Her heart squeezed at the pain in his voice. That was why she hadn't turned up. "Is it bad?"

"Yes."

He needed her. She wanted to be with him. She glanced at Adnan. "I'm at Henk's translating for Border Force, but I'll be there as soon as I can. Which hospital?"

"Albany." He cleared his throat. "Annisa must be happy to see you."

She didn't want to burden him. "We'll talk about it later."

"I've got to go. We've arrived at the hospital."

"Take care of yourself."

"You too." He hung up.

"Who'd you call?" Adnan asked.

"My friend Jeremy attended the crash. His sister was in one of the cars."

Adnan swore. "Was Henk there?"

"I didn't ask. His sister is being rushed to hospital."

She desperately wanted to leave, go to Jeremy and comfort him, but Annisa needed her too. She wasn't in the crash, which meant she was still out there somewhere. Only Zamira could question the men to find out where Henk had taken her. She had to find her. Annisa could be in real danger.

Guilt filled her. Zamira should have insisted Annisa go with them on Sunday. Then she would be safe and Zamira wouldn't be torn in two by her desire to go to Jeremy as well.

She sighed. Jeremy had other friends he could call. One of his crew was probably already with him.

Another migrant was brought over. She clenched her hands. She had to stay. Had to find Annisa.

"What do you want to know?"

****

The ambulance pulled into the emergency department and the doors swung open. Jeremy's mother stood there, arms wrapped around her waist, fear in her eyes.

She had aged, more grey in her hair and lines on her face, and her lips were pinched in an expression he remembered. She wasn't happy. Next to her hovered Heather and Ollie, all their focus on the stretcher being rolled out.

He waited until Moira was wheeled into the emergency department before he followed. If only Zamira was here. He'd desperately wanted to tell her he needed her with him, but her dream was to work for Border Force and this was the ideal opportunity. He couldn't stuff it up for her. And he couldn't let himself rely on someone who was leaving soon. Better he make the break now.

The paramedics took Moira straight through double doors which closed behind them.

"Wait!" his mother yelled. "That's my daughter."

A nurse hurried over. "Please, take a seat, ma'am. The doctor will be out as soon as possible to give you an update."

"I should be with her."

"That's not possible. The doctors need to assess her condition."

"I want to see my daughter." Every word rose in volume and Jeremy winced.

"Tracey." Ollie put an arm around her. "Moira's in good hands."

She shook him off and spotted Jeremy. "You!" Somehow she made the single word an accusation.

"Mum." He nodded as Heather gasped.

"You had something to do with this."

Jeremy stepped back and the breath left his body. He swallowed. "I responded to the accident," he said. "My crew extracted Moira from the car and put her in the ambulance."

Ollie strode over. "How bad is she?"

He closed his eyes briefly and then focused on Moira's fiancé. "The paramedics thought she had a fractured pelvis," he said. "She was conscious and lucid when I arrived and answering questions. The paramedic gave her something for the pain."

"And then?"

The guy was sharp.

"She coughed up some blood. Might have been a cut in her mouth…"

"But you don't think so."

Jeremy shook his head. "Her skin was pale and she lost consciousness after we got her into the ambulance."

"Internal bleeding?"

He shrugged. "I'm not a doctor, but there's trauma

of some kind."

"Where did the crash happen?" Heather glared at him.

He shouldn't be surprised — she'd always been their mother's favourite — but it still cut him. "On the road between Albany and Blackbridge. Another car T-boned hers and pushed it into a tree."

"What was she doing there?" Tracey asked. "She should have been at work."

Jeremy glanced at Ollie.

"She had patients to visit in Blackbridge," Ollie said. "She left early so she could stop at the bakery."

Jeremy gave a tiny nod of thanks.

His mother stared at him as if wondering how she could blame him. And maybe he was to blame. If Moira hadn't been meeting him, she wouldn't have been on the road so early. He should steer clear of all his family in future.

Guy and Cynthia walked into the waiting room. Jeremy pushed past his mother and Heather, and strode over. "How is she?"

Guy glanced at the others behind him. "They've taken her for scans. Her vitals are good, but it's likely she'll need surgery."

"What kind of surgery?" Tracey demanded.

Guy shook his head. "Depends on what they find. They'll send someone out after the scans are done to update you." He smiled. "Thanks for your help, mate. You kept her distracted so I could do my job." He shook Jeremy's hand.

Jeremy had no words. To be appreciated, especially after the grief from his family, made his throat close over. He blinked rapidly.

Guy's radio blared with dispatch requesting an update. "I've got to go. See you at football on Sunday."

He nodded and let out a breath. Moira was in the right place. The doctors would fix her. The doors opened again and a doctor walked out. "Are you here for Moira Mendelson?"

"Yes." His mother pushed in front of him. "I'm her mother."

Jeremy winced at Ollie. It wouldn't be long before Ollie was Moira's next of kin.

"She's stable but she's got a ruptured spleen and a broken pelvis. We're taking her into surgery now."

"Will she be all right?" Ollie asked.

"We'll do the best we can," the doctor said.

"How long will it take?"

"A couple of hours," the doctor said. "I need to get back in there. I suggest you get a coffee while you wait." He walked back through the doors.

Jeremy tugged on his beard. He wasn't waiting here. Not with his family's death stares.

"You want to get a drink?" Ollie asked him.

"Ollie, this is Moira's brother. We don't speak to him," his mother said.

Jeremy shook his head. Still, after all this time…

Ollie lifted an eyebrow. "He helped to rescue my fiancée and that deserves a drink at least."

Tracey gaped at him.

Before she could respond, Jeremy said, "Thanks, but I'd better get back to work. I'll call for an update in a couple of hours."

"Typical," Tracey muttered.

He ignored her.

"I'll call you if anything changes," Ollie said. "What's your number?"

Jeremy gave it to him and then glanced at his family. "I'll see you later."

They said nothing, though Heather gave him a slight

smile.

He walked out of the emergency department and stopped. He didn't have a car.

Adding a large taxi fare to his day was just perfect. He sighed and made the call.

Chapter 16

Jeremy turned into his driveway, relief oozing from his pores. Talk about a shit day. He needed a cold beer and to forget about everything.

After leaving the hospital, he'd returned to the caravan park and finished his work there. Ollie had called him around midday to tell him Moira was out of surgery and doing well. He'd invited Jeremy to visit, but Jeremy didn't have the energy to face his mother again today. He'd go tomorrow when he hoped they would be back at work.

Even after thirteen years they hadn't forgiven him. He used to dream the next time he saw his family they would welcome him back, apologise for abandoning him. Today proved it wasn't going to happen – not with his mother and Heather at least.

He groaned and parked his truck. The wind blew straight off the Antarctic tonight, so he pulled his jacket tighter around him as he headed inside. "Miri?"

No answer.

He'd sent her a message when he'd left the hospital, but she hadn't replied.

The fire in the pot belly was almost out and Fetch

lay in his bed, snoring his head off. Great guard dog. Jeremy checked the house, but Zamira wasn't there. He stoked the fire, let Fetch out to relieve himself and went into the kitchen. He should think about dinner, but he wasn't hungry.

The house felt so different tonight. Empty. He frowned. And clean.

Had Zamira tidied up?

He wandered into the laundry and discovered his washing machine full of wet clothes. She must have put it on before Border Force called. He set the machine on a rinse cycle and walked back into the living room, but Zamira didn't magically appear. How had he got so used to her being here? He missed her.

What would it be like when she left? Instead of thinking about it, he dialled her number.

"Jeremy, are you already home?"

"Yeah. Where are you?"

She sighed. "I've finished translating for today. I'm walking back to your place."

It was freezing outside. "Via the road?"

"Yeah."

"I'll come and get you." He hung up before she could protest. He grabbed his ute keys and hurried outside. The wind was definitely fierce, and the light was fading.

He reached the road and a car drove towards him, the headlights bright. It was going way too fast. The car's lights highlighted Zamira hurrying through Henk's gate, her head down, arms wrapped around her waist.

The car swerved, heading straight for Zamira.

His heart lurched. No!

Zamira turned, saw the car. She leapt towards the one tree on the side of the drive.

The car swerved away and passed Jeremy. Grey

sedan, two inside — the driver and someone in the back seat. Too dark to see their faces after the glare of the headlights.

Jeremy turned into Henk's drive, jumped out of the car and ran to where Zamira was sprawled on the ground, unmoving. "Miri!"

She groaned as she sat up. "Ow." She brushed off her hands and relief filled him.

"Are you all right?"

She nodded. "Did you see who it was?"

"No." He helped her to her feet, held her close for a moment, his heart still thumping hard in his chest. "Shit, that scared the life out of me."

"Me too. Do you think the driver was drunk?"

He shook his head, wrapped his arm around her waist and led her over to his ute. "We'd better tell Agent Franklin what happened."

She gasped. "Were they aiming for me?"

"Looked that way." He helped her into the passenger side and then drove down to Henk's house. A uniformed man met them at the front door.

"Did you forget something, Zamira?" the man asked.

She shook her head. "Someone just tried to run me over, Adnan."

Adnan's eyes widened and he gestured them in. "You'd better talk to Franklin."

They were led into Henk's lounge room where the agent was going through a mound of paperwork. Border Force had taken over the house. Franklin glanced up. "What happened?"

"Someone tried to run Zamira over," Adnan said.

Franklin gestured for them to sit and Zamira told her what had happened. Something didn't add up. Who would want to hurt Zamira?

"It has to be Henk," Jeremy said.

"Or it could have been an accident."

He shook his head. "No, they swerved deliberately. My neighbours would have stopped if it was an accident. This road isn't a throughway to anything. You're only on it if you live here or are visiting someone."

"Who lives on the other side?" Franklin asked.

"Alyse Wilson and her partner Mark," he said. "There's plenty of bush on her property. Henk or someone he works with could have been hiding in there." It wasn't too far to walk from the crash site.

"And risk getting caught?"

Jeremy shrugged. "Maybe they left something behind."

Franklin got her phone out. "What did the car look like?"

He told her and she phoned it in. When she hung up she said, "Zamira is staying with you tonight?"

He nodded.

"Stay alert. This might have been opportunistic and they won't bother her again."

"Why go after her at all?"

"If it is Henk, then he might blame the raid on her. She was here before we were and now she's helping us."

Jeremy swore and Zamira played with her necklace. "I'll take care of her." The words resonated with him as he helped Zamira to her feet. Nothing could happen to her. He cared for her too much. It didn't matter if she was leaving him. He had to protect her.

They drove in silence back to his place and as they walked up to the back door, Zamira threw her arms around him. "Thank you." Her voice was muffled against his chest.

He wrapped his arms around her and held her. "You're all right. You'll be safe with me."

She clung to him, her body shaking and he picked her up, carried her inside to the couch and carefully lowered them both onto it, so she sat straddling him. He brushed her hair off her face, kissed her forehead.

She raised her head and tears glistened in her eyes. "I'm sorry. I'm OK. It's been a hard day, but you've had it worse than me. How's Moira?"

He'd prefer to comfort Zamira than think of that. "Stable. She broke her pelvis and ruptured her spleen but she'll be fine."

"Good. I'm sorry I didn't come to the hospital. I was the only one who could translate and we needed to know what happened to Annisa."

"Wasn't she there?"

"No. One of the migrants said Henk and another man took her away yesterday."

Shit. That wasn't good. "Do you know where?"

She shook her head. "Does Henk have another place?"

"Not that I know of." He used his thumb to wipe away her tears before pressing a kiss to her mouth. "Word will have spread that his place was raided. If anyone knows something, they'll come forward."

She snuggled into him, warm and minty and his heart swelled. "Why don't you have a shower while I make dinner?" He could find the energy for her and it would help him forget about his day.

She glanced up at him. "Will you shower with me?"

His body hardened. "Ah, you probably want to have a soak." And he wanted to bury himself inside of her.

Zamira shook her head. "No. What I want right now is to be with you."

He wouldn't deny her anything. He could keep his

urges under control. "Then let's go."

She squealed as he lifted her up and carried her down the hallway to his bathroom.

***

After they'd showered, Jeremy cooked Zamira dinner — if you could call heating up tomato soup from a can cooking. She sat at the kitchen bench watching him.

"Did you get any information from the migrants?" Jeremy asked.

She nodded. "Henk should go to jail."

"And no one could tell you where he took Annisa?" He put a couple of slices of bread in the toaster.

"No. Franklin showed the workers the driver's licence photo of the man who died in the crash. He was the one who'd taken Annisa."

"Crap." He hadn't seen who the dead man was, had been too distracted to ask Lawrence if it was someone they knew.

He buttered the toast and then dished up the soup, and they sat at the table. "What was it like translating for them?"

She beamed. "Fantastic. I felt useful and Adnan actually respected me."

"I'm glad. Isn't this what you want to do?" Maybe this would help her transition to the job she wanted — maybe even find one in Western Australia. He crunched into his toast. Is that what he wanted — for her to stay?

She broke off a piece of toast and slipped it to Fetch who'd come to sit by the table. It warmed his heart, softened his insides.

He liked having company… he liked having *Zamira* with him.

She glanced up and flushed at being caught. "He looked hungry."

"He always is."

Her expression grew sombre. "So, tell me… did you see your mother?"

The warmth fled his body. "Yes." He stared at his bowl, his teeth clenched.

She hesitated and then asked, "How did it go?"

"Not great." He looked at her. "She thought I must have been at fault, caused the crash."

She covered his hand with hers. "Did you set her straight?"

"Moira's fiancé, Ollie covered for me. Didn't tell them Moira was driving to meet me." He swirled his spoon around his soup.

"That doesn't mean it was your fault."

"She wouldn't have been on the road if I hadn't agreed to meet her."

"And the car wouldn't have been speeding if Border Force hadn't raided Henk's property," she shot back. "This isn't your fault."

It felt like it.

"Jeremy."

He sighed. "I know."

Zamira studied him before gathering their empty bowls and carrying them through to the kitchen. When she returned, she wrapped her arms around him. "I'm sorry you had to go through that. I'm sorry I wasn't there for you."

He couldn't let it matter. She was leaving on Sunday. "You had your own stuff to deal with." He got to his feet. "I'm used to attending car crashes. I'm just glad she didn't die."

Zamira gasped. "But someone did. I can't imagine what that's like. Do you want to talk about it?"

He shook his head. "I didn't have to deal with him." But suddenly memories of past crashes hit him like an out of control strobe light. The blood, the crumpled cars, the screams and moans, the tears. Moira's face replaced the countless others he'd seen, her eyes wide and unseeing. He shuddered and stumbled over to the couch.

"Jeremy?" She sat down next to him, her hand on his arm. "Are you all right?"

His chest was tight, it was hard to breathe. He gasped for air, as pain pummelled him.

"Jeremy!" Zamira shook him and some of her panic pierced his mind.

He had to get control.

He gripped her hands, saw the concern in her eyes. Cupped her face, needing to touch her. The tightness eased, his breath slowed as the images faded.

But the pain of those pictures remained and tears flooded his eyes.

"I'm here for you, Jeremy." She kissed him gently. "What do you need from me?"

Her eyes grounded him, keeping the agony from taking over.

He wanted to get lost in her, to taste her, to forget all the memories haunting him. He dragged her closer, kissed her, all the desperation and pain pouring out, and she kissed him back. He ran his hands under her top, caressing her soft, smooth skin and needed more. He broke the kiss, ripped her jumper up and off.

Her eyes were dark as she undid her bra, threw it on the floor and he pulled her towards him again, shifting so she could lay on the couch beneath him.

Then he covered her body with his, kissing her sweet lips and sliding lower so he could lick her breasts. She moaned, arching up towards him. He was so hard he could cut diamond.

Zamira clutched at his jumper, tugging it towards

her and he ripped it off and then slid off his pants. He needed her desperately, had to forget everything but her. She was his salvation.

He undid her pants, slid his hand to her core and she was hot and wet, waiting for him.

"Please, Jeremy. Now."

He tugged her pants down, fought to get them off and then thrust deep inside her.

"Yes." Her words echoed everything in his mind. She was perfect, this was perfect, he needed her again and again. He moved, the sensation sending tingles throughout his body as he focused on her. He thrust, kissing her neck, her chin, her mouth, and her legs wrapped around his waist, drawing him closer.

She drove him wild and he thrust faster, responding to the core need, his core desire deep within him.

She screamed his name as she came, her head thrown back, her body arching, the most beautiful thing he'd ever seen. With a final thrust, his world exploded.

***

Slowly Jeremy's senses returned. Zamira's warm body under him and the wooden support of the couch base dug into his knee. He'd just had sex with Zamira like some kind of crazed animal. No finesse, no thought for her satisfaction, no condom.

Fuck.

He climbed off her and reached for his pants, guilt rushing through him. "I'm so sorry." He couldn't bear to look at her.

She grabbed his arm, and when he met her gaze, she wore a satisfied smile. "I'm not. That was amazing."

Her words slowed the guilt. "I was too rough. We didn't use a condom…"

She sat up, tugged him back down to the couch.

"You weren't rough." She ran her hand through his hair and he leaned into her. "I wanted this as much as you did." She kissed him and caressed his beard. "And as for the condom, I'm on the pill so as long as you're clear, we're fine."

"I am." He'd never lost his mind like that before. Why wasn't she running?

"Then I'd say we just had incredible sex." Zamira got to her feet, pulled him up. "Which is a fantastic way to end such an awful day." She kissed him again. "Let's clean up and go to bed."

He followed her, not quite comprehending. He'd used her to forget about his pain. Shouldn't she have a problem with that? Or was she really that understanding, that amazing? Her bottom jiggled nicely as she walked down the hallway to his bedroom, distracting him. The one sock she still wore featured The Hulk. He smiled. He loved everything about her.

His footsteps faltered. *Loved?*

She was going back to Melbourne on Sunday. He couldn't possibly love her.

"I won't be a second." She let go of his hand as she went into the bathroom and closed the door. He stared after her for a long moment before he shook his head. It must be the sex talking. His defences were low.

After he cleaned himself, he went into his bedroom. The bed was made and the floor clear.

He turned as she walked back in. "Did you clean up?"

She screwed up her nose. "Yes, I hope you don't mind. It was either clean or drive myself crazy wondering if you were all right."

He frowned. "Why wouldn't I be?"

Zamira got into bed, patted the place next to her and he lay down. "Your sister had stood you up and then you had to go to a traffic accident. I was worried."

Her concern soothed him. He pulled her closer. "You don't need to worry about me, I'm tough."

She laughed. "You're a marshmallow. You might look tough on the outside," she fondled his beard. "But you're all soft on the inside." She kissed his cheek. "It's one of the things I like about you."

Her words lifted his spirits. "What else do you like about me, aside from my ruggedly handsome good looks?"

Zamira gazed into his eyes. "There're too many things to list."

His heart expanded. Maybe this could somehow last past Sunday.

She yawned, covering her mouth. "Sorry. It seems being thoroughly satisfied makes me sleepy." She winked and then tucked herself into his side. He wrapped his arm around her, loving her warmth curled into him.

And for the first time since he could remember, he fell asleep immediately.

Chapter 17

Jeremy strolled along the white sandy beach, his eyes on Zamira in the water, her bikini top only just covering her enough for decency's sake — a pity. She smiled, gesturing him towards her with the smallest crook of her finger. Hell yes. As he moved towards the ocean, the scent of smoke tickled his nostrils. He frowned. There shouldn't be any fire near the beach in summer. He wavered between turning to check and not wanting to lose focus on the gorgeous woman in front of him. He sniffed, the smell stronger this time, but still his feet moved towards the water. As he touched the waves, the scene changed, morphing into a fire and rescue training session.

Part of his mind swore as he fought to return to Zamira, but the scent of smoke wouldn't leave him. He struggled to consciousness, the pitch of night telling him it was way before morning. Running a hand over his face and beard, he sat up, found Zamira in bed next to him, sound asleep, but the smoke lingered.

He climbed out of bed and went to his window. His breath hitched and he swore. Smoke poured out of the front door of his shed, and orange flames lit up the windows. He spun, grabbing his phone from the nightstand. "Zamira!" He shook her awake and dialled triple zero.

"What's wrong?" She sat up as he switched on the light.

"The shed's on fire." He told the dispatcher his address and then handed her his phone. "Get dressed. Put Fetch in the ute and move it away from the shed." If he was quick, the fire shouldn't spread, but he didn't want to risk it. Where was his gear?

Zamira was already dressing so he ran down the hallway to the laundry and pulled his gear on. He charged out of the house, straight to his generator and started it. Then he uncurled the fire hose.

Grey smoke billowed out the front door and inside was well alight. Pain hit him. Everything he had would be destroyed. He shut down his emotions and focused. What had started it? He hadn't been inside all day. Nothing could have still been smouldering, and nothing would automatically combust.

But the undeniable truth was all his projects, all the piles of wood he had stacked up inside, were fully ablaze. Even as he directed the water through the door, he assessed the situation. Windows closed, no overhanging trees that would cause the fire to spread, it was currently contained. The house should be fine.

Behind him the ute engine growled to life and he glanced over as Zamira backed it up, leaving room for the fire truck. Fetch sat on the front seat. At least he didn't have to worry about his dog.

He faced the fire again. The heat was incredible, stifling hot, radiating out of the structure and the flames roared and crackled. The wood wouldn't have burnt this fast, this hot on its own. He sniffed and smelled something sharp, something like petrol.

Had one of his jerry cans tipped over? Still it needed something to ignite it.

Shit. He had a whole bunch of aerosol cans inside, they could start exploding at any second. He directed the water at the shelves, hoping to cool them down enough. The fire hadn't spread to that side yet.

He moved the spray back to the base of the fire, all the beautiful Tasmanian oak he'd been saving for a special project, now completely ruined. He squeezed his eyes shut. It didn't matter.

He could get more.

The side window of the shed cracked and then broke and the wind howled through, feeding oxygen to the fire. The flames leapt higher, twisting, and ash swirled around inside, blowing out the front doors towards him. He coughed, wishing he had a breathing apparatus on hand.

Where was his crew?

The roar of the fire and the hum of the generator filled his ears. He glanced at the sky but the clouds that had been there all day were gone and stars shone mockingly down on him. Mother Nature wasn't going to help.

A high-pitched shriek sounded. Jeremy turned one ear away from the fire to check if it was a siren. Nothing. He must have imagined it.

Moving closer to the window that had broken, he directed his water through it, getting a better angle on the flames than he could at the entrance. He wouldn't risk Lawrence's wrath again by going into a burning building without the proper gear. Besides, there was nothing he could save.

Everything would be destroyed.

***

Zamira forced the sleep from her brain as Jeremy handed her his phone and the dispatcher asked for more information. She answered on auto-pilot and threw on some clothes and her boots.

Where was Fetch?

Still snoring in his bed, oblivious to what was going on.

The scent of smoke was stronger in the living area. What had Jeremy asked of her? Take Fetch, move his ute away from the shed.

Where was the key?

She found it in her bag as the dispatcher told her a fire crew was mobilising. It was midnight. How quickly could they get here? Stopping in the laundry, she took a treat out of the cupboard and then woke Fetch. She tucked the phone between her shoulder and ear, held onto Fetch's collar in one hand so he didn't run away, and waved the treat in front of his face with the other. "Come on, Fetch."

The dog groaned and lurched to his feet.

"That's it."

She went out the front door, adjusting her hold on the phone now she had Fetch's attention, and scanned the yard for Jeremy. The shed's interior glowed orange and Jeremy was dragging a long fire hose towards it.

He had everything under control.

She opened the ute door and threw the treat inside. Fetch scrambled inside and she shut the door behind him. "Do you still need me on the phone?" she asked the dispatcher.

"What's the status?"

"Jeremy's got a fire hose. He's fighting the fire and it's contained in the shed for now."

"Good. The fire crew's ETA is fifteen minutes."

"OK. I'm going to hang up and help Jeremy with

the fire." She thrust the phone into her rain jacket pocket and zipped it up.

How fast could a fire like this spread?

She glanced around the gravel yard. She needed to leave room for the fire truck, but the ute should be fine on the far side.

Getting in, she pushed Fetch back to his seat. She reversed the ute as far as she could from the shed, but stayed in the wide turning circle in front of the house. She pointed the ute forward so it could be moved quickly if needed.

Now she needed to help Jeremy.

He must have another hose somewhere.

She wound down the window a crack so there was enough air in the vehicle and got out, stopping Fetch from following her with some difficulty. "Stay." Fetch would be fine in the ute.

She scanned the area. Jeremy's truck was still close to the shed and might cause an obstruction when the fire crew arrived. The key would be inside. She should shift it as well.

Zamira moved forward but someone grabbed her arm, tugging her back. She shrieked and turned as a heavy hand covered her mouth. Her heart raced as a second person lifted her legs from under her and in the firelight she recognised Henk. Shit.

She struggled, kicking and punching but their hold was too tight. She yelled, her voice muffled against the salty, dirty hand. They carried her away from the house.

What the hell?

From the dark, a grey sedan appeared. She struggled harder, twisting to see where Jeremy was. Still fighting the fire, his back to her.

Henk dropped her legs but before she could kick out, he trod on her feet. Pain shot through her. He bent and fastened a plastic tie around her ankles.

No. They couldn't take her. She had to get free. The second man took his hand away from her mouth. Her scream was muffled as Henk stuffed a rag in her mouth. It tasted oily.

She lashed out, punching Henk and though he grunted, the second man captured her arm and wrenched both of them behind her back. Her muscles screamed and the plastic tie snapped into place.

No, no, no.

Henk opened the car boot. "In you go."

She pressed back against the man who held her, tensing her body, fear filling every cell. It was no use. The man lifted her up and Henk grabbed her legs. Together they shoved her in and then the boot closed. Pitch black.

There was no telling what Henk would do. She kicked her legs but the ties were too tight for much movement. She tried her wrists and the plastic chafed.

The car doors slammed and the engine started, straining a little before the car bumped forward over the rough ground.

Terror gripped her. Zamira couldn't get enough oxygen, the gag pressed into her mouth and rested against her nostrils.

She rolled as the car accelerated and then managed to brace her feet against the side. Her skin hot, her hairs standing on end, she wanted to scream and scream and scream.

They turned a corner and her head bumped the side, the pain breaking through her panic.

She had to get out of here.

She shifted, feeling around with her hands but her movement was limited. Aside from the grit, the carpet was bare. Nothing she could use to cut her bonds.

Loud sirens pierced the air and her heart leapt. The police!

The sirens passed in a wail.

Not police — the fire brigade. At least it meant they'd soon be at Jeremy's, they'd help him. Then they might notice she was missing.

She hoped.

But she couldn't rely on them to save her.

Straining her shoulders back as far as they could go, she shifted her hands under her butt. Her muscles tensed and the car went around a sharp bend, rolling her to the side again.

Damn it.

Lying on her back, she put her knees in the air and lifted her hips. She'd done bridge pose many times in her yoga practice. She bit into the rag as her arms reached towards her butt. Almost there. Her shoulders screamed but she got her hands under her butt.

She panted, drawing in what little breath she could as her body balanced in an abdominal crunch position. Step two, her feet between her hands. If she got out of this, she'd thank her grandmother for teaching her yoga.

Another rough bump in the road and she was flung to the side. She could do this. She had to.

Rolling onto her back she squeezed her legs close to her and stretched her arms away. Her feet touched her fingertips, then her wrists and then they were through.

Her muscles ached as she pulled the gag down and sucked in air. The pressure in her chest lessened. She twisted, reaching for anything she could use to cut her ties or as a weapon in the small, cramped area. Nothing.

She kicked and scissored her legs, trying to break the ties, but there wasn't enough room to move.

What else?

No way to access the spare tyre cavity with her lying on top of it.

But there had to be a way to access the back lights. They were made of glass.

Her fingers pried around the carpet above her head and she found the edge. She tugged hard, shifting back and the carpet came away. The red from the rear light glowed through the grille that protected it.

The car slowed. Her heart seized. She was running out of time.

She ripped at the grille, tearing it off and pulled one of the light globes out, gritting her teeth at the heat. Closing her eyes, she smashed it against the side… it didn't break. She hit it again, harder this time. Still nothing. Damn it.

The car stopped. Doors slammed.

The boot popped open and she enclosed the globe in her fist.

A light shining nearby illuminated Henk. He scowled at her. "How the fuck did you get the gag out of your mouth?"

"Help!" she screamed. "Help!"

Henk laughed. "Scream as loud as you want. No one's going to hear you out here." He grabbed her wrists and hauled her out of the boot, her head hitting the lid with enough force to make her wince.

She inhaled deeply, the sea air howled. Nearby, waves crashed against the shore. Behind Henk was a small beach shack and surrounding it was thick beach scrub too dense to run through. Henk hefted her over his shoulder and carried her inside.

The rickety wooden steps had protruding nails and the floor inside was grimy. He walked her through a tiny living room, lit only by a gas lantern and then unlocked another door and dumped her onto a single spring bed.

"What do you want from me?" she demanded.

"You ruined my operation," he snarled. "Where you're going, no one will find you. You'll wish you never stuck your nose into my business." He slammed the door and then the lock snicked into place. Darkness filled the room with only a little light from the small window.

"Zamira!"

She sat up and her eyes widened. "Annisa?" As her eyes adjusted to the dark, she made out two more beds, both with lumps on them.

"Why are you here? What's going on?" Annisa asked in Malaysian.

Relief filled Zamira. She'd found her. Now they had to escape. "Henk kidnapped me." Zamira open her fist and placed the globe on the ground. Using her boot, she crushed it gently and picked up a piece of glass. "Can you come here?" This had to work.

"I'm tied to the bed and so is Bethari."

Movement on the other bed revealed another woman lying there.

Zamira hopped over to Annisa and discovered her hands were tied above her head to the bed with plastic ties. She clenched one hand to give herself more space to saw at Annisa's ties. "How long have you been here?"

"This is the second night."

She glanced at the other woman. "What about Bethari?"

"Same. She was at Henk's too," Annisa said.

The glass slowly cut through Annisa's tie. Almost there.

"Do you have a phone?"

Zamira stilled. She'd forgotten about Jeremy's

phone. She'd shoved it in her pocket before she'd moved the ute. She placed the glass on the bed and withdrew the phone from her pocket.

No signal.

She held it up high and moved it around. Not even SOS only. She shoved it back in her pocket. When they got free, they'd walk until they got reception.

She kept at Annisa's restraint, and Annisa pulled her hands as far apart as she could, putting tension on the tie. Finally it snapped.

Yes!

Annisa rubbed her wrists.

"Help Bethari," Zamira instructed, handing her the glass. She picked up another piece from the floor.

Annisa worked on Bethari's ties as Zamira turned her attention to the restraint around her feet.

She jerked her feet apart and the plastic snapped with a satisfying pop. Now her hands. They were going to get out of here. She turned the glass around, wincing as it cut her wrists.

Footsteps clomped outside the door and the lock rattled. No. She needed more time.

Bethari whimpered.

"Annisa, can you get out the window?" Zamira shoved the phone at her cousin and then enclosed the piece of glass in her fist as she moved to the side of the door, ready for it to open. She had to catch them unaware. Had to knock Henk out and then they could run.

Annisa struggled with the window, but it didn't budge.

The door opened, light flooding the room and Henk swore. "Where—"

Zamira launched herself at him, swinging her fists, but she couldn't get much momentum with them tied together and the glass cut into her palms.

He grunted as she hit him, and he stumbled back a step but recovered quickly and grabbed her. "You little bitch."

She fought hard, kicking, trying to knee him in the groin. He was so strong, his muscles not flinching as she hit him.

Something cold and hard pressed against her head. "Stop moving or I'll shoot."

She froze and Henk knocked her to the ground. Her head spun as she looked up at the second man whose face was covered with a black balaclava and then focused on the gun pointing at her.

Her heart stopped and then resumed its beat in triple time. She panted.

"We're going for a walk," Henk said. "You run and he'll shoot you." He gestured to the other two women. "Make sure they understand."

His meaning was pretty clear no matter what language he spoke, but Zamira translated for the women. Bethari sobbed.

"Get up," Henk ordered.

Zamira slowly got to her feet. There had to be a way out of this. The key was getting the gun from the hulking great big man. Like that would be easy.

"Follow me." Henk walked out the door and the guy with the gun gestured her to go first.

She gave Annisa and Bethari a reassuring smile. "We'll be fine." She walked out of the little room into the living area where there were a couple of couches. Through another door was a basic kitchen. It was the kind of shack surfer hippies would have lived in, just the basics, not even electricity.

How long had she been in the boot of the car? How far were they from Blackbridge?

Surely Jeremy would have noticed her missing by now.

Outside the stars were bright, filling the sky. The waxing moon gave more light and the wind whipped around her. Henk switched on a torch and the beam illuminated a narrow, sandy beach track. Bushes lined either side of the track, about two metres high which restricted her view and prevented her from making a run for it. Behind her Bethari continued to sob. Zamira opened her hand, felt the warm blood from the cut. Carefully she manoeuvred the glass so she could work on her ties. She was the only one still restrained.

Was Henk going to kill them?

The track sloped down and the crash of the waves grew louder. The path opened up to a sandy beach and an aluminium dinghy waited in the small bay beyond the break, rising and falling with the swell.

Her breath caught and her pulse thumped slow and heavy. No one would search for them on the ocean.

She stopped walking and Annisa and Bethari huddled around her. She wrenched her wrists apart, but the tie didn't give. She kept cutting.

"Keep moving," the man behind her ordered.

"We're not getting into the boat."

"You'll do what Henk says."

Henk turned around, shone the torch in her eyes. She shut them against the glare and turned her head away. "I only promised them two women," he said. "You're a bonus. But if you don't get in the boat, I'll kill Annisa and then force you in there." He retrieved a gun from his waist band and pointed it at Annisa's head.

Annisa shook, tears pouring down her face.

Zamira's throat closed over and she stumbled forward. "Where are we going?"

"We're meeting someone who pays very well for

women of a certain age."

Her skin crawled. "Jeremy will be looking for me."

He laughed. "He's busy with the fire."

Henk must have lit it. The bastard. All of Jeremy's work was in that shed. How dare he hurt someone she loved?

She inhaled sharply.

She barely knew Jeremy, but she knew enough. His generosity to friends and strangers alike, his dedication to his work, the way he'd listened to her without judgement, and was genuinely interested in what she had to say. The little things he'd done for her like finding her painkillers when he noticed she was sore, blow-drying her hair so she could make a good impression, and taking the time to make sure she was ready when they made love. It was impossible not to love him.

Would she ever see him again?

The man in the balaclava pushed her forward as the boat pulled onto the shore.

Determination stiffened her resolve. She would see Jeremy again. She'd get them out of here. She'd had enough of arrogant men ruling her life. It was time to put a stop to it.

The gun was the biggest problem. She couldn't run without risking Annisa being shot, but once they were in the water… "Can you swim?" she whispered.

Bethari shook her head and Annisa said, "Not in these waves."

She let out a breath. There had to be another option. Her boots filled with water as the waves washed over them. She glanced back. No lights, no trace they were there, except for the footprints the waves washed away.

Henk grabbed her arm and jerked her over to the dinghy. The ties snapped. Yes! One step closer to escape.

"Get in."

As long as she was alive, she could escape. Something would come to her. She wasn't letting this self-entitled asshole ruin her life. She swung her leg over the side of the aluminium boat and sat on the middle seat, on the far side. A man sat by the small outboard motor, a beanie over his head and his face covered with a black scarf. He wore all black like the other man. She faced away from him, wanting to see where they were heading, and helped Annisa aboard. The waves splashed over the sides of the boat, wetting her pants and the wind blew colder. Henk lifted Bethari in and the three women huddled on the seat together as Henk climbed in the front. The man holding the gun pushed the dinghy away from the shore and walked away.

The motor roared to life and wind throbbed around her ears as the dinghy slowly made its way through the waves and swell. The slower they went the better.

Annisa clung to her and Zamira patted her knee. The little boat couldn't travel very far or very fast. By the time they reached the shore again she'd have a plan.

They headed directly out to sea, past the waves breaking, not turning to hug the coastline. Probably rocks close to shore.

All along the coastline it was dark, not a single car headlight or house. Henk held the gun loosely in his hand. She twisted, pretending to lean in to say something to Annisa and glanced at the skipper. One hand held the side of the dinghy and the other was on the motor. No gun.

Which left Henk. How fast could she pounce? Could she get the gun from him?

Bethari moaned and Annisa hugged her.

A dark shape coalesced in front of the dinghy. A fishing boat, one of those trawlers that went deep out to sea to catch their livelihood. No lights shone aboard but as they approached, Henk flashed his torch three times.

An answering flash.

Her muscles stiffened. Not good. A boat like that could take them further and faster, it could handle the big waves the Southern Ocean threw at them. But she might not survive the swim back to shore, not in these waves and the others wouldn't either.

The dinghy pulled alongside the fishing boat and Henk threw out a line. Someone on board caught it and Henk switched his torch on. "Time to get off." The light illuminated the metal ladder on the side of the boat. He hauled Bethari to her feet. She swayed, moaning again and then vomited all over him.

Zamira's smile froze on her face as Henk backhanded Bethari and she fell overboard with a splash. Henk wiped at his jacket. "Looks like it'll be only two after all."

Bethari's head popped above the waves and she shrieked, splashing hard before going under again.

No. Zamira couldn't let her drown.

She dived in after her. The ice cold hit her, compressing her lungs. Her clothes immediately soaked up the water, weighing her down. She fought to the surface and gasped, a wave filling her mouth with water. Coughing and struggling against the pull of her clothes she scanned frantically for Bethari.

A hand.

She swam hard, fighting the swell and took a deep breath as the hand disappeared. She dived after her, reaching, stretching, the water pitch black. Her fingers brushed skin and she kicked again, clasping Bethari's hand. Her lungs squeezed and demanded air. She changed direction, swimming up to the faint glow from Henk's torch. Her clothes battled against her, pulling her down.

With another hard kick, her head breached the water and she gasped, pulling Bethari above with her. Bethari sucked in air and clung to Zamira, mumbling in panic, trying to climb on top of her.

Zamira fought her, fought to stop going under, but it was no use.

The water closed over her.

Chapter 18

The shrill wail of a siren pierced through the roar of the flames and Jeremy turned as the fire truck pulled to a stop and his colleagues jumped out. That didn't take long. How long had he been standing here?

Lawrence strode over while others worked to get the hoses out. "What have we got?"

"It's contained. I don't know what started it, but I smelled petrol."

"Deliberately lit?"

He shook his head and then fear gripped him. Henk! He shoved his hose at Lawrence. "Where's Zamira?" He scanned his yard. Fetch was in the ute watching proceedings, but Zamira wasn't with him.

Surely she wouldn't have gone back into the house. He ran towards it, burst through the back door. "Zamira!"

No answer.

Quickly he searched the rooms. Empty.

He fumbled in his jacket pocket for his phone. It wasn't there. He'd given it to Zamira.

He ran back outside to Mai who was manning the pump. "Mai, I need your phone."

She handed it to him. "Code's one three zero seven."

He plugged it in and dialled his number. "This phone could not be reached. Please leave a message."

He swore. He had reception around his house. Where could she be? He tried again as he checked behind the shed. Nothing.

"Zamira's missing," he reported to Mai.

"She might be finding another hose."

He shook his head. "She's not answering my phone. The fire was deliberately lit and whoever did it has taken her."

Mai scowled and reached into the truck to grab the radio. "We've got a missing woman."

He needed the number for Agent Franklin. Mai would have Lincoln's number. He scrolled through the contacts until he found the sergeant's number and dialled.

"Mai, do you know what time it is?" Lincoln's voice was raspy with sleep.

"Lincoln, it's Jeremy. Henk torched my shed and he's taken Zamira. I need Agent Franklin's number."

Lincoln swore. "Repeat that slowly."

Jeremy could hear him moving about. "Zamira's missing. Someone set my shed alight and while I was hosing the fire, she moved my ute out of the way and now I can't find her." He took a torch from the back of the fire tanker and strode over to his ute. Fetch wagged a greeting, but Jeremy walked past, scanning the ground for footprints. The gravel provided nothing, but the grasses next to it were flattened. He followed the trail.

"What makes you think it was Henk?"

"Someone tried to run her over when she was walking back to my house this evening after helping Border Force. Henk's the only one with motive."

"Has she got a phone on her?"

"She was using mine to call the fire brigade." He gave Lincoln his number and continued towards the road. He stopped as he discovered footprints in the grey soil and deep tyre marks as if the car had had trouble getting out of the soft sand. "Lincoln, there's been a car here."

"I'm on my way. I'll call Agent Franklin and see if we can get a triangulation on your phone."

He hung up. Zamira had his phone and he had location tracking enabled on it. He was also connected to an app that linked him to the rest of his fire crew in case they got separated while they were fighting a bush fire. He swiped through Mai's apps as he strode back towards the house.

There.

He clicked on it, held his breath as it came up.

Six red dots hovered around his house and one red dot east, near the coast. Nothing out there except a couple of fishing spots. Definitely no buildings, no reason for her to be anywhere near there.

Keys. He patted his pockets. No, Zamira had them. He checked the ute, but they weren't inside.

Shit.

He strode over to the crew. "Lawrence, I need the fast attack."

Lawrence glanced at him. "We're using it."

"I need to go after Zamira."

Concern crossed his face. "Mate, I can't let you take it. We've got hoses all over the place."

Jeremy called Lincoln again. Busy.

He checked the app. The dot was out over the water. Was the signal dodgy, or had the person who'd taken her put her on a boat? He wasn't chancing it.

He scrolled through Mai's numbers and called her

brother, Kim.

"Mai, what the—?"

"It's Jeremy. I need Marine Rescue."

"Is Mai all right?"

"She's fine. She's at my place putting out my shed fire. Zamira's been kidnapped and she's on a boat heading out to sea."

Give his friend credit, he didn't ask stupid questions. "Where?"

"Around Old Man's Blowhole."

Kim swore. "No boat ramps in that area. We'll have to launch from town."

"I'll meet you there. Lincoln's on his way." He hung up and a car drove into the yard.

Jeremy ran over, opened the door. "Don't stop. She's on a boat." He showed Lincoln the app. "I've called Kim and he's mobilising Marine Rescue. We've got to get to the boat ramp in town."

Lincoln handed Jeremy his phone and accelerated away. "Call Franklin back. It's the last number I called."

He dialled and relayed the information.

"Where's the boat ramp?" Franklin asked.

He gave her directions.

"I'll meet you there."

Lincoln turned onto the main road and put his foot down, accelerating fast. "You think this is payback?"

"Maybe." But why take her onto the ocean?

His blood went cold. Had they killed her? Were they dumping the body?

He checked his phone again. The dot still moved away from shore. "Can't you drive any faster?"

Lincoln grunted, but didn't answer. As they reached the town, Lincoln drove straight past the turn off to the boat ramp. "It's that way!"

"I need my gun." He pulled up in front of the police

station and ran inside.

Jeremy's foot tapped on the ground. What was taking him so long?

Lincoln returned, wearing a vest and carrying another. He tossed it at Jeremy. "This is for you."

A bullet proof vest. "You think we'll need it?"

"I'm not taking any chances. I'd leave you behind if I didn't think you'd steal the first boat you found." He drove fast through the quiet streets and pulled up at the Marine Rescue boat ramp. Lights illuminated the area and the boat was in the water, people aboard. Jeremy and Lincoln ran down the jetty. Three Border Force agents were on board and Kim was behind the wheel.

Lincoln called out, "Kim, you don't have to come. This isn't Marine Rescue business."

Kim glanced at Jeremy. "I know. But you won't find a better skipper."

Lincoln nodded. "All right. Let's go."

Jeremy handed Mai's phone to Kim. "Thanks, mate."

Kim grinned. "I can't let you have all the fun." He turned to Lincoln. "Cast us off."

Jeremy shrugged off his heavy fire jacket and fastened up the bullet proof vest to wear beneath it. Kim handed him an inflatable life jacket. "Put this on too."

The others already wore them. As he did as he was told, he moved over to where Franklin and Lincoln were speaking.

"I've called it in, but it could be more than an hour before we get air support." Her voice was raised above the engine and the wind.

"Why take Zamira?" Lincoln asked.

Franklin glanced at Jeremy. "Henk might be involved in a trafficking ring as well. Some of the men we interviewed mentioned women often arrived at the property but never stayed long — a month or two at most — and they didn't see them again."

Jeremy froze. "What happens to the women?"

"Probably sold to brothels. We've got some evidence that women are traded, those taken from Australia are sent overseas and they get foreign women in return."

His teeth clenched hard enough to shatter and he hit the side of the boat.

No. He wouldn't let that happen.

He would save her.

Jeremy spun on his heel, returned to Kim. "Can't you push this thing faster?"

****

Zamira struggled, prying Bethari's hands away from her shoulders, gritting her teeth and kicking towards the surface. As her head broke through the waves, she yelled, "Don't panic."

Hands grabbed Bethari's jumper and hauled her aboard the dinghy. Zamira trod water, fighting the drag of her clothes and the swell of the waves. She panted, the chill seeping into her bones and reached for the side of the dinghy, but it shifted in the waves. She wiped the water from her eyes as she met Henk's gaze. Would he leave her here?

He only needed two women.

Her body shook in the cold.

She lunged for the boat and this time caught the side. Bethari was being helped onto the fishing boat so Zamira pulled herself along the side towards the trawler.

Henk followed Bethari up the ladder and tossed the rope back.

Shit. Stay with the dinghy, or go after Annisa? Her arms trembled. She couldn't pull herself up. The dinghy skipper pried her fingers off the edge of the boat. She lunged for the trawler ladder, her fingers closing around the cold metal. She panted as the engines next to her roared to life. She had to move. Reaching up, she found the next rung and lifted her feet. Slowly she climbed as the trawler motored forward.

Her foot slipped on the ladder, her shin crashing into a lower rung and pain bursting through her. She gritted her teeth and hauled herself up and onto the fishy-smelling deck. She lay there panting and Henk smiled down at her. "Well done. Now come with me."

Where were Annisa and Bethari?

As the boat motored through the waves, Zamira followed Henk below deck. The lights were on and for anyone paying attention it appeared to be a fishing boat going to work.

There must be a radio on board.

A cramped bunk room off the corridor contained Annisa and a wet, bedraggled Bethari. Annisa threw herself at Zamira, hugging her.

"I'm OK."

Henk threw a couple of towels at them. "Make yourselves comfortable. You'll be in there awhile." He shut the door.

Zamira reached for the handle… nothing. The door sat flush against the wall and was the width of one of the panels. If she hadn't seen it open, she would have thought the room had no exits. It was probably invisible from the other side — the perfect smuggler's room.

Shit. What other options did they have?

Two bunk beds had rugs on them, but there were no windows and only a tiny vent in the floor.

She shivered. First they needed to get dry. She stumbled as the waves rocked the boat side-to-side. Bethari moaned, her face pale.

Then she vomited all over the floor.

***

Salt water and vomit was all Zamira could smell. Bethari had thrown up until she had nothing left and now the vomit moved over the floor with the crash of the waves. Annisa sat on the bottom bunk with her knees hugged to her chest.

Zamira used one of the towels to wipe Bethari's mouth. Bethari shivered, her skin pale and goosebumps on her arms. She had to warm them both up, otherwise they could freeze to death.

She ignored the vomit and squeezed Bethari's arm. "You need to take off your clothes."

Bethari glanced at the door and shook her head.

"If you don't, you could die." She unzipped her rain jacket and hung it on the bunk ladder and then stripped off her wool jumper. She hadn't taken the time to put on a bra or a shirt. She squeezed out the wool and Annisa helped, taking one side and twisting it in the opposite direction.

Zamira dried her top half quickly and ran the towel through her hair. To really warm up she should get under the bedsheets naked, but she wasn't willing to risk being so vulnerable. She dressed again, her teeth chattering so hard together they might break. She had to get warm. Quickly she slid off her shoes, taking off her pants and socks and wringing them out. Her hands shook as she dressed, her skin like ice. Bethari watched, still shivering.

"Your turn." This time Bethari raised her arms so Zamira could pull her jumper off. They repeated the process, squeezing as much water as they could out of Bethari's clothing before she dressed again and lay down under the sheets on one bed. Zamira dragged the rugs off the top bunk and piled them on top of her as well.

She wanted to join her but they had to escape. She held a hand against her stomach. The bump of the hull against the waves rattled her teeth further and the sway made her nauseous. She breathed deeply, and then retched at the vomit stench. She clenched her teeth. Now wasn't the time to be weak.

What else was in the room?

The bunks were made of sturdy wood. She lifted the mattress on the top bunk, looking for anything that might help. A couple of pillows, sheets and a rug. Nothing sharp, no kind of weapon.

The cotton pillowcases were probably too breathable to suffocate Henk even if she managed to hold it over his head for long enough.

Bethari moaned and retched over the side of the bunk.

Zamira winced and checked her temperature. Warmer. Her skin was no longer covered in goosebumps.

"Zamira!" Annisa waved Jeremy's phone at her.

Her heart leapt. It had a signal. She hit the emergency link and dialled triple zero.

It rang.

"Do you need police, fire or ambulance?"

Her heart racing, she said, "Police."

Chapter 19

Jeremy scanned the ocean around him, but he couldn't see any lights, any boats, anything at all.

They had to be somewhere.

Kim touched his shoulder. "The sea's rough tonight. It's easy to miss a light in the waves, but we'll find her."

A radio crackled behind him and Lincoln moved forward into the cockpit. "Can you repeat that?"

"We've had an emergency call. A woman says she's been kidnapped and is on a fishing boat with two other women."

Jeremy's heart leapt. "Did she give a name?"

"Zamira Musa."

She was alive. Thank God.

Lincoln flashed him a smile. "Roger that. Do you have a location?"

Coordinates came through and Kim adjusted the direction they were heading. "How far are we?" Jeremy demanded.

"About ten nautical miles," Kim answered. "But this boat can move faster than a trawler."

Lincoln went to relay the news to the team of Border Force officers while Jeremy continued to scan the ocean. Ten nautical miles was still a big distance. How far out before they hit international waters? Would they be forced to turn back?

His grip on the side of the cockpit tightened. Whatever happened, he wouldn't let them return without Zamira.

About twenty minutes later, a dot appeared on the radar. "We've got them," Kim said.

Jeremy's eyes strained in the darkness and finally a light flashed between the waves. "Over there!" He pointed.

Kim nodded. "That could be them."

Jeremy strode over to Agent Franklin. "What's the plan?"

She raised her eyebrows. "The plan is for you to stay on this boat while we board and search the trawler."

He shook his head and opened his mouth to protest.

"You shouldn't even be here," Franklin snapped. "You do as I say."

"She's right, Jeremy. We're trained for this." Lincoln handed him a radio. "Once we're on board, you need to watch. They might panic and throw the women overboard."

Jeremy grabbed the radio, his jaw tight. He nodded once, but he wasn't going to make promises he couldn't keep.

As they neared the vessel, it became clear it was a fishing trawler. The Marine Rescue boat shone its spotlight towards it and Franklin hailed it over the radio. "This is Blackbridge Marine Rescue One to the vessel Hera, over."

A long silence before, "This is Hera. Go ahead, Blackbridge Marine Rescue One."

"You need to stop your engines and prepare to be boarded."

"What's this about?"

"I repeat, stop your engines and prepare to be boarded. All personnel should come out on the deck."

"Roger that."

The spotlight illuminated three people as they came out onto the deck dressed in wet weather gear. Henk wasn't among them. Was this the wrong boat?

On Franklin's command, Kim pulled the Marine Rescue boat next to the fishing trawler and the three Border Force officers and Lincoln transferred and then Kim pulled back.

The officers searched the men on deck and then Franklin went to the wheelhouse and the others went below deck, out of sight.

Jeremy gripped the side of the boat.

Where was Zamira?

***

The boat rocked and banged as it went over wave after wave. It seemed like an eternity since Zamira had called the police. She had to hope they could find the boat in the middle of the ocean. She wrapped the rug tighter around her shoulders and stroked Bethari's head. The poor woman lay groaning on the bed, clinging to the side, her face pale. Annisa sat on the opposite bunk watching Zamira as if she could make anything happen.

Zamira couldn't let them down. They would get out of here alive.

At least neither of them was still shivering.

Suddenly a loud announcement over the ship's PA. "We've got trouble. A boat's approaching... looks like Marine Rescue."

Yes! They were saved.

Footsteps pounded past the door and then the door flung open. Henk held his gun. He screwed up his nose as the smell of vomit reached him, but he strode in and someone shut the door behind him.

"If anyone speaks, I'll put a bullet in them," Henk said.

Zamira shuffled away from him and Annisa scooted to the other end of the bed, closer to her. Poor Bethari groaned, not moving.

"Shut up." Henk swung the gun towards her. "You give us away and you'll be dead."

Tears ran down Bethari's face, but she was silent.

"What's going on?" Zamira asked.

Henk scowled at her. "It will be a pleasure to kill you, so don't tempt me."

"They'll hear it if you shoot me."

He grunted.

The PA again. "Marine Rescue are boarding. Everyone up on deck."

Zamira's heart beat fast. "They'll search the boat."

He grinned at her. "But they won't find this room."

Her stomach dropped. They couldn't be this close and not be rescued.

A few more footsteps pounded down the steps and voices yelled, "Clear."

They were searching.

She needed to call the police back. Tell them they had the right boat. She needed a distraction.

Bethari pulled herself up and retched silently over the bed. Henk moved back, his face a picture of disgust.

That was it. If she could fake being sick, Annisa could cover her for long enough to make the call.

She tugged on Annisa's arm and whispered, "Stand in front of me. Help Bethari."

Annisa turned, and Zamira slipped the phone out of her pocket. Then she retched and Henk swore under his breath. Hands shaking she opened the phone and scrolled through the contacts. What was the policeman's name? Lincoln. No number for him. Who else? She closed her eyes, concentrating. One of Jeremy's friends volunteered for Marine Rescue. It wasn't Jamie… it had to be Kim.

She retched again, and dialled Kim's number.

"Zamira?"

Relief filled her. He must know what was going on. "There's a hidden room on the boat you're searching," she whispered. "Henk's with us and he has a gun." Annisa shrieked and then Zamira was yanked backwards. The phone flew out of her hand and landed on the floor. She looked up into Henk's red, enraged face.

She had only seconds to register his fist coming towards her before it hit her.

Pain exploded through her head and she fell against the bunk.

Henk picked up the phone and swore. "You bitch!" He yanked her towards him, pressing the gun against her head.

Fear coursed through her veins. "If you shoot me, you'll be up for murder, not just kidnapping."

He narrowed his eyes. "It might be worth it."

She prayed they would find the room quickly.

He moved his gun towards Annisa. "Or perhaps I should kill your friend instead."

"No!" The words came out before she could stop them. "Henk, please."

"I've got nothing else to lose. They're going to put me away for a long time and I don't do well in confined spaces."

More footsteps and the door clicked open. Two Border Force officers stood there, guns pointed in the room. "Drop it," one demanded.

Thank God.

Henk pushed Zamira in front of him, the gun to her head. "I'll shoot her."

Bethari sobbed on the bed, not moving.

The room was too cramped, and if people started shooting it would not end well. Particularly not for her.

"Hands behind your head," the officer ordered.

"No. Move out of the doorway." Henk pressed the gun harder into Zamira's temple and she winced in pain.

"How about you let the other women go," the officer said, his gun not wavering.

"I want the Marine Rescue boat," Henk demanded. "Tie it to the front of the trawler, no people on board."

"Give us one of the women as a show of faith."

Henk growled low and yanked Zamira back. "Get out of here." He nodded at Bethari.

Annisa looked at Zamira.

"Take Bethari and go," Zamira said in Malaysian. "Quickly now."

Annisa pulled Bethari up, encouraging her to move. Bethari was incredibly weak but she stumbled out the door. Henk grabbed Annisa and jerked her back. "Not you."

The officer pulled Bethari through the door and continued to train the gun on Henk.

"Mr Jennings, put down your gun."

The cold barrel pressed unwavering against her head. "No. You've got two minutes to have the boat in place."

If they didn't obey the order, Zamira was pretty sure what the consequence would be.

"Move back," Henk demanded. "We're coming out."

One of the officers glanced down the corridor where

Bethari had gone and then stepped that way. The other man followed, his eyes not leaving Henk's, his gun still trained on them.

"Do exactly as I say," Henk told Zamira. "Move forward slowly and stop when you get to the door."

Zamira translated for Annisa and added, "When you get to the door, run towards the officers."

Annisa's eyes widened and Zamira nodded in encouragement. Henk didn't have the right angle to shoot Annisa.

Henk tightened his grip on her arm. "Move back," he ordered the officers.

They stepped back, only one still visible. Annisa shuffled to the entrance and as she cleared it, she leapt to the side.

Henk roared. "I'll shoot this bitch."

The gun pressed painfully against Zamira's skull.

"The Marine Rescue boat is waiting for you," the officer still in view said.

"You try anything, you flinch at the wrong moment and I will kill you," Henk growled.

She believed him. Fear spread through her. This couldn't be the end. She needed to see Jeremy again, tell him she loved him. There had to be another opportunity to escape before Henk got off the boat.

Henk shoved her through the door, using her as a shield, his strong grip around her waist keeping her on her feet. The two officers stood in the corridor, guns out facing them, ready.

"Walk backwards," Henk said.

She had no choice as he dragged her back, the rocking of the boat making it hard to walk in a straight line, but the corridor was narrow and braced them.

Henk stopped. "Reach up," he said. "Open that hatch."

She glanced at the hatch above her head. Wide enough for two of them to fit through. A ladder was attached to the wall underneath it. Henk couldn't possibly keep the gun on her while he climbed out. The officer furthest from them spoke quietly into his radio. There had to be more people above deck.

Did Henk really think he could escape?

She climbed up a ladder rung, pushed the hatch open and Henk shifted the gun to the middle of her back. "Slowly now, we climb out together."

She glanced at the officers and the man nodded. Trust.

The metal rungs were thin but wide and Henk stepped on the same rung as her, holding her in place next to him. She effectively screened Henk from the officers below deck as they moved up the ladder. Moving up another rung enabled her to see above deck. The Marine Rescue boat hovered off the trawler's bow, its lights shining directly at her. Agent Franklin and Lincoln moved into view, guns out. The boat rocked and water washed over the bow, making the deck slippery. The wind blew through Zamira's wet clothing, freezing her. This was her chance. If she moved fast enough, the officers could get a clear shot at Henk. She hefted herself out of the small space as a huge wave washed over the bow. The water hit her, knocking her off balance and she rolled along the deck, letting the wave carry her away from Henk.

A shot rang out and she hit the railing of the boat, her legs sliding under. She lunged for it, but it was too wet, her hands unable to grip. With one more desperate reach, her fingers brushed the metal. The boat's bow dipped, meeting the ocean, and water sucked at her legs, pulling her under and off the boat.

No. She reached for the railing, but it was no use.

She managed a single gasp before the freezing cold ocean closed above her again.

***

Jeremy was going out of his mind. The officers had been on the trawler for a good ten minutes, but no Zamira. The crew were handcuffed on the deck and Lincoln stood guard over them.

Zamira was on board. She'd called Kim to tell him. So where was she?

Movement at the main door caught his attention and Lincoln rushed over to take a woman from Agent Franklin. Not Zamira or Annisa.

Lincoln moved the woman to the side of the boat and gestured them over. The deck height difference between the trawler and the rescue boat was significant.

"Jeremy, go help," Kim ordered as he manoeuvred the boat into place.

He gritted his teeth as he threw the line to Lincoln and then grabbed the woman's waist as she straddled the edge of the boat. He half lifted, half fell, pulling the woman with him, but managed not to hurt either of them. "Where's Zamira?"

No answer. The woman was pale, soaked to the skin and shaking. He wrapped his arm around her waist and helped her into the cabin below as Annisa ran out on the deck. She spotted them and raced to the side, not needing any instructions.

Jeremy left the other woman with Kim and went to help Annisa on board. "Where's Zamira?"

She pointed back to the trawler. Not helpful.

"Get to the front deck." The words were murmured over the radio. Lincoln gestured for Kim to shift the boat away and move to the front of the fishing vessel. Jeremy hustled Annisa down into the cabin area. He shoved towels at both women, glancing through the windscreen.

Moments later a hatch opened and Zamira's head popped out.

His breath left his body. She was alive!

She climbed out, Henk right behind her, a gun pressed against her side. Jeremy froze, his hands clenched. If Henk shot her, Jeremy would kill him. He didn't blink as Zamira crawled onto the deck, swaying with the motion of the boat. A wave washed over the deck, knocking Zamira over. She rolled towards the side and grappled for the railing. A bang. Henk's gun pointed directly at Zamira.

No.

The water swept her legs under the railing and she reached for the bar.

She wasn't going to make it.

Jeremy was already moving as Kim yelled, "Man overboard."

In two steps he was at the railing, scanning the water.

There. Zamira reached for the side of the fishing trawler. A wave crashed into her and her head hit the side. She stopped struggling and slid under the water.

No!

Jeremy dived in, the ice-cold water hitting him like a brick. The waves pummelled his body, throwing him this way and that, but he swam towards where Zamira had disappeared. Taking a deep breath, he dived under. The Marine Rescue gave a little light, but not enough. His heavy fireman gear helped him down, dragging him under.

His lungs screamed for air. She had to be somewhere, but she could be right next to him and he wouldn't see her. He stretched out in all directions and his fingers brushed something. He kicked hard and found her hand.

His throat closed up, and his body demanded he breathe.

Changing direction, he kicked upwards. There wasn't even a speck of light from the boats above. He wasn't going to make it.

He dragged Zamira to him and brushed the life jacket he wore.

The *inflatable* jacket.

He tugged on the tags, holding Zamira close and the jacket inflated, drawing him up. Frantically he pushed towards the surface. A light appeared. Not far now.

His face breached the surface and he inhaled deeply, water and air filling his mouth. He turned away from the waves as his head spun and he gasped. Zamira's eyes were closed, her face pale.

"Zamira!" He shook her. No response. Pulse. He needed to check for her pulse.

Waves crashed over them as he struggled to keep them both afloat.

"Jeremy, catch." Kim threw out a life buoy. It landed within arm's reach and Jeremy placed it over Zamira's head, threading her arms through. Her pulse was thready, but she wasn't breathing. He tilted her chin back and breathed into her mouth once, twice.

Her lungs inflated and then she coughed, water spilling from her mouth and he turned her to her side, his heart beating again as she spat and spluttered.

"Jeremy?" Her voice was low, croaky.

"Yeah. You're all right, Miri. I've got you." He held her in place as Kim pulled them in.

They'd drifted some way from the fishing trawler, and Jeremy couldn't see what was happening on board. He kicked hard to help Kim. The freezing water soaked through his layers and he shivered. Zamira's eyes were closed again. They reached the edge of the boat and Kim leaned over and grabbed Zamira under her arms. He hauled her up and into the boat. Seconds later he was back, helping Jeremy aboard. Then they both huddled over Zamira slumped on the ground.

She lifted her head. "Annisa? Bethari?"

"At the front." Jeremy pulled her into his arms, hugged her tightly. "You scared the life out of me."

She held onto him, shaking. "Out of me too."

Kim wrapped a thermal blanket around their shoulders. "Come on. Get out of the wind."

Jeremy helped Zamira to her feet. They moved forward and Annisa and Bethari shuffled around to give them more room. Jeremy glanced over to the trawler as he stripped off his life jacket. All the Border Force officers were on deck with the crew in handcuffs. Good. As he turned around, he frowned. Was that blood on the deck? He checked himself and then turned to Zamira. "You're bleeding."

Kim was already on the radio requesting an update from Border Force.

Her rain jacket had a hole in it and was rapidly turning redder. He pushed it up and his heart stopped. A bullet wound. "Where's the first aid kit?"

"To your left."

Jeremy found some gauze and pressed it hard into her side. "You've been shot."

She hissed. "That hurts."

"Lay down," he ordered. "Kim, we've got to get her to a hospital."

There wasn't a whole lot of room in the cabin, but he helped Zamira to lie down.

"I need to check with Lincoln."

Jeremy's teeth chattered as the cold spread through

him, but Zamira had been in the water longer and he had to stop the bleeding, which was already soaking the gauze. He grabbed some more bandages but her clothing kept getting in the way. He unzipped her jacket. "Take it off."

She struggled to do what he said and Annisa helped her, then covered her top half with a blanket.

Kim pulled alongside the fishing trawler and Lincoln climbed on. He hurried to the front. "We can go. The others are staying on the fishing vessel. They'll motor it back to shore."

Kim turned the boat and let the engines roar.

Lincoln crouched at the entrance of the cabin. "How are they?"

"Zamira's been shot."

Lincoln swore and reached for the radio, called for an ambulance to meet them at the boat ramp.

Jeremy wrapped the bandage as tightly as he dared around her waist, his hands shaking — from cold or fear, he wasn't certain. The bandage turned red even as her skin had a bluish tinge.

He prayed.

Chapter 20

The boat trip took an eternity, Zamira's bandage getting bloodier despite Jeremy applying pressure. She shivered violently.

Damn. She still wore her wet pants. He removed them and wrapped a blanket around her lower half. On the other side of the cabin, Annisa huddled with Bethari who clutched a sea sickness bag in front of her. Although they were going with the waves this time, it didn't seem any faster. He glanced out of the cabin window. The hills that marked the entrance to the inlet were getting closer. Good. "Almost there." His teeth chattered.

Kim glanced at him and his eyes widened. "Shit, Jeremy, are you still wearing wet clothes under the blanket?"

He nodded.

"Lincoln, monitor Zamira while he gets out of the clothes."

Lincoln moved him out of the way and he was too cold to stop him. His fingers shook as he stripped off his clothes and boots. Lincoln handed him a blanket and he wrapped it around his shoulders.

Not far now.

Over at the boat ramp, two ambulances were parked, their lights flashing. Kim slowed and pulled up along the jetty where the paramedics waited with stretchers. Jeremy helped Zamira to her feet and she swayed, slumping against him. He dragged her out of the cabin.

"Let me get her," Lincoln said. "You're too cold." He picked up Zamira and passed her to the paramedics. Guy made her lie on the stretcher and pushed her towards the ambulance.

"You next." Lincoln helped him off and Jeremy stumbled after Guy. Cynthia intercepted him. "Let me examine you."

Jeremy shook his head. "See to Zamira first."

"Guy's got her. Were you injured?"

"No."

"You're wet. Did you go for a swim?"

"Zamira fell in, went under." The words caught in his throat. He could still see her disappearing. Guy loaded her into the ambulance as the other paramedics ran down the jetty to Annisa and Bethari.

"OK, we need to warm you up."

He ignored the woman and climbed into the ambulance. "I'm going with her."

Cynthia took one look at him and then nodded. "Strap in."

In moments the ambulance was on its way, racing towards the hospital. Guy put an IV into Zamira's arm and then handed Jeremy another blanket. "Wrap yourself in this."

It was warm inside the ambulance and his skin hurt from the change in temperature. He huddled in his blanket as Guy monitored Zamira.

The ride to the hospital was fast and then Zamira

was wheeled away from him. He tried to follow but Fleur stopped him. "You need to stay here," she said. "Let me check you over."

"No—"

Fleur put a hand on his chest. "Yes. You'll only get in the way. The doctors have her. They'll stabilise her before taking her to Albany." She took his arm and led him over to a bed. "How long were you in the water?"

"A while."

She raised her eyebrows at him and he blinked, bringing himself back to where he was. She was right. He needed to warm up so he could see Zamira when she came out.

"About five minutes."

He answered Fleur's questions and submitted to her prodding, his gaze on the door Zamira had gone through.

She had to live.

***

Zamira was warm. She slowly opened her eyes. Bright lights assaulted her and she squinted.

"How are you feeling?"

She turned to the female voice and saw a woman dressed in scrubs. She frowned. "Am I in hospital?"

The woman nodded. "In Albany. Can you tell me your name?"

"Zamira Musa." She closed her eyes, pushing past the fatigue, trying to remember. She'd been cold, so cold… and wet. She'd fallen into the ocean. Henk. Being kidnapped, then shot. Jeremy had rescued her.

She tried to sit up and her side pulled. "Where's Jeremy?"

The doctor smiled. "He's in the waiting room," she said. "Tell me, do you feel any pain?"

Zamira put her hand to her head. "No."

"Good. You were shot, but the bullet missed anything vital. You're very lucky."

She remembered the gunshot, but not any pain. She'd been too focused on not falling off the boat. "Are Annisa and Bethari all right?"

The doctor nodded. "Jeremy told me to let you know they're fine. They were taken to Blackbridge hospital."

It was over. Annisa was safe. She lay back down. "What time is it?"

"Almost seven in the morning. Are you up for visitors?" the doctor asked. "A number of people want to talk to you. Jeremy's been driving the nurses in the ED crazy asking about you."

Zamira smiled. "Yes." She needed to see him too.

"I'll let them know."

Zamira shifted to a seated position. She had to tell him how much joy he'd brought into her world. His smile brightened her day, filled her with such hope, such love. Her chest squeezed and she let out a breath. He twisted her up in so many knots.

Could there be a future for them?

Jeremy walked in wearing jeans and a dark grey hoodie. He had rings under his eyes and his hair stuck out at all angles but he was alive and well. His face split into a huge smile. "Miri." He strode over and pulled her into his arms and she hugged him back, inhaling deeply. Jeremy was here, he was safe. He kissed her softly.

"I'm so glad you're all right," she whispered.

He snorted. "Me? You're the one who was kidnapped, shot and almost drowned."

She frowned. She didn't remember the almost drowning bit. "What happened?"

"Jeremy, what are you doing here? I told you we

needed to talk to her first."

Zamira glanced up as Agent Franklin and another Border Force officer walked into her room. Neither looked like they had slept.

Jeremy shrugged, unconcerned. "You were too slow."

Franklin smiled at Zamira. "How are you?"

"I'm fine."

"We need to interview you about what happened. Are you up for it?"

Zamira shifted to a more seated position in the bed. "Yes. Can Jeremy stay?"

Franklin shook her head. "Not this time."

Jeremy sighed. "I'll be in the waiting room. Come and get me when you're finished." He kissed Zamira and walked out.

Her heart ached. She wanted him with her, wanted to talk to him about their future. Now Annisa was safe, she had no excuse to stay. She was due at work in four days. She had at most three more nights with Jeremy, three nights in this lovely town where most of the people were so friendly.

"Tell us what happened last night."

Franklin's question brought her back into the room. Right. They wanted answers.

She told them in as much detail as she could. When she spoke about the shack, Franklin said, "So aside from Henk, there was the dinghy skipper and a man who helped Henk kidnap you?"

"Yes. He stayed behind."

"Can you describe him?"

"Taller than me, about a hundred and eighty centimetres, and broad across the shoulders. His face was covered."

"We'll hopefully get some fingerprints from the

shack when we find it."

Zamira couldn't help them with that. "They were taking us to another boat," she said. "Henk said we were meeting someone who pays well for women of a certain age."

Franklin nodded. "We've been monitoring boats in the area," she said. "But with Henk not making the rendezvous, they won't wait around for long."

"Did you find any information on the trawler?"

"Not a lot. The crew don't know much about the smuggling. They get paid well to transport the girls back and forth."

Zamira scowled. "They'll go to jail though, won't they?"

Franklin nodded.

"Good." They had to be stopped. "This isn't the end of the investigation, is it? It's got to be far bigger than Henk and his crew."

"We believe so." Franklin studied her.

"Where's Henk now?"

"He's under police guard at the hospital," the officer said. "He was shot after he shot you. He'll go to jail as soon as he's discharged."

That was a relief. "Has he said why he's been doing this?"

Franklin shook her head. "He's not talking yet."

"Let me know when you need me to testify against him."

Franklin tilted her head to the side. "You kept it together last night," she said. "You saved those two women. Have you ever considered moving into operations? We need a new person in the region."

Zamira's mouth dropped open. "I've tried, but never got an interview."

Franklin frowned. "You're from Melbourne, aren't

you?"

She nodded.

"I'll have a word to my colleagues over there."

Zamira grinned. "Thank you. I'd appreciate it." She hesitated. "I'm open to moving to Western Australia if there's a job available." And then she could stay with Jeremy.

Franklin smiled. "I'll be in touch next week." She glanced at her notepad. "We've contacted Annisa's family. We haven't got much information out of Annisa or Bethari as yet, but they'll both need to go into detention."

Zamira gritted her teeth. It was the correct procedure for someone who was illegally in the country, but she didn't have to like it. "Do you need me to translate?"

Franklin shook her head. "It's best we get a neutral party." She stood. "We'll let you rest."

"Thank you. Could you send Jeremy back in?"

Franklin smiled. "Of course."

Moments after Franklin left, Jeremy walked in with Annisa by his side. "Look who arrived."

"Zamira!" Annisa flung her arms around Zamira.

She hugged her back. "How are you?"

"I'm safe. You rescued me."

Someone had given her a change of clothes and she looked rested. "How did you get here?"

"A Border Force woman brought me."

That was nice. "Have you spoken with your mother?"

Annisa nodded. "She's happy."

"Good."

Jeremy sat on the other side of her bed and took her hand. She had so much she wanted to say to him, but not with Annisa there.

Annisa continued to talk, telling her Bethari was well and about everything that had happened since she'd arrived in Australia. All the while, Jeremy stroked her hand, seemingly content to be by her side.

A couple of hours later, Franklin returned. "The translator has arrived and we need to question Annisa."

Zamira translated for Annisa and she frowned, stepping away from the agent.

"It's all right," Zamira said. "They'll take care of you."

"You won't leave without me?"

She shook her head. "No."

After Annisa left, Zamira closed her eyes. She was tired.

"Do you want to sleep?" Jeremy asked.

"No." What she wanted was for Jeremy to hold her and tell her he loved her. She opened her eyes again. "I'm a little hungry though."

"Let me ask if you're allowed to eat." He jumped up and left the room, freezing right outside, the smile disappearing from his face

"Jeremy, are you finally here to visit your sister?"

The angry tone had Zamira sitting up. She couldn't see the woman talking.

"Mum." His voice was flat.

Zamira gasped and shifted, cautiously swinging her legs off the bed. She couldn't let Jeremy face his family alone.

"Miri, don't get up." Jeremy rushed to her side and footsteps clicked closer.

"Who's this?" The woman standing in the doorway was in her fifties, significant grey through her short hair and her face pinched.

Jeremy glanced at Zamira, uncertainty in his eyes. With a deep breath he faced his mother. "Mum, this is my friend, Zamira."

"What happened to you?" the woman asked.

Zamira narrowed her eyes. This woman had abandoned her son. "I was kidnapped, shot and nearly drowned. Your son saved my life." She squeezed Jeremy's hand.

"Oh." His mother blinked, her face hardened. "Fallen into a bad crowd, have you?"

Jeremy flinched.

Zamira clenched her teeth. "How dare you?" Before she could give her a piece of her mind, a guy in his twenties joined Jeremy's mother. "What's going on?" He spotted Jeremy and grinned. "Hey, Moira just asked me to call you." His gaze drifted to Zamira. "Oh, sorry, I'm interrupting."

Jeremy's mother huffed and walked away. Jeremy watched her go, the pain clear on his face.

"I'm Zamira." She held out a hand to the guy.

"Ollie." He shook it. "I'm Jeremy's soon to be brother-in-law."

She'd forgotten all about Moira's car accident yesterday. She touched Jeremy's arm. "You should go visit Moira." Jeremy needed to speak with his sister. They had unresolved issues. "I could do with a nap." She looked at Ollie. "Can you take his mother for a coffee?"

He smiled and nodded. "We were heading to the café anyway."

Jeremy glanced at her. "Are you sure?"

She nodded. She could wait to tell him she loved him. They had time now.

He let out a sigh. "OK. I'll ask the nurses about some food for you on the way." With all the pain he must be feeling, he still remembered she was hungry. No wonder she loved him.

He brushed a kiss on her cheek.

"Take your time," she whispered.

***

Zamira snuggled down under the covers and smiled at him. With her support, he could do this. Jeremy left the room with Ollie. "Which way?"

"Next door."

Ollie went in first and Jeremy stopped a nurse in the hall, asking her for some food for Zamira.

When Ollie came out a moment later, he said, "Moira's alone. I'll keep Tracey away for a while."

"Thanks." His chest tight, steps uncertain, he walked into the hospital room. Moira wore a cotton nightgown and had small cuts all over her face.

She grinned. "Hey, Jeremy."

He swallowed hard and shifted closer to Moira's bed. "How are you?"

"Sore," she said. "But alive. Thank you for getting me out of the car."

He shrugged. "It's what I do."

Moira sighed. "I should know that." She studied him, took a deep breath. "Sorry isn't a big enough word. I can't apologise to you enough for not speaking to you for thirteen years."

His throat closed over and he stepped back. He hadn't been expecting an apology. "It is what it is."

She frowned. "What it is, is inexcusable. I'm surprised you agreed to meet me."

"You're family."

"Family who has treated you like shit."

It was strange to hear his sweet little sister swear.

She shook her head. "God, I've got no excuse. I believed everything Mum said, I blamed you for killing Dad for so long."

He clenched his teeth. "I did kill him."

"It was an accident," she said. "It took me so long to realise it. It wasn't until I almost got run over while texting that I understood how a moment of inattention could kill."

His heart lurched. "Were you hurt?"

"No. I managed to stop in time." She tapped her thigh. "I met Ollie right afterwards and he asked about my family and I thought about you, about what had happened." She glanced up at him. "I looked you up, I had your number, but I was too scared to call. Then I saw you in the hardware store and I knew it was you. You look so much like Dad."

He gritted his teeth against the pain.

"I am *so* sorry for how I treated you. I lost my father and brother that day."

"You were just a kid. You didn't know any better."

"So were you. How did you manage? Where did you go?"

There was so much she didn't know. "Pete took me in."

She opened her mouth. "He never said."

"I asked him not to. Didn't want to cause any trouble between him and Mum." They'd all been good friends. Whenever Pete had invited her and the girls over, Jeremy had made himself scarce and had moved out as soon as he could afford it.

She was silent for a moment. "So how long have you lived in Blackbridge?"

"About five years. I opened my business there."

"Mendelson Construction. You've got some great reviews on your website."

She really had been checking on him.

She touched his hand. "I'd like to have you back in my life, Jeremy." She screwed up her face. "If you can forgive me."

He couldn't blame her. At only ten she would have believed whatever their mother told her. "I'd like that too."

Her eyes watered and her smile was shaky. "I'm so glad." She used the sheets to dab her eyes.

Jeremy hesitated. "What will you do if Mum doesn't want you to see me?"

She frowned. "Tell her I'm going to have a relationship with you whether she likes it or not."

Moira was no longer the little girl eager to please.

His heart swelled and he gently hugged her. "It's nice to have you back, Moi-Moi."

"Ditto."

***

Jeremy's eyes felt like lead and frustration filled him by the time Zamira was discharged later that afternoon. He hadn't had Zamira to himself at all. Nurses had come and gone, Moira had wanted to know everything about him and about what had happened to Zamira, and just as his mother had returned and Moira had declared she needed a nap, Annisa had returned from being questioned by Border Force.

He was desperate for sleep, but he wasn't leaving Zamira's side again. Not for a long time.

Finally, the doctor had come around to discharge her. Though he hadn't wanted the company, he'd invited Annisa and Bethari to stay at his place and was relieved when Agent Franklin had insisted they stay with them because both women were illegally in Australia.

He scanned the carpark for his ute. Kim had found the key in Zamira's jacket, which had been left on the boat, and had dropped it off earlier so they could get home. Zamira yawned as she got into the car.

"Why don't you nap on the way home?" His heart squeezed. She'd changed his place from a house into a real home since she'd been there.

She smiled. "You don't mind?"

He shook his head. It would give him time to get his head together.

It didn't take long for her breathing to become regular and he concentrated on the road, battling his fatigue. Finally he turned into his drive and his stomach twisted at the burnt remains of his shed. The double doors were wide open revealing the blackened interior, charred wood, ash and water. The roof had a hole in the centre where the flames had burnt it out. It would take some work to fix it.

After the arson investigator went through, Jeremy would see just how much work. He didn't want to mess with any evidence. The longer Henk and his gang stayed behind bars the better. He got out of the car and helped Zamira out.

"I'm so sorry about your shed," she said.

He shrugged. "I can buy new stuff."

She gasped, her hand covering her mouth. "What happened to Fetch?"

"Mai took him home with her after they finished mopping up the fire. He's apparently terrorising her cat, Calypso."

She chuckled.

He wrapped his arm around Zamira's waist, needing to hold her, to reassure himself she was fine. They walked inside. "Do you need any more pain killers?" he asked as he switched on the kettle.

She shook her head. "What I need is you." She hugged him. "I want to forget about everything that's happened, forget about going home on Sunday and just be with you."

He ached. Only three more nights.

It wouldn't be fair to ask her to stay. Her life was in Melbourne. He bent down and kissed her, savouring the taste of her lips.

Mindful of her gunshot wound, he slid his hands down her side and pulled her closer, kissing her forehead. She fit so perfectly against him. He didn't want to let her go.

The kettle boiled and he stepped back, swallowing down the words he wanted to say. "Do you want a cuppa?"

"I'm still exhausted. I need sleep more than anything." She held out her hand. "Will you join me?"

That sounded perfect. He slid his hand into hers and they walked down the corridor to his bedroom. Slowly he helped her undress and she climbed into bed, her short, dark hair like a halo on the pillow.

He got in next to her, pulled her close, and she nestled her head against his chest. This was where she belonged. He squeezed his eyes shut as the pain in his heart increased. He wanted her to stay, wanted her to be part of his life.

"Sweet dreams," she said, a smile in her voice.

"I love you." Jeremy's heart stopped as the words slipped out of his mouth and Zamira's body tensed. Idiot!

Zamira tilted her head up, her eyes wide. "What did you say?"

He gritted his teeth, what else sounded similar? Fuck it. It was out now. He shrugged his shoulders. "I love you."

She sat up, pursed her lips, studying him.

His face heated. "Sorry. I didn't mean to say it. It kinda slipped out. I know you're going home on

Sunday…" He shifted on to his elbow.

She put a finger on his mouth to stop him speaking. "Did you mean it?"

He nodded, ran his hand through his beard, his chest tight. Like he'd say something like that as a joke.

Her smile lit up her face. She placed her hand on his cheek, brushed her lips against his. "I love you, too."

Hope speared through him, but he controlled it. "You don't have to say it back."

She laughed, rolled her eyes at him and kissed him hard. "It's true. I've been miserable about the thought of leaving." She kissed him again. "Franklin said there's a job with the Task Force over here… I could move, I just need to find a place to stay…"

He ran his hand through her hair, pulled her closer, touched his forehead to hers. Joy filled him. "Move in with me. Please. When you went missing, and then when you fell off the trawler…" He huffed out a breath. "I've never been so scared. I want you with me."

Her smile widened. "OK." She kissed him again.

Was it that simple? His heart swelled. He would never get enough of her kisses, of her. His mind raced. He could make space in his wardrobe — hell, she could have a whole spare room if she needed it for her things. "I'll finish my office." Except he had no equipment anymore. His spirits fell. It would take time to replace everything that was destroyed.

She laughed and his spirits lifted again. "Hey, there's no rush. We'll work it out." She squeezed his hand. "Besides we need to rebuild your shed first. I'll help if you can teach me what to do."

The thought of having Zamira with him while he rebuilt, teaching her, sharing his life, filled him with such incredible joy. "I can do that."

Whatever life threw at them, they would get through it together.

Epilogue

It had been fourteen days since Jeremy had last seen Zamira in the flesh and fourteen very lonely nights. His weekend trip to Melbourne to meet her parents was far too long ago and Skype calls weren't quite the same. He smirked. Though some had been very entertaining. He tapped his foot on the ground while he waited at the gates of the airport for her to disembark.

People walked past and he stood straight, scanning the faces, waiting to see the one who brought so much light into his life.

Why were there so many people on this damned flight?

He waited, and he waited and then finally he saw her beautiful face. His spirits lifted and he pushed past people and picked her up, spinning her around.

Zamira squealed. "Put me down!"

He lowered her to the ground, keeping her body pressed against him. "I missed you." He kissed her and she pulled him closer, kissing him back, one leg wrapping around his. He groaned.

"Get a room," someone yelled.

That was a very good idea. He wanted to bury

himself inside her and never let her go.

He broke the kiss and grabbed her hand. "Let's go."

Zamira laughed. "I need to get my bag."

Right. Of course. He'd helped her pack up her apartment and the things she'd wanted to keep were already on their way, being shipped across the country, but she needed clothes in the meantime.

They walked over to the carousel hand in hand. "What colour is your bag?"

"Red."

He scanned the baggage claim but there were no red bags. He stepped in front of her, kissing her. "It's not here. You might have to go naked."

Her tongue teased him and he went hard as jarrah wood. As she went to pull away, he held her in place. "Give me a minute," he murmured. Now he wished he hadn't arranged what he had at his house.

She glanced down and grinned. "Oh look, there's my bag."

"Minx." He breathed out, doing his thirteen times table and then let her go. "Which one?"

He picked it up and together they went out to his ute. "Mum and Dad dropped me at the airport," Zamira said. "They've accepted my move. It helped that you charmed them so completely when you came over."

He squeezed her hand. "Thank you."

She frowned. "What for?"

"For moving here for me. I know it's going to be hard at first and I know what you've given up for me." No one had ever done anything like that for him before.

"Jeremy, I'm happy. I can't wait to start my new job and get to know all your friends."

That was going to happen sooner than she thought.

He drove out of Albany Airport and towards Blackbridge.

In what seemed like no time, he turned into his driveway and swallowed his smile at all the cars in front of his house.

"What's going on?"

He parked and got Zamira's case out. He took her hand. "Shall we go and see?"

They walked inside to find a huge WELCOME TO BLACKBRIDGE sign hung along one of the walls in the living area and his friends standing underneath it. Mai and Nicholas, Kim, Jamie, Adam, Elijah, as well as Fleur and Will, Kit and Lincoln, Hannah and Ryan. Even Moira and Ollie had made it. Mai stepped forward. "We wanted to be the first to welcome you to Blackbridge." She smiled at Zamira.

Zamira brought a hand up to her mouth, her eyes glistening. "Thank you." She glanced up at him. "Did you know about this?"

He smiled. "I wanted you to feel at home here."

She kissed him hard. "Anywhere you are is home to me."

His heart squeezed. He felt the same way.

Thank you for reading!

I hope you enjoyed the book. It would be super awesome if you could leave a review wherever you bought it, because I love to hear what you thought of the story.

ACKNOWLEDGEMENTS

Thanks as always must go to the people who helped me research this book. Derek Stone from the Denmark Marine Rescue was kind enough to show me around their base and answer a bunch of questions, Matt Hartfield and the Water Police answered policing questions for me, and Rania answered my Muslim queries.

A huge thank you to my production team: Lana Pecherczyk for the cover, Ann Harth for the structural edits and Teena Raffa-Mulligan for the copyedits.

Shield

The Blackbridge Series #6

His life is in danger. But the only man who can protect him is afraid to go public…

Blackbridge, Western Australia. Jamie Zanetti holds his secret close to his chest. Fearing that coming out as bisexual will ruin his small-town teaching career, he represses desires he'd rather explore. But when his handsome high-school crush Elijah returns and joins him in the volunteer emergency service, the attraction may be too much to resist.

Elijah Johnson knows where his heart lies. And after eight years of soul-searching across Europe, he's finally ready to settle down with Mr. Right. But Elijah refuses to have a clandestine relationship, no matter how delicious Jamie's lips feel.

While they're thrown together in dramatic rescues, Jamie is torn apart as he fights to hide his growing feelings. But the truth might be the only thing that saves them both when Elijah stumbles upon a sinister local crime ring…

Can Jamie and Elijah expose a deadly gang of thieves and move their love into the open?

Shield is the sixth standalone novel in the page-turning Blackbridge romantic suspense series. If you like deep characters, sweet attractions, and thrilling emergencies, then you'll adore Claire Boston's captivating story.

Buy *Shield* to bring passion to the rescue today!

www.ingramcontent.com/pod-product-compliance
Lightning Source LLC
Chambersburg PA
CBHW060916190726
48286CB00002B/527